THE STREETS

An LP Novel

Franco Book 1 of 3

Tom Sheridan

Streets Creations

Published in the United States by Streets Creations.

ISBN: 1-7321758-1-0
ISBN-13: 978-1-7321758-1-5

FOR TNZ

With love from coast to coast

FOR MDKS

Made in Woodbridge

TRACKS

1. Intro   1

2. The Fighter   5

3. The Kid   31

4. Docked   47

5. Frogger   65

6. Bunns Pain   75

7. Ray Day   85

8. Yogi   103

9. Don't Call It a Comeback   121

10. (W)Rapped Up   147

11. Corrections   159

12. Warnings   167

13. Woodbridge   185

14. Battle of Newark   201

15. Everything I'm Not   221

16. Life After Death   237

Bonus. The Streets   241

TRACK 1. INTRO

BACK IN THE DAY, Franco told T they were gonna take this trip. Hop the Turnpike straight outta Jersey. Fill up on Philly cheesesteaks. Run the Rocky stairs. Blaze through the dirty dirty. Push a hunid thirty thirty. Refuel at a bodega in Talladega. See the city serenade that is a Nawlins jazz parade. Next to West Texas. Watch them Friday night lights burn bright. Rent a Stang, a '66, on Route 66. Eat enchiladas in East LA. Cruise Crenshaw with Dre. Catch a Little Tokyo drift and coast up the coast. Raid a Raider game. Mosh in a Wash mosh pit. Hit a rodeo in Colorado. See the Cubs in Chicago. Walk eight miles on 8 Mile. Believe in Cleveland and steal through Steel City. Ship up to Boston. Stomp through them mean towns of Beantown. Then catch the Bombers in the Bronx. A Chappelle show at the Apollo. And cross the Hudson River line. In a Jersey state of mind.

Breeze back to their own blue-collar melting pot that was a little like all of the above but exactly like none. Exit 11 along that oil tank Turnpike stretch of Jersey. The one Tony Soprano leaves in his rearview as his Escalade escalates to greener pastures. A place too small to be a city. Too broke to be a burb. Too rough to be rural. Just a town. A tough little Turnpike town. The last of a line of them tucked underneath Newark. Elizabeth. Linden. Carteret aka Carteruff. Rahway. Where the inmates get it the raw way. And the town where the iconic prison actually resides. Woodbridge. Aka Hoodbridge. The Wood. The Hood. By any name, a town. Surrounded by a steel cage of bridges and refineries, warehouses and highways, rail yards and jail yards.

A town set in the eastern pinch of the state. Where the North Jersey head, the South Jersey body, the NYC shoulder, and the Long Island arm all meet. The armpit. Where the Turnpike (aka I-95), the Parkway, (I-)287, and US Routes 440, 9, and 1—the nation's longest north-south highway—all converge. When Franco would sail his Stang over the Driscoll Bridge at night, he and little T would have a bird's-eye view of the whole thing. A town laced with hundred-year-old highways hauling cars anywhere but there. Taillights on the Turnpike North to New York. Taillights on the Parkway South to Sea Bright. Taillights on 287 to suburban heaven. Taillights hightailin it on Highway 9. Taillights on highways headed anywhere but there. Woodbridge. The strained heart of Jersey. Pushing taillights along aging arteries.

Franco was one of the exceptions. Mainlining his blue Mustang into whichever vein brought him back to his hometown. The one full of cramped cottages, brick boxes, aging apartments. A bi-level if you were ballin. Occupied by residents who mowed their own lawns. Painted their own places. Helped friends move for a six-pack and a pizza. Boys from the hood rocking hoodies. Girls from around the way wearing stunner shades. All playing spades. Little tykes on their bikes. Cutting through old-timers. Immigrants. And everyone in between.

Franco saw the whole world in Woodbridge. A township

of nine baby boroughs. Firefighters affording houses in Fords. Indians integrating Iselin. Hispanics hooping in Hopelawn. Hippies n homies smokin Ls in Avenel. All kinds of crazies in Keasbey. The classy in the colonials of Colonia. Backyard weddings in Port Reading. Double-shifted longshoremen snorin in Sewaren.

All that and more in the primogenitor. The borough of the township's namesake. Woodbridge. To distinguish Woodbridge borough, one of nine pups in the litter that was Woodbridge Township, people referred to it as "Proper." To Franco, it was anything but.

It was a town older than America that had grown as motley as today's America. The crossroads of the state that was the crossroads of the colonies that was, as Franco figured, the crossroads of the country. Connecting north to south. Red to blue. Old to new. Either a perfect alchemy. Or an insane stew.

In March of '08, it was looking like the latter. One that would swallow up Franco and T both.

TRACK 2. THE FIGHTER

FRANCO AND T walked the streets of Woodbridge that
mad March day. Albeit in separate ways. As it was these days.
Franco gettin ready for a fight. T hoping to avoid one.

Franco broke into a jog despite the weather hitting the
northeast trifecta—cold, rainy, windy. His dark hair damp. A
single curl defied the downpour. His soaked black thermal
barely trapped his traps. Ran along his ripped arms as he ran
along the ripped-up roads. Getting to the matter at hand. The
matter that had him up at six in the morning. Training for the
last fight of his contract. His last, period, if he didn't come
correct. *Six in the mornin.* Joggin in jacked-up weather while
Snoop and Dre were drinkin gin n juice.

Franco must've ran Main Street a million times. But he'd
still get nostalgic. He breezed by St. John's. His favorite
building. The Catholic church looked like somethin outta the
Renaissance. The peak. The spire. The bell tower. The stained
glass and statues giving it a pizzazz the two Protestant
churches lacked. A real work of art. Ah. Who was he kiddin?
It was his favorite building because he married Julie there.

Coulda looked like the three-story brick box of a school they had across the street and it still woulda been his favorite building. The school him[1] and Joey Yo would go to once a week as kids. The CCD lessons going in one ear and out the other. Kinda like how they'd walk in the bathroom door at one end and hop out the window at the other. Then hit up the karate supply store Franco jogged past next. The Martial Fist. Ten years old and they were buyin Chinese stars, chuckin em into trees. Franco bobbed past The Barber Shop. The barbers in the plain-named place saved all their creativity for their ill cuts. Fades, brooks, hawks. Sketches that garnered gawks.

Franco breezed down the remaining block. As a boy, Main was a grand old ave with every place he could imagine. As a man, it was two blocks of shoddy shops. Could cover it in a minute. Even with the hitch. Fucking up the otherwise lean machine. That ailing fuckin ankle. That one slip in the cage that led to seven years bad luck. But. He had come full circle. In the same position at 33 as he was at 26. That's why when he beat feet past Palermo's, he could glance in the plate-glass pane and carry on without wanting the baked ravioli too badly. Soon as Franco won his next fight, he'd order em times two. Or would he roll next door? Get Tito's tacos al pastor. Yeah, he'd hit both places. Followed by the chicken n waffle joint Brazil was always braggin about. And the Thai place Taz's family owned. Knock down some curry like he was Dell Curry. Oh, and how the hellal could he forget the Halal? That lunch when Lama signed him. Not to mention Demitri's and the Iberian. He had to show them

---

[1] Or should it be "he?" Franco wondered. Didn't he learn somethin about subject vs. object back in the day? Ah who the fuck knows what school would say. Anyone on the street would say, "him." And don't even get Franco started on lay vs. lie and that vs. who and further vs. farther.

love. It would be all of the above. Yeah, he was gonna buffet for days. Make up for all the days of training. All the days of stale cut oatmeal and browning bananas for breakfast. Canned tuna and turnips for lunch. Chicken breast and broccoli for dinner. All for a couple cauliflower ears.

Franco worked his way past the Woodbridge train station. A brick throwback with a classic clock tower. Like that one in *Back to the Future*. If only Franco had a DeLorean. Of all the dates he'd fly back to fix, and there were plenty, he'd fly right to that fuckin fight in '01. The Split Decision. The one that split his ankle. Split his family. Split his whole existence in two. The Life He Was Supposed To Have. And. The life he did have. But the clock's hands were only moving forward. Fast.

Franco kept his feet going likewise. He pressed past Parker's Printing Press. The landmarked cottage still standing since the 1700s. The fighter still standing seven years later. Two weeks from his first Pay-Per-View. They slotted the local fan favorite as the first fight of the Newark card. And pitted him against an undefeated up-and-comer. The 24-year-old number-four fighter. With a win, they'd have to give Franco a new contract. He'd be able to hang up his side hustle once and for all. And maybe down the road, a title shot with the champ headlining the card. A loss, meanwhile, and Franco would slip out of the rankings and into oblivion. A fall too far for a fighter far too old.

Franco picked up the pace along Amboy Ave. He jogged toward G-Dub, his old teammate. Joey Yo may have been Franco's best bro, but every high school soccer season, Franco, G-Dub, and Young (aka Youngin) were as thick as thieves among the fall leaves. Three wrong side of the track kids on a team of college-track kids. They got real tight as they balled all fall. But now? Now it was winter.

G-Dub rested outside a historic colonial. Against the base of a memorial sign offering little shelter from the storm. Sipping from a Dunkin' Donuts cup. Something colored toffee and other than coffee. Franco fist bumped G-Dub and patted the memorial. Franco had the Cross Keys Tavern sign committed to memory:

> *On April 22, 1789, George Washington stayed the night at this Tavern on his way from Mount Vernon, Virginia to New York City, for his inauguration as the first President of the United States.*

The situation was so familiar, Franco would breeze by and almost forget that G-Dub shared much more than the memorial with the Father of Our Country. He also shared his name.

The more Franco pondered America then and now, Woodbridge then and now, his own ancestry then and now, the more his legs pumped. As if he was trying to outrun a growing monster. Franco wrapped up his run with a sprint down the middle of Bunns Lane. The project bricks of his past breezed by on his right. The cramped cottages of his present unpacked on his left. Tricked-out rides and burned-out beaters to his right. Work vans and dogs barking to his left. Hail hammering it all. Franco sucked wind. His cut quads cut into his sweats. Pounding harder than the hail. Until he touched his beat-up blue Mustang. Parked in the driveway of the last house on the left. The claustro Cape with the chintzy chain link fence. With the off-white vinyl siding turned off-off-white over the years. Franco doubled over. Huffed and puffed.

There was an even greater wheezing across the street. Coming from a burgundy Astro Van. With the work van on the project side of the street and Franco's beater on the house side, he lost his bearings for a beat. The burgundy Astro Van wheezed again, but the engine wouldn't turn. Six Hispanic laborers were packed into it. Two more inspected the situation under the hood. One looked over to Franco. Said something in Spanish. Franco couldn't understand the words, but the guy's weathered face and bloodshot eyes said it all.

It wasn't the first time Franco was taken for Hispanic. He was taken for everything. Joey Yo said he looked like Prince. *Ya know, pumped up n without the pumps.* The Frog called him a young Sly Stallone. T had him for a mean street Mario Lopez. Taz messed with some Messi-Pacquiao-Master Blaster, and he even got The Rock when he rocked a shaved head. In support of Julie's mother's lung cancer. Two more who had an answer. Julie thought him Black Irish while Julie's mom thought him half-black half-Irish. Just last week, Franco was buying an iced tea and got Ice-T. It was at a 7-Eleven. This shit happened 24-7. Shit, Ice-T was born in Newark, too. For all little orphan Frannie knew, they were fuckin brothers. Maybe he'd change his name to Lemonade.

Then again, Franco couldn't blame people for guessing. The orphan's identity was on his own mind, too. Even the national pastime couldn't pass the time. Other than Mattingly, his favorite players were the Francos. The paisan John and the cocoa Julio. One in the batter's box with the unorthodox stance while Franco pondered his life's unorthodox stance. The other a relief pitcher offering no relief.

Whatever Franco was, he knew what the guys before him were. The half as big, work twice as hard kind. The get half the pay, give twice the thanks kind. Mexicans, some would say. Even though they coulda been anything from Mexican to Manautian. Even though Franco saw light-skinned six-foot

9

Mexicans mixing it up at the World Cup. And even bigger ones on their ball team. The guys before him were maybe Mexican, but they were definitely, what was that word from *The Motorcycle Diaries?* Oh yeah. Mestizo.

Franco asked in his best Spanglish, "Necesitas un...jump?"

The laborers nodded. Mucho sís and thank yous.

Franco finished giving the guys a jump a few minutes later. Their thank yous resumed as Franco's hot rod rumbled away. Hail pelted the Mustang's heavy metal mold. Rat a tat tat. A chirping brake pad soon joined the band. An unrelenting duo known as Father Time & Mother Nature.

Franco usually tuned this looming act out with the radio. Rock or rap. Some in Woodbridge would only listen to one or the other. But Franco was always torn. As if the gods wrestling for control of his soul were Bruce Springsteen and Biggie Smalls. As if he were simultaneously born to run and ready to die. The guys with the initials BS. Who spit nothing but Truth. Like Ice Cube, Creedence, Cash. Dylan, DMC. Joel, Jay, Dre. Marley, Meth, Mellencamp. From Thorogood to Nas, so thoroughly good. Petty, Pac. Santana, Seger. Sublime, Slim. From Eric Church to *It's Dark and Hell is Hot.* From "Who Shot Ya" all the way to Frank Sinatra. To Franco, they were all singin songs from the streets.

But Franco was running behind. No time to turn the dial. Couldn't be late for Nelly. Coach Nelson. Wrestling coach turned athletic director. Woodbridge royalty. By way of a currency more powerful than position or paycheck. Blood. Thomas Nelson the Ninth. Numbers One through Eight all buried right behind Woodbridge's first church. Or was it the second of those two prehistoric Protestant jobs? Franco could never remember. What he did remember was that Nelly's was the one that, upon in its founding in the 1600s, had accepted all faiths. Sure, back then that just meant different denominations of Protestants. Still, unlike the Wu who said as much, the church brought together the English and the Dutch.

Franco had been in the fight game for a few years before he got going with Nelly. Had been hittin the mats with Youngin. His soccer homie whose best sport was wrestling. Youngin beat everyone in the county. Save for his own demons. Died of a heroin overdose the first time he tried it. Worked up the moxy after a year on Oxy. When they filled Youngin's grave, Franco filled his shoes. The red Asics Aggressors Youngin's mother handed to him. He could still feel Mrs. Young's cold fingers clutching his wrists. *While Robert's up there— You give em h—*. She broke down in tears, but Franco got the message. It was the same day Franco crossed paths with Coach Nelson. Outside the funeral home. Coach asked the up-and-coming Woodbridge fighter who he'd wrestle with now.

Franco was 25 in 2000 when he ran in those Aggressors to his first session with Coach Nelson. Franco was running behind that day too but sprinted across campus and hopped a construction fence to make it to the mat on time. Still, Coach Nelson told him he was late. Before Franco could rebut— *Ten years too late,* gnawed Nelly. Where was Franco at 15? When the rookie coach could've used the frisky freshman. In the very same spot they were then. Sans mat.

Balling. Five-nine with no future as a hooper. But Young Franco was balling. Balling because his foster father signed him up for basketball. Balling because his foster father loved the game so much, he'd drink brown-bagged Bud Heavys and shout at little Franco to shoot the fuckin ball. Balling because there was a basketball court on Bunns Lane. Balling because the Iowa-Ohio State wrestling match didn't make it to the ten channels of Franco's ten-inch TV. Balling because the UFC wasn't founded until just after his high school graduation.

So here Franco was in '08. Fifteen years from graduation. *Still* trying to make up for the mistake of his first fifteen years of life. Here Franco was trying to scratch a few bucks together at the bottom of the MMA barrel. The only difference between him and the top guys being time. The top guys having all grown up in one discipline or another while Franco was balling. Perfecting their craft while Franco was at Pearl Street playing pickup games. Balling. The top guys crossing over into boxing, Jiu-Jitsu, Muay Thai. While Franco was crossing up Joey Yo for lazy layups. Balling. Not that Franco thought about it that much. He wasn't much for bawling.

Despite the slick roads, the bald tires, and the lack of front wheel drive on that winter day in '08, Franco sped over the speed limit. Navigated potholes like a pro. Knew the ave like the back of his Don Mattingly rookie card. Both of which had seen better days.

The high school had also seen better days. A behemoth brick job with rusted window frames. Franco parked in front of the tennis courts where he used to give Julie a hand with her game. The ones now rendered unfit for varsity play. A home court of cracks and weeds. Now used to smoke crack n weed. Franco hustled past a busted-out brick wall on the forever-under-construction ass end of the school. He yanked open a dented metal door that banged against brick as he jogged over to the gym.

Franco was soon feeling high as he crouched low. The highlight of his day was getting his mat work in. And if he was lucky, he'd just so happen to bump into T on his way out. Julie couldn't complain about a coincidence.

Franco circled. Ready to pounce. It had been eight years

since that first session when Nelly pinned him more times than a bulletin board. Franco had been making up ground on the ground game ever since he decided to fight. Formally. Street fights and bar fights, Franco had been having those his whole life. One was finally fuckin worth it back in '97.

Young Franco was 22 and on a pickup for The Frog. At a dive gym called The Power Plant. Franco breezed past the dude at the desk hooting and hollering about how Franco needed a membership, this and that.

"I'm thinkin of joining," Young Franco offered as he carried on toward the back.

The Power Plant was full of yuge dudes. Goliaths of all grayscale who'd been rocking spiked-out hair, fresh fades, and black beaters well before *Jersey Shore*. Tatted arms pumped out-of-date free weights. A dude maxed out in Air Maxes. All while The Game strained the training room's speakers. His ethnically eclectic "Westside Story" telling the gym's story.

Franco cut through the coral reef of cock D like Henry Hill bouncing through the Bamboo. There was Willy Momo. Cuz he always wanted to eat mo mo. There was Whitey Bulger. A buff blond. And there was Little Benny. The samallest of his Samoan brothers at five-ten, one ton. There was Five For Five. A five-foot-five five-hundred-pounder. There was Conway. His real name was Tito Chang, but he'd con his way into the squat rack. And there was Bluto. From when he dropped a 45-pound plate on his foot. There was Peggy. A million calf raises wasn't gonna outdo his DNA. Working out with his wide-shouldered wife, Peggy. And Brother Darryl. Pushing plates with the power of his sermons.

Franco headed to the back of the congregation. Rolled on the alpha hitting the heavy bag. An HGH experiment who went by the name of Herc. All mohawk and mouth. Barking.

Strutting. Bobbing to his Bose headphones. Franco had his money on "Whoomp, There It Is." And hey, what do you know, Herc actually does a set. To much congratulations by his two bros.

One bro, the bantam ball of muscle, clocked Franco walking over. Gave Herc a tap.

Herc sneered. "Kid's not even a gangster. He's a fuckin goon."

Young Franco bit his lip. "Ay Herc. You owe six hundo. Let's not make it a big deal."

"You want my money, tough guy?" Herc pulled his pockets out. "Kiss the rabbit between the ears."

Franco looked at the three juiceheads before him. His mind flashed back to *Cape Fear*. When DeNiro beats the shit out of a gang of guys. Franco learned a long time ago that shit didn't go down like that in real life. In real life, there were only two ways shit would go down. Either A: Franco would hit Herc and get jumped. Or B: Franco would hit Herc and simultaneously stun the other two mahfuckas.

Franco was betting on B. Herc might've had everyone else in the gym fooled. But Franco saw his old classmate. The pre-steroid fat-fuck[2] that wrestled heavyweight. The heavyweight that always went last when the team's outcome was on the line. Franco would watch from the bleachers as Herc—Seamus Herkle back then—folded every time. The no-heart hump would lie on the mat, his pale skin puffed from black tights like he was a beached killer whale. Except the only thing this whale killed was his team's chances. Shamu Herkle.

And when Franco saw Herc's goons, he saw past their biceps to their shrunken balls. Their lack thereof evident in

[2] Franco would have you know that not all fat people are fucks. But in Herc's case, he was definitely fat. And most definitely a fuck.

how they not only got cut from the wrestling team but doubled down by showing up to matches and shouting drunk shit talk from the back row of the bleachers. Franco, the fiery point guard from the ball team, would try to support the wrestling team with cheers and hollers while Herc's goons— "Cray Z" and "Smooth B"—would be yelling, *The other guy's got a boner!*

Truth be told, Franco and Joey Yo would crack up at the bar back in the day as they recounted those incidents. But the older Franco got, the less funny and more depressing such shit became. Life's a party in your 20s and a hangover in your 30s, Franco figured.

But back in those young 20s party days of '97, those piss n vinegar days, Franco was as freewheelin as Bob Dylan. Had as much juice as Tupac in *Juice*. He squared up with Herc, flared his right shoulder forward—look over here—boom. Hit Herc with a left cross that left his eyes crossed. Caught him on the button with the kind of magic trick a boy learns on Bunns Lane. The sleight of hand of throwing hands.

Next thing ya know, the steroid head's staggering out, eager to pay. "I'ma go find an ATM."

Word around town was that Herc's boys came out from behind the ellipticals. Hours later.

Franco strolled out past the dude at the desk with the bad news. "I decided not to join."

Out front, Joey Yo caught up to Franco. (Every time Mr. Moran called his name for attendance in eighth grade, Joey would say, "Yo.") "I was just comin outta the locker—that was fuckin awesome, yo!" gushed Franco's Boricua goomba as they handshake-hugged. "You should do MMA, yo!"

"What? Like where the karate guy fights the boxer?"

"Nah yo. The whole game's changin. Everyone's doin everything. Kinda like your scraps on the street. Kinda like how you box with me and wrestle with Youngin. Just with some Bruce Lee martial art-type shit mixed in."

The realization hit Young Franco like a ton of bricks. He had Joey Yo show him all about it on AOL. That night in '97, he saw it clear as day. As he dreamed of the big time over Bud Lights at Big Times. Franco was athletic as hell. Fit as hell. And fought like hell. Things he'd never go around saying sober. But as his blood alcohol crept up, so did his boasting. He was a three-sport athlete back in high school, wasn't he? Naturally. No guidance, no personal trainers, no nothin. All-County no less. And since then boxing with Joey Yo, a bona fide amateur, and wrestling with Youngin, first team all-county. Franco's homies helpin him out so he could bring the heat on the street. And cuz the crazy fuck liked it. Liked going blow for blow with Joey Yo despite the 20-pound weight disadvantage. Liked giving Youngin a better run for his money than the Joe Blows he blew away in high school. Not to mention Franco also hit the weights like a beast. Yeah, Franco could see it now back then. Add some martial arts training at 22. His first fights in AC at 23. Regional rep at 24. The Show at 25. Top contender at 26. By 27? Biggie wouldn't be the only one makin sure his crew was loungin. It was all so Juicy.

The next morning in '97, reality set in alongside Franco's hangover. Alongside his three-year-old son asking Dada to wake up. Alongside his wife reminding him to put on his knit socks. To hit the docks.

Still, Franco flung himself into the fight game. Got after it every spare minute. Roadwork before hitting the road for work. Workouts as soon as work was out. The wrestling mats on Monday and Friday mornings. Muay Thai on Tuesdays. Weights on Wednesdays and weekends. *Thursdays* was the worst days. Had to box his beefy bro Joey Yo. Then thought he'd die on Fridays. When Jiu-Jitsu replaced drinking at Friday's. All because he finally knew, at 22, what he was born to do. Even if he was a bit behind the curve. Even if the mortgage and meals for the family came first. Even if he didn't have the cheddar for the right trainers. Even if he had to endure injuries—especially hell without the healthcare.

And Franco had success early on. When he started knocking around in the late '90s, from underground gyms in Brooklyn to hotel halls in AC, it was nothing his street fights ain't seen. A bunch of twentysomething ex-wrestlers, cocky kickboxers, and street toughs. A bunch of Kimbo Slices all fighting for their slice of power. Young Franco jacked unskilled juiceheads and one-dimensional dudes alike. And yeah, there were those who brought the heat. But they either lacked the heart to perfect their art or the insistence to go the distance. At the end of the day, the new jack cleaned up Atlantic City like he was the star of *New Jack City*. The regional banger racked up a record of 6-0. And was headed to The Show.

By 2000, as The Show grew and its fighters improved, Franco had his first failures. Even then though, it was two steps forward for every one back in his first tries beyond the Tri-State.

The first true mixed martial artist he ever mixed it up with was a young buck from Bucks County, PA. A square-jawed buzz cut kid. All-American wrestling pedigree along with a top-shelf team. Even his cutman had a PhD. It was enough to give Franco a PhD. (A playa hatin degree.)

The young buck had trotted his way across PA. Was giving Franco fits in Pittsburgh. Almost beat Franco every which way—knock out, submission, points. The young buck had refined his craft in all capacities. Except one. Not even sparring can get you ready for a cold-cocking. Either you have a chin or you don't. As round two wound down, Franco caught the clean-cut kid clean. The uppercut rung his bell at the bell. Franco hunted the bewildered buck in the third. Shot at the deer in headlights and hogtied him with a hammerlock.

While Pittsburgh's black and gold faithful gave it up for the Jersey kid black and blue, Franco's get was barely enough to get his team paid. Still, as the Mustang stole away, he'd take the steal in Steel City.

Franco's second fight for The Show was a barn burner in Birmingham. They pitted him against a good old Alabama boy. A husker from the hay throwing haymakers. Franco had crimson tides of blood flowing from his face before he finally encountered a chance to counter. Franco would've lost on points, but his left hook was on point. *Roll Tide*, Franco and Joey joked as they coasted up the coast in the Stang. Nelly and Taz meanwhile packed in the back. All to save a few bucks after claiming their second buck.

By the third fight for The Show, Franco and his coaches flew coach. For a battle in Seattle. Franco's ground game was gorilla. He'd never had better hands. But. That fuckin Pride Fighter from Japan. It was one thing to tangle with Taz on a Tuesday in a rundown gym in Woodbridge. It was another to be pitted against a Pride champ and come up with a win in Washington. Franco was unable to work in past the foreigner's flying feet. He was handed his first defeat.

The fight had hurt his pockets, too. After all the training leading up to the fight, the travel expenses for his whole team, and the fees for the lawyer, Franco coulda cried uncle when he got to Uncle Sam. But his only bottom line was the outcome of the fight. And it was less than a wash in Washington.

After that, Franco and Taz straight stepped up the kicks. Worked on straights and step-up kicks. Roundhouse clocked each other around the clock.

Two more years and 20,000 more miles on the Mustang, Franco had two more wins. His first by kicks on Route 66. Even won the Rage of The Cage Award. It was a nice little payday in Santa Fe. Then a win by submission in Michigan. He was looking pretty adroit as he left Detroit. Sitting at 10-1 overall and ranked tenth in The Show.

They next pitted Franco against Walid Al-Jassim. Saudi by his sire's surname. Mixed by his American mother. Brit by birthplace. And a millionaire by any measure. A young old-money millionaire who, at 22, was already accomplished. National team boxer. Jiu-Jitsu world champ. First round finish in his first go in The Show. Sent a distinguished veteran away like he was the VA. Same in his second. So impressive, he had skyrocketed to a tie with Franco for tenth.

The phenom with the backstory to boot. His father an oil sheik who brought the fight game to his homeland. His mother an Olympic medalist who also meddled as a Rhodes Scholar. The diver met the ox of a man at Oxford. Then dove into the sheets of his London loft. The Saudi and the San Franciscan birthed a British boy. A pampered lad who had it all. And took what he didn't. When a reporter made comparisons to him and boxing's "Prince" Naseem Hamed, he responded with a wag of the finger. *I fancy I am no Prince Naseem. I am a true prince. I am THE Prince.* The London lord ripped the nickname right off the lad from the slums of Sheffield. Like a Redcoat carrying out a search and seizure.

And Franco would have to match dukes with the duke in London. It was a make-or-break match for the up-and-comers. The winner on the fast track to superstardom. The loser to go from fledgling to flailing.

Franco was feeling good, his Juicy dreams right on track, as he had his first interview at the weigh-in. The reporter, who reminded him of Julie, asked him what the hardest part of preparing for the fight was.

"Uh. Gettin a passport," deadpanned Franco.

The bantam beauty guffawed. *Just like me Julie,* thought the Ali G fan as his mind drifted back across the Atlantic.

Franco prided himself on running to the cage in a rage. Fuck the walk. Fuck the hop step. Let's fuckin do this. Once there, he'd continue to run and circle. A pitbull marking his territory. For four or five laps. But he barely finished one upon the arrival of The Prince. There was something about Franco's opponent as he hot-stepped down to the cage and swung his long legs over the edge. Something about the son of the medalist mother in the front row draped in jewels.

Jewels. Franco's own Jewels was across the Atlantic with a front-row seat to her mother's hospital bed. And looking after T. And on-call for work of course. But a win would change all that.

Still, it was something else about the son who had his father and fourteen other Saudis on hand to lend a hand. Something else about the royal with the regal shoulders and behemoth bank account. *And* the gift of good looks to boot. Like he grew up with a genie that granted him unlimited wishes. *Something* about it all. Something Franco couldn't quite figure that day. Something else that halted him as he copped a look at The Prince and his copper eyes. His eye-popping muscles. As he popped in his corner. Like a rocket ship about to takeoff.

In his pre-fight interview, The Prince was asked if he would look to lean on his Jiu-Jitsu to take away Franco's edge as a slugger. The Prince sneered at the notion that Franco had any edge at all. *I fancy I'll smoke the bloke in round one. Take a vacation in Jersey. The real one. The dog's bollocks. Not the "New" one. The one that smells like a dog's bollocks.*

When the round-one bell rang, smoking the bloke is exactly what The Prince sought to do. Franco was an aggressive fighter. One who came forward, unafraid to engage. The Prince was a fighter who preferred to counter. Preferred to let his opponents do all the work. Lay out their own rope. Then hang them with it.

But for Franco, The Prince made an exception. He came forward. Darted from edge to edge. Hit Franco from various angles. Even with Franco's guard up, The Prince pinpointed jabs that sliced in like a lowercase i and dotted Franco's head. All at a speed Franco had never seen before. He had taken pride in his fists, but it was The Prince's causing fits. On top of the angles and the speed, The Prince had cutting combinations. Combinations that anticipated Franco's reactions. Like Franco was a brand-new Master Lock with the code still stuck on his chest. One The Prince spun into duress. He landed jab after jab. A cross here. A hook there. Franco's blood everywhere. The Prince had dialed up all the right numbers. But. The Master Lock refused to crack.

The bell rang. The home crowd cheered their emir's aggression. Still, the chap was chapped. The Prince swatted the water bottle out of his henchman's hand. Heel-kicked his stool. Stood with his hands on his hips. There, too, was something about the mauled man across the cage that made The Prince stare. The mauled man who should've fallen to the mat minutes ago. The mauled man with all of three guys in his corner. Them telling the mauled man in earnest that he was still in the fight. Could they bloody see his bloody face? Already the lad huffed and puffed. Already his face was cotton stuffed and puffed. Already the man was wrecked, The Prince reckoned.

Round two began with more of the same. Only The Prince's flurries never materialized into a blizzard. Flurries that were enough to cause a delayed opening, but not enough to cancel Franco's school day altogether. Flurries that were, instead, enough to make The Prince fatigued and frustrated.

Franco absorbed the combinations and finally sent back some blows of his own. He'd weather a flurry then bomb back with a snowball. Quality over quantity. Then the avalanche. The Prince was too busy attacking to take proper note of Franco switching his stance. Franco informed him with a right hook that split his eye open. A hook that both blurred The Prince's vision and made the judges see more clearly. And when Franco took an angle outside The Prince's narrowed periphery and dropped him with an elbow, the judges' vision was 20/20. Round two was Franco's.

The Prince backpedaled. In a hurry to find fence before he fell on his bum like some Jersey bum. He landed somewhere in between—one-hopped off his arse and bounced up off the cage.

Despite the punishing blow, The Prince went on the offensive. Franco shook his head. *Should've dropped him.* Still, he kept The Prince at bay and took the round. He went to his corner with the match all tied up.

As Franco sat in his stool, he liked his chances in the third and final round. Momentum was on his side. As he hyped himself up, Taz wiped him down. Joey urged him to fight his fight. *Keep dictating the action.* Then Nelly reminded him of patience. Like he was Phil Jackson.

The Prince's corner meanwhile was quite cantankerous. His father Hakeem put his paws on his refusing-to-sit son. Pushed him onto his stool. The imposing Saudi had enough of the gaudy. "Stop trying to knock heem out! Do you hear me?"

The Prince looked away. Scowled as he fought being toweled.

The sultan swatted his son's face like he was the Sultan of Swat. That got the message through. Americans. Trying to talk to their little ones until they're blue in the face. *Hagh!* No wonder they're so spoiled. Hakeem meanwhile spoiled his son with a plot to take the fight. The Prince looked up at his baba. Took in every word. Like a baby drinking his baba.

As they marched out for the final round, Franco was confused by the conflicting advice from Joey and Nelly. So he, too, turned to advice from family. Uncle L. Tellin him, "Mama Said Knock You Out."

Franco worked toward the song's climactic hook with a series of hooks. But he couldn't quite land a haymaker. He angled in closer—whack. The Prince's kick took Franco's leg out from under him.

Franco found himself fighting from his least favorable position. On his back. From the guard.

The Prince mounted him like a London bobby mounting his horse. He worked the reins and tried to submit his steed any which way. Franco barely broke the arm bar attempt. Barely slipped out his tri when The Prince tried a triangle. Between each attempt, The Prince worked in some ground and pound. But when the London bobby went for a kimora, his bronco finally bucked him.

Franco got up and again went right after The Prince. Like 50 Cent and Tony Soprano once said, *I am what I am.* To keep The Prince guessing, Franco mixed in some kicks. He landed a kick to the calf here. A kick to the knee there. Kept The Prince off guard enough to mix in some jabs. Put the fight back to a toss-up.

Franco then shot on The Prince. Put him on his back. More easily than anticipated. Franco didn't even have to go down with him. The Prince looked content to lay on the canvas all night. Two minutes left and he's lying there like a turned-over turtle. Franco had yet to see anything like it. This turned-over turtle he should've left for roadkill. To be run over by the judges' cards.

Franco then got distracted by another animal altogether. The boo birds that infested the London arena. Franco imagined the booing crowd as a horde of angry soccer hooligans. Hooligans who put up their hard-earned pay only to get a shit show. Franco circled The Prince. Tried to work in past the gangly palace gates. For a clean shot to the crown. The clock winding down. Franco angled in farther. Dropped a couple hammers. Then got caught up in The Prince's scissors. Franco had slipped the slightest bit. On a mixture of the very blood and sweat he beat from The Prince. Or. From the very blood and sweat left in the wake of a cunning snake.

The Prince's legs went taut as they taught Franco a lesson. *Don't fancy me for a turned-over turtle. Or any other reptile I reckon. I'm a Venus flytrap.* The flytrap from another planet twisted Franco to the ground. Twisted on Franco's ankle. Twisted as Franco refused to submit. Twisted as the winner of the third round twisted. Twisted as the trajectory of Franco's entire life twisted. Twisted until the pop at the bell.

Franco didn't even need to hear the announcement. That The Prince won by a split decision. As Franco lay there with a split ankle. Just two minutes ago, he had the win wrapped up. As the EMTs strapped Franco to the stretcher, it looked as if his career was wrapped up. Franco would never forget the date. Saturday, September 8, 2001.

Franco was laid up in a London hospital for the next few days. He spent the time outside of surgery sleeping and staring at the specks in the ceiling tiles. Counting the craters as his career cratered. He finally got so homesick that he turned on the TV. Tuesday. Another day he would never forget.

The damage done that day lingered in Franco's ligaments seven years later. Nonetheless, Franco was ranked number ten once again. After seven years of sideways like he was Paul Giamatti. Worse than sideways if he was being honest. He was post-surgery. Post-prime. Post-divorce. And on the final fight of his contract.

The last time Franco was sitting at ten, The Show had given him a shot to turn into a top contender. This time? It was a kiss of death match. The Show had their young stud, Rafael Barbosa, all set for his own pop at The Prince. All Barbosa had to do was fly into Newark and blow away some local bum they called The Bunns Lane Brawler. Then, after the fight, the victorious Barbosa could call out the headlining Prince and create some bad blood that would fuel the next Pay-Per-View. The Show wasn't doing Franco any favors by putting him on the Newark card. They were sending a hitman to bury him in the swamps of Jersey.

But The Bunns Lane Brawler had other plans. He had plans of pulling a Micky Ward, who after many setbacks, reached the fight game's highest award. Franco had made big changes since his fight with The Prince. As soon as his plane landed back at Newark in the wake of the chaos caused by 9/11, he took his loser's purse and went right to the top Jiu-Jitsu academy in the area. (Before that, an instructor had been coming to the high school mats to teach Franco the basics. Didn't even make 'im take off his Asics.) The owner, Bobby Bogans, tried to cast him off. At least till Franco got his cast off. But Franco crutched over and folded himself in a folding chair. And watched.

If Franco had ever seen a genius, it was Bobby Bogans.

Fuck that nerd Francis Freeman that—or *who* as that fuck would tell Franco—locked himself in his room for four years until he knew how to spell every word in the dictionary. Then rubbed it in to fifth-grade Franco when he bounced him in a spelling bee. Bobby was a born genius. From his flipper-sized feet to his mile-long legs to his concrete core to his almond eyes to the top of his bald brown dome. A genius from Bunns Lane who didn't discover his ability until his 20s. Bobby came up as a track runner (the only sport he could afford) and a self-defense fighter (the only way he could afford to survive on Bunns Lane). He had looked out for little Franco on the Lane. Until Bobby ghosted the day after his high school graduation. Never even bragged about going to Fort Bragg. Served eight years for the country that served him Section Eight. He came back and tagged along to a Jiu-Jitsu tournament with an army buddy. Bobby entered on a whim. And walked away with a win.

He worked graveyards in the graveyard as he honed his Jiu-Jitsu. Until about 32. When he was so fuckin brazilliant they started calling him Bobby Brazil. The African-American with the South American name. Teaching an art from Asia. By 35, Bobby had fulfilled his father's wishes of being a man who could stand on his own two feet. By opening a business tying people up with his own two feet. He never once lamented what might have been. If it was a different situation he came up in. He loved what he did. Had his academy open around the clock. Yet he'd always say he hadn't worked a day since he dug his last ditch. Not to mention he had found a channel for all his professional fighting ambitions. The kid from the Lane. Who came to him. Saying fuck the crutches. Let's do some clutches.

And there Franco was in '08 circling Coach Nelson. Sizing up the coach only seven years his senior. With a bit more height and hulk. A gorilla as they'd call him in the Jersey clubs. Not that the Ninth would go to one. Between the AD job, the family of five, and all the coaching and community service, Coach Nelson barely had enough time for the fighter before him. He batted Franco's head with bare hands that felt like bear hands. Tried to knock Franco off-kilter and set up the kill.

Franco's lead ankle was ailing. If only he could borrow the legs of the brick shithouse before him. Built upon behemoth calves that only God could give. Of course God was good to Coach Nelson. He had been good to God. Good to The Wood. Good to his family.

Franco switched his lead leg from right to left to alleviate the ankle. He took the opportunity to surprise Woodbridge's archangel as he shot from a new angle. Coach Nelson sprawled. His tree-trunk legs planted roots as deep as his family's. He tried to bear hug Franco at the hips. But Franco dove even deeper. Like a sub on the hunt for Red October. He torpedoed in. Scored a direct hit.

Nelly scrambled to his feet. Upped the aggression. Pawed at Franco's head. Grabbed at his arms. Deked forward.

But when the bull charged, Franco sidestepped and hip-tossed him. A martial arts matador back at the height of his craft. Franco's fight was fifteen days away and couldn't come fast enough. Julie would be watching with T. He was sure of it.

At the current moment, though, someone else was looking for attention. The Frog had hopped in. The Frog with his Armani suit, Ferragamo boots, and pockets full of loot. To keep them full, he'd hired Franco. Fourteen years before. Told the kid from the closed-down restaurant he'd get him some temp work down the docks. Franco, the 19-year-old with the newborn, couldn't be more grateful. Of course he'd take the shifts. And yeah, sure, of course he'd do The Frog a favor.

The first favor was so fuckin easy. *Ay Franco. I gotta pick up an envelope, but I ain't got the time is all. You go get it. Keep a C-note for yourself.* Easiest hundo Franco ever made.

But it's all about the comeback. Fourteen years later and The Frog is still coming back. "I need you down the docks."

Normally, Franco wouldn't mind getting down the docks. MMA was still finding its legs in the aughts. For the fifty fighters who made a living in the cage, there were five hundred ham n eggers who could barely afford ham n eggs. Five hundred ham n eggers on day jobs. Busting up buildings. Busting up bar fights. All busting their humps. All in the name of getting in the cage and busting someone else's. At that moment, that's exactly what Franco wanted to focus on.

The Frog kicked back against a padded gym wall. Watched as a brother bouncing through the halls popped his head in. *"Nelly!"* called the brother with a deep voice and a departing peace sign. *Nelly.* What a joke. When The Frog went to school, they called their coach—the current one's father—Coach Nelson. Always. Over the years it had devolved to Coach. Or Nelson. Or, at the very least, Coach Nelly. Now? Just...*Nelly.* Same name as that clown rapping with the Band-Aids on his face. The Frog could practically hear Thomas Nelson the First turning over in his grave.

The Ninth meanwhile gave the kid a wave and took Franco aside. The veins in his neck bulged like a sequoia come to life. His beet-red head a volcano ready to blow off his buzz cut. Like Franco was Beavis and he was Buzzcut. "The heck you think Barbosa is doing right now?"

"Got my roadwork in. Got some good mat work in."

"While you're down at the docks doing whatever the heck you're gonna be doing, Barbosa is gonna be practicing seven ways to submit you."

Franco couldn't look Coach Nelly in his emerald eyes. Fuckin things looked like they were gonna shoot lasers. Franco looked down at Coach's paws. On his hips as he sweated through sweats. Waiting on a response. Franco clocked the clock. If he left now, it'd be too early to catch T. Franco then snuck a glance at The Frog.

The Frog's Ferragamoed foot rested against the padded gym wall as his gold medallion rested against his chest hair. His cavernous eyes cruised the cave of a gym. Save for the glance at his Rolex that took place at the exact moment Franco glanced over. The Swiss watchmaker wasn't the only one with precision timing.

Franco's eyes sunk even lower. To Coach Nelly's red Nikes. "I'll get a workout in tonight. Tomorrow gonna get an extra throw with Yo. Right now, I gotta get down the docks."

The wrestling session was over. And it was The Frog who scored the final takedown.

TRACK 3. THE KID

TJ (AKA T) WALKED the streets that same wicked winter day. Concerned about his beef with Ray. His journey began not on Bunns Lane but on the other side of town. TJ now lived at the same house Julie grew up in. The one on Bucknell Ave she had boomeranged back to. With T in tow and without Franco.

TJ wiped freezing rain from his eyes as he walked down Rahway Ave alone. Far removed from his old friends on his old side of town. He strolled past apartments that arose out of the swamps of Jersey. Past the vinyl-sided Marco's Hair Hut. Where TJ would nod with approval despite the butcher job by ole Marco Soto. Cutting hair like he was playing Marco Polo. TJ walked past the little church with the little congregation and the little sign that read: *Ye shall be born again.* Wasn't reincarnation only for Hindus? TJ then wondered what he'd turn into after Ray stomped him to death. Hopefully a bull. If it wasn't all bull.

The five-foot 14-year-old freshman wanted to think about anything but what lay ahead. Ray threatening he was fuckin dead. So TJ's mind drifted, as it often did, to when he was a kid. To 1998. When life was great.

It wasn't just him, right? All of America was doing better back in '98. The peace. The prosperity. The country was doing so good, in fact, that all anyone worried about was Slick Willie's willy. Then again, Pac and Biggie didn't make '98. That's the thing about the streets, TJ figured. Always gotta watch your back on the streets. At least 2008 TJ wasn't worried about handguns. Just Ray's guns. Those buffed-up biceps. Choked by chain link ink. On a dude six-two without shoes.

So as the winter wind blew TJ down the block, his mind blew back. He felt like he had the perfect childhood. *Childhood.* He loved that word. When he heard it, a highlight reel of images ran through his head. He saw his memories from a distance. Like they were out-of-body experiences. Was that magic? He didn't know. The time was.

TJ's first image: Franco and Julie. Each of them holding one of TJ's hands. Standing on the Seaside boardwalk in front of one of those balloon dart games. Sun shining down on their smiling faces. Franco and Julie were only 23 at the time. Older adults adored the young couple taking the kid for the day. The cool young aunt and uncle. Getting some practice in. That little boy standing between them. Wearing the Yankee cap. Squinting in the summer sun. Smiling his missing-tooth smile. He couldn't be theirs. He was. Before anyone could even imply accident, they'd call him their miracle.

Dad's hair—faded to a shave on the sides no doubt—glistened in the summer sun. A few curls higher than the others as if they were little masts atop the *SS Franco.* Atop aviator shades copped for a copple dollars. Ray could ban the sun but not knockoffs, Dad would joke. His smile accentuating his chiseled jaw. Softening his hardened look.

TJ cringed as he trekked up the trestle over the tracks. *Ray-Bans*. If only they'd ban Ray. Back to back in the day. Those Seaside summer days. Even Mom would be tan. Darker yet was her long hair that dangled down, constantly threatening to pop her bubble butt.

Franco would slip his arm around her waist and give her a squeeze. Then say what he liked most about her, with his hand in front of his own chest, was her big...heart. He'd use that one if he wanted to see her smile. The one she kept hidden. Cuza the front tooth gap that revealed her social gap.

And if Dad really wanted to win the A-student over, he'd say her most beautiful body part was her brain. Although TJ suspected Dad had her brain number two to her eyes. Franco was always saying how hers put his own to shame. Those haywire hazel jobs he had. A smattering of brown, blue, gray, green. A blotchy battlefield where Franco's entire ancestry met. Fighting for survival.

Julie meanwhile had big blues that, from little TJ's vantage point, took up half her head. Especially on days down the shore. When the summer sun would shrink her pupils to pepper. Inflate her irises to blue moons. Blue moons that, off the ocean's reflection, would turn turquoise. It was a day like that that Franco came up with his nickname for Julie. His Jewels. Cuz she had one in each eye.

Meanwhile, 2008 TJ's big browns batted as he cut away from the cutting wind. Into the clay pits. A wooded patch once home to Woodbridge's clay economy. TJ had learned in fourth grade about the shift from farming to industry in the late 1800s and how the Woodbridge clay pits were the basin for the manufacturing of millions of tons of bricks that built Newark, Elizabeth, and beyond. The bricks that built The Bricks. Must've been pretty good bricks, too. Local brick houses still stood stout as ever. Still, TJ preferred the clay pits' current function. A haven of kid bike jumps, teen fire pits, and adult magazines.

TJ hobbled down uneven terrain onto the soaked soccer field. He hopped puddles. Mucked through mud. Grasped for grass. He continued onto campus, wishing like hell it was back in the day. But all he saw was Ray. Wearing a T despite the cold day. Chain link ink on full display. So back went TJ. To back in the day.

The second image from TJ's memory: Franco's brand-new blue '98 Mustang. The sparkles in the fresh factory paint. The alloy wheels. The Armor-All'd tires. In the ten years following, TJ came to know that Franco didn't care much for material shit. But he splurged on that Mustang. TJ eventually figured that Franco got it for what it stood for. Whether he realized it or not. American made. Tough and fast. Meant for the streets. No hood ornament. No bells. No whistles. No bullshit. It was Franco's Ferrari. No. To Franco, it was better than a fuckin Ferrari.

Franco told TJ on one of them lazy boardwalk strolls that he could afford it because he was getting a lot of dock work back then. And once Franco, fresh off his first wins, started figuring the fight money in his future...*forgetaboutit.* He'd rap along to Biggie blasting out of a t-shirt shop, strut along the planked wood, and tell TJ, *It's allll good.*

Save for the Mustang's expired meter. A sentimental reminder to TJ that the family was too busy having fun to get back on time. Julie would work herself into a panic over the expired meter as they doubled back on the boards. She always knew what time it was, even before her first cell phone. The sun's directly overhead on a July day, it's about 1:15. The lifeguards are packing up, it's 4:00. The rides are lighting up the night something special, it's 9:00. Time to get to the car.

Julie would drag TJ as her flip flops clacked along to her little strides. Franco would trail behind, telling her, *Relax. It's a beautiful night. Have a soft serve.* Soft serve sounded good to TJ, so they'd outvote her. Then Dad wouldn't even get one! That cracked little TJ up. TJ and Mom would chow down on their half-orange *(arr-inge)*, half-vanilla *(vanella)* custard cones while the fledgling fighter fasted. Then they'd all cram into a photo booth and get a strip of four photos. It would start with Julie giving an annoyed look at Franco. The next two would be snapshots of them tickling and hugging the ice cream-mustached TJ. The last would be one of Franco and Julie kissing. The top half of TJ's mug poking into the picture.

One time, they slipped out of Seaside at sunset. Cruised over the Tunney-Mathis at magic hour. Cabin cruisers cut through the Barnegat below. The cottage-clustered coastline lay ahead. Backlit by an amber sky. Little TJ would swear he was in the Mediterranean for a minute. While the moment moved Dad to music,

> *Forget Vegas n all the lights*
> *Miami n those white hot nights*
> *Just gimme a summer*
> *In Seaside Heights*

TJ would ask Franco where those lines came from. Franco said he couldn't remember where he'd heard it. TJ knew. Franco heard it in his own head. It was born in his bones. A hereditary trait that just waited for the right moment to reveal itself.

They'd sail away from Seaside, hit the Parkway to the Turnpike, and head back to The Bricks. To TJ's third image from his memory: the cloud maker. A mass of vats and pipes on the edge of town. Dad would park the Mustang in an abandoned lot. Franco and Julie would sit in lawn chairs and tailgate. A stemmed plastic cup of *pinaht griggeo* for her. (Pinot Grigio wasn't on Julie's high school vocab lists.) For Dad, it used to be a Bud Light. Then H2Only when he started to fight. Readying for his own plane to take off as they looked up at the underbellies of those landing in Newark. Like a couple of deep-sea divers admiring great whites. TJ meanwhile would sit "Indian style," as he learned it back then, on the hood of Franco's Mustang. And watch those pipes pump brand-new clouds into the clear blue sky.

Days so clear Franco, Julie, and TJ could make out the Twin Towers. They'd gaze at the beacons of the far-off land. Like the Scarecrow, Dorothy, and the Tin Man staring upon Oz. Only Franco, Julie, and TJ had no intention to go. They already had it all.

TJ would follow his parents across the lot for a better look. He'd look up at Franco and Julie in front of him. Two side-by-side silhouettes in the sun. So big. So strong. So indestructible. His very own Twin Towers.

TJ now walked toward another tower altogether. Worst fuckin part about it, he didn't even know why Ray had it in for him. Did TJ say the wrong thing? Do the wrong thing? Was Ray jealous? Of TJ's raps? His good grades? Maybe Ray was just fuckin bored. Whatever which way, the worst part of it all was that TJ was rolling up alone.

Five-year-old TJ could've sworn he'd be walking to high school one day with Lance, Blanco, and Alp. The old Oak Ave Army—TJ having joined as the Bunns Lane Boy from around the block. An army whose mission was to play football at the park. Ride bikes until dark. Hit the candy store on a lark. The little Yankees would then head back to the barracks and watch the Yankees. Or the G-Men. Hell, they were so indiscriminate, they'd also root for the Mets and chant for those J-E-T-S. Cooling since kindergarten. Four precocious kids blessed with book and street smarts. The witty kids in class who knew it all. Then concluded it was all a fuckin joke. The kind of kids who, in kindergarten, were inspired to name themselves the Oak Ave Army after hearing the self-proclaimed name of a clan of kids on one of Franco's CDs. From the black nylon case forever between his Stang's bucket seats. The CD about a clan of kids from right across the river. In Staten Island. Or as the precocious kids on the CD called it, and thus the precocious kids in kindergarten called it, Shaolin. The good old Oak Ave Army. The kind of kids capable of great success. Or great failure.

But nah, Mom had to flunk Franco and take TJ across town. Worse, TJ couldn't even fuckin hang out with his old Oak Ave friends when he got to school.

Lance was the first one to bail. After eighth grade, he signed up for St. Joe's. Home to Jay Williams and other hoop pros. TJ figured it was to play basketball. When he found out over slices at the mall. Lance was the best baller in their rec league—the best league around considering their middle school had no athletic teams whatsoever. But nah, Lance told TJ he was gonna play lacrosse. Then explained to TJ what the fuck lacrosse was. Some sorta soccer meets hockey ultimate white boy shit. Lance was gonna cross over into it like he was the next Serena Williams. The next Tiger Woods. Lance's dad, a local insurance broker, which made him Warren fuckin Buffet in TJ's mind, had masterminded it all. He was going to be the next Richard Williams. The next Earl Woods. He led Lance to the light. Explained that Lance wasn't gonna be just another B-level baller when he could be an A-plus Ivy League lacrosse recruit. Only problem was, the local high school lacked lax. So Lance was off to St. Joe's. TJ was down the first of his bros.

Alp meanwhile was at the same high school but over in honors classes. Though these classes existed somewhere in the halls of the high school, for all TJ knew, a "BLB" (Bunns Lane Boy) as he once overheard his middle school counselor refer to him as, the honors classes might as well have been on Mars. Alp was always all stressed out with assignments out the ass anyway. TJ would try to talk to him in the hall but Alp would just go on about how his parents were on his ass and how he had to get going. And his parents had set a high bar for Alp right from birth. They named him Abraham Lincoln Patel.

Then there was Blanco. Busy with Diverse Horizons. And its SAT tutors. Guest speakers. Intern opportunities. Him[3] and TJ would still say hi in the halls. Then TJ's white-as-a-ghost friend would ghost. Off to haunt his next meeting. TJ had tagged along recently and tried to join. But he got bounced on the account of his (unverifiable) color. Or lack thereof. Either way, TJ could care less. One less hassle.

Mom wasn't so smiley about the whole thing. Julie unshackled from her desk for her exactly thirty-minute unpaid lunch break which would give her exactly ten minutes to get over to the high school, exactly one minute to park, exactly eight minutes to talk to the principal, exactly one minute to leave, and exactly ten minutes to get back. She breezed into the office waiting area, dragged her son into Mr. Mulligan's office, and wondered aloud why the school wouldn't offer such good things to all of its students. When Mulligan gave her some jazz about white privilege, Julie cut him short. *TJ's not exactly the son of Daddy Warbucks. Furthermore, his father is diverse anyway.* But that was docked due to little orphan Frannie's lack of documentation.

---

[3] Or "He" as Blanco's tutor would stress.

Julie then jested about how it was marvelous that Marvin Miller's kid from the mansion on Maple gets to be in the program. Marvin Miller who turned his minimal time on the Minnesota Vikings into making a mint as a mutual fund marketer for Metuchen millionaires. Yeah, his kid really needed a break. *Give me one*, Julie jeered. When Mulligan gave a final go about white guilt, Julie went on about how the whites in Woodbridge weren't exactly the ones you saw on TV. Unless you were talking about *Roseanne*. Julie, the student Mulligan once gave the creative writing award on senior night for a poem she wrote, hit him with the words of another poet. About the poor whites in "Only a Pawn in Their Game." The poor white then concluded that white guilt must mean she was guilty of being white. With a sentence to be carried out by her son.

The warden could only shrug.

Frozen out from Lance, Blanco, and Alp, TJ walked in a freeze as cold as the Alps. The four kids with heritages from five continents, once brought together like Pangaea, were now broken apart. And there was no panacea.

As TJ rolled across the quad, he clutched the English paper rolled up in his hoodie pocket. He had bailed on a backpack after getting jacked for his Jansport. He had stayed late one day. To complete his tarea for Mrs. Barea. Then headed home alone. Hood rats who hung around school until one of their grandmoms picked them all up decided to kill time and live a little. They lifted the backpack off the little guy with one punch to the eye.

TJ learned his lesson. Less cargo, less of a target. It was all good, though. He'd always finish all his homework in study hall anyway. Except for those English papers from Miss Lane. Had to finish hammering those out at home. Still, balancing books and the streets was all no sweat. He was a double kid. Like Costigan in his favorite movie. *The Departed.*

TJ reached the hordes of high schoolers cooling in the cold. The latest ingredient to be dropped into a melting pot hot with hormones, homeboys, haters. Bookworms, athletes, skaters. White, black, Dominicun. Every race under the sun. One ethnicity blending into the next. The part-Irish kid looked like the part-Polish kid looked like the claims-to-be-all-Italian kid looked like the half-Greek kid looked like the Iranian-Indian kid looked like the majority-Mexican kid looked like the three-fourths-Filipino kid looked like the Chinese kid looked like the Turkish kid looked like the 100 percent Dominican kid (who was 100 percent part African, part European, and part New Worldean) looked like the "African-American" kid from Georgia looked like the neither African nor American kid from Georgia (the country) looked like the Puerto Rican kid looked like the ethnically Arabian religiously Christian mistakenly Jewish kid looked like the who-knows-who-cares kid looked like the aforementioned part-Irish kid and on and on and on and. However much time they spent making that Michael Jackson "Black or White" video, they could've shot it outside TJ's high school and been done before the morning bell.

Ill Co, a cohort of about twenty street kids, claimed the concrete by the auditorium entrance. Metro and rugged as all hell. "Wood Zoo" and other ill shit shaved in their heads. Ice in ears, grills in teeth, shaved lines in eyebrows. Hoodies and flat brim caps. Girls with teased-up hair, tiny jackets, exposed midriffs. Straight-up gangsta gals, too. Hoodies and haggard teeth. Dudes slap-boxing, breaking, skating. Girls gossiping, flirting, spading.

Ray and TJ belonged to opposite ends of the Ill Co spectrum. Ray and his big dog bite. Always down to fight. TJ and his little dog bark. Those raps he'd spark.

TJ figured he had three allies in Ill Co. The first was UN, whose heritage rivaled that of the entire Oak Ave Army. His IQ not so much. His sword-tipped sideburns were hella, doe. TJ could only manage a fist bump with his beefy boy who was busy running a high-stakes spades hand of his own. A doughboy focused on dough, boy.

TJ's second ally was an ally by proxy. A friend of UN's who therefore fucked with T. Screws. A 19-year-old fifth-year who once drank a fifth before fifth period. His Elmer's skin stood in stark contrast to his coarse black hair. His hairline so low, it turned his forehead into a threehead. Always a day unshaven, too. Looking like someone threw a pocket full of pepper at his paste face. TJ tried to make eye contact with Screws, but Screws was busy sneaking drags from the lit cigarette cupped in his hand. He was the fuckin man.

Dragon, the third of TJ's allies, swooped in. "You got that rhyme ready?" said Dragon with hopeful hickory eyes. Set below the illest haircut TJ had ever seen. A frohawk dyed red and shaped into triangles. Dragon's mane.

"I don't know..." T mumbled before his bro. "Should work on it some more."

"Work it out then," snarled Dragon.

TJ snuck a glance at Ray. The big dog was already doggin him. The A-Rod fan's flat brim Yankee hat and chinstrap facial hair merged into one. The headbreaker's helmet. His beef busting out of his T as he grilled T. Fuck the cold. And the kid before him.

There was Dragon. Nodding for his boy to bust a rhyme. There was Ray. Grilling T like he was George Foreman. Torn by each guy, T had to break the tie. He looked to Lenore. Five four. Poofed hair and hoop earrings. A cheek mole so endearing. And that caboose crammed into white capris. T could drop to his knees. Then a wind swell. The smell of her

Chanel. *Mmm.* Fuck Ray. T's about to slay.
"Yo."
Dragon cut the music on the breakers' boom box.
"Yo."
All eyes on T. His own bronzes narrowed. In search of silver and gold. Below spikes tilted forward like a million bayonets. But there was no army. Just a lone wolf. Ready to howl. "Yo. Listen up.

> *This town'll*
> *Knock ya socks off*
> *Blow ya hair back*
> *Like ya did two-twenty in a Maybach*
> *Exited on*
> *Amboy Avenue*
> *Seen shit you never knew*
> *Existed*
> *Asian Marines enlisted*
> *White dudes digging ditches*
> *Homies double-shifting*
> *Buncha punch the clockers*
> *Take they pain*
> *Stuff it in hurt lockers*
> *Dogs with no dish*
> *All barkin*
> *Tryin to roll ten*
> *Land on Free Parkin*
> *This New York overflowed sloppily*
> *Welcome to Wood Zoo*
> *The purple monopoly."*

Everybody OHHHHHED over T's verse. Errrbody. Save for Ray.

Dragon handshake-hugged T. Hopped on the verse. "Uh—

Landin on Boardwalk the best
Ho rentin out her community chest
But we in jail not a guest
Bunch of Woodbretians
A new breed
Fuck the Phoenicians—"

Then. The sting of the bell ring. For that moment, for that single fuckin moment, TJ had it made. Was sharing smiles with Lenore. Rhymes with Dragon. Now? Everyone bailed from the yard as the sleet came back hard.

Like a gentleman, Ray held the door open for Ms. Wayfe. "After you." Then turned to the last kid trying to creep in. "Bumpin into me, son?" Boom. Ray backed TJ up with punch to the chest.

T's adrenaline jumped—bladder almost pumped. The last of four friends from five continents. Concerned with incontinence.

"What's your hoodie say? Zoo York? Corny-ass bitch."

"Sorry Ray, gotta bump." TJ winced. *He's* the one that's gotta apologize.

"Shirt's too big for a little bitch." Ray wrangled TJ by the hood of his sweatshirt. Ripped it off.

"Come on, R—"

Ray jabbed TJ in the throat. Settled the collar of TJ's hoodie around his own throat. And Ray had to say. He looked good in gray. He felt the paper in the pocket. "The fuck is this doing in my hoodie?" The ripped fella ripped it up. Made sure to toss it in recycling. Because he was a gentleman like that. Although on his way in, he did forget to

43

leave the door open for TJ.

The late bell rang as TJ pulled on the door. Fuckin automatic locks. He beat feet through the sleet.

TJ flew through the main entrance of the old school, down its cinder-blocked halls, and up its plastic-coated stairs. TJ turned the rusted knob of a classroom door that creaked open. Interrupted Miss Lane's lecture from the overhead projector. TJ once again garnered *ohhhhhs*.

Miss Lane lowered her glasses. Gave T and his soaked T a long look. *Hood rat*, she thought but dare didn't say in these teacher-must-pamper-the-pupil times. If only it was the '70s and she could put the little punk in his place. Poke a finger in his face. Berate him before everybody. Or at least the early '90s. When she could pull a kid in the hall and let him know he's no good. Like she did with TJ's father. But even that was a no-no these days. Instead, she had to settle for, "A little light for the winter weather."

TJ would've loved to question Lane's own look. Her hair dyed blonde despite going gray years ago. Her reading glasses with the designer name noted on each side. *Subtly* noted, but you better believe it was there. Her frumpy dress that made her look like a character out of *Hamlet* or some shit. Like she was too good for The Wood or some shit. But the pupil could only sit. On the linoleum floor. Despite open seats. Reserved for special ed aides. As the cold wall of concrete. Received T's shoulder blades.

Miss Lane fired a-gain. "Do you have your essay?"

TJ's throat throbbed. He tried to talk—had to settle for a shake of his head. His line of vision toggled between charcoal chalkboards and washed-out windows. The universally accepted symbol for no.

Universally accepted save for Miss Lane. "I can't hear you."

TJ took a breath. Eked a hoarse, "No."

"Where is it?"

"Ho-home," submitted TJ.

"Oh snap! TJ just said, '*Ho, home!*'" noted his dear friend UN.

"Well." Miss Lane paused. Waited for all eyes on her. Like she was 2Pac dropping his fourth album. "I'll just call your mother."

More *ohhhhs.*

Miss Lane and her fuckin rough drafts. To be done in pen to improve penmanship. If it was a final draft, TJ's mom *could* print out a new copy and bring it in.

"Actually..." TJ debated telling the truth. Lane was not only his English teacher but also the advisor for Future Problem Solvers. A club that was invitation only. A club that Julie was on TJ's ass to join. Especially after the Diverse Horizons fail. TJ looked to his homies, Dragon and UN. Considered mustering the courage to put it all out there. Then. He looked to Lenore's elbow partner. The one with his arm around her seat back. Her partner not only in the class but apparently elsewhere, too. The one with the gray hoodie. And that grilling look. *I fuckin dare you.*

"I didn't do it," admitted TJ.

TRACK 4. DOCKED

AS TJ ARRIVED at school wanting to be anywhere but there, Franco approached planes leaving Newark headed anywhere but there. Wiseguys around town would joke that the opening of *The Sopranos* follows Tony getting the fuck away from Woodbridge. Take the Turnpike North from Woodbridge, you'll do exactly what he does. Drive past the oil tanks. Past planes taking off from Newark. Past the toll booth and off to greener pastures. The made man who made it, man.

Only Franco took a different exit. Into the swamps of Jersey swamped with infrastructure. Exit 13. (*Of course it was 13*, Franco figured long ago.) He headed for the expansive harbor area known as The Port.

The conglomerate added up to one of the largest on the Atlantic with annual containers numbering in the millions. Cargo valued in the billions. As Franco's car slipped toward his slip, he imagined The Port as the mouth of America. The harbor lips opened to the ocean. Let in freighters like an endless supply of supper. The cranes then carved up cargo like incisors mincing meat. Meat that was packed into eighteen-wheelers and stuffed down asphalt esophagi. Off to feed and fatten all of Uncle Sam.

When Franco pulled in past the checkpoint, he was still holding out hope that it was for a day of dock work. The average longshoreman would tell you machine operators had it made. Whether working a crane, a truck, or a forklift, the machine was the muscle. The run-of-the-mill runners had it okay. Tie up a ship. Uncover some cargo. Gauge some gauges. Then there were the backbreakers. The truck loaders. The hull hosers. The mess moppers. Franco was a backbreaker. A temp backbreaker without a pension or benefits to boot.

Fourteen years and Franco was still filling in. Fourteen years of taking every and any shit shift while everyone else called out and went on paid vacation. Fourteen years of midnights. Zero-degree days. Hundred-degree days. (Which were even worse. Any longshoreman will take zero over a hundred hands down.) Downpours. Sunpours. Christmases. Fourth of Julys. Emergency shifts of sorting through maggot-infested meat. Raking up rat shit. Working next to guys getting double the time and half the supervision. All by choice. All for the fight game. So he could take his leaves without losing his job.

The other longshoremen got a kick out of Franco. They'd watch a game at the Elks back in The Wood, drink, and bullshit about what's good. They'd say Franco was the only fuckin guy that liked doin the fuckin job no matter the fuckin day no matter the fuckin weather. And how the fuck could he like it so much? Not only was it a fuckin hump buster to begin with, Franco got all the worst fuckin shifts. Franco would respond by asking if they all suffered from a speech impediment. Fuckitis. It was easier than telling them what he really thought. That they were the true heroes. All in on the gig. All in on socking away college and retirement cash. Walking the line like they were Johnny Cash.

Franco in '08, meanwhile, was starting to lose the gig altogether. The economy was in the toilet, and hours for temps were now few and far between. The hours Franco did get were thanks to The Frog. So there were the favors for The Frog. Pick up some pesos here. Prop up a poker night there. Rough up some roughnecks anywhere. No big deal. Franco figured the favors like the dock position. Temporary. All until he made it in MMA. A jack of all trades. Trying to master one.

Franco pulled into the dock parking lot. Had it really been ten years since he first entered a cage? *Ten years.* Fuck. Ten years since 23. His Michael Jordan year. When he was on top of the world. Married to the baddest B in the world. (He could never bring himself to call Julie the B-word.) Father to the cutest kid in the world. Clocking dough down the dock. The Frog's favors on lock. And. Embarked on creating the capstone that completed the Great Pyramid of Franco: Full-time fighter.

Now? Parking the same Mustang he bought back then. *Thirty*-three. His Larry Bird year. And it had been bleak. The Great Pyramid of Franco suffering a seven-year sandstorm. The broken ankle. The broken family. The broken bank account. The pyramid's capstone decapitated. And not only unsettled at 33, *less settled* than he was at 23. Living in reverse like he was Benjamin fuckin Button. Once he had wrapped his Jordan year, he had set his sights to 33. His Larry Bird year. The year he always had in mind when he imagined his future. Imagined down to a single image. A still shot of him with his arms around Julie and T. All smiling in front of a big-ass house in Bridgewater. Just kickin it. Instead, life was doing the kicking. And on March 30, it would kick his ass another year down the curb. Thirty-four. His fight set for the night before.

Franco moseyed over to his slip where a handful of longshoremen stood and stewed at the locked entrance. Franco's skull-capped compadres exhaled cold breath. A brotherhood that looked nothing like brothers. Fat, skinny. Tall, short. Dark, light. They filled Franco in. A freighter of Colombian coffee was waiting to dock. Yet they were locked out.

Then the gate opened. The longshoremen were about to herd in when they heard the officer. On a megaphone from the lead car of a police escort. Droning about how the dockworkers were not permitted onto the slip and to please step aside. The borough police, under orders of the slip owner, had to escort in the newly hired help. The newly hired help packed into a burgundy Astro Van. Its occupants nodded at Franco for the second time that day.

Franco bit his lip. *Fuck.* What a Lemony Snicket. Franco had no idea who the fuck Lemony Snicket was, but that's what he called a series of unfortunate events. Never saw the movie but caught the commercial a couple thousand times. And labeling a shitty situation something silly helped take the sting out of it.

None of the docked dockworkers noticed the nods to Franco. They were too busy shouting—*How am I gonna feed my family! Fuckin illegals!*—as they shook the van.

"Can you believe these fucks?" croaked The Frog, having hopped up the highway behind Franco.

Franco was pissed no doubt. Felt bad for his fellow longshoremen no doubt. But he also remembered when he was 18 and needed a job. He walked into the old C——'s on Route 1 over by Woodbridge Mall. Got made waiter like that.

Walked right into the gig slinging food alongside middle-class college kids. Carry some trays around. Listen to the surround sound. Bang a shot with the bartender. Trade shifts, bullshit, count tips. It was nice in the front. But Franco spent just as much time in the back. Helped out with the dishes when it was slow. With the grunts in the fluorescent lit, steaming, ' stinking kitchen. Backbreaking work back there. Cleaning cauldrons. Frying food. Bleaching bathrooms. And who was doing it? "Mexicans." Every single one of them. It was funny to Franco. No one in the front gave a shit about their great jobs while everyone in the back took great care with their shit jobs. People with seniority back there. One day off a week. Supporting families whether they be in an overcrowded apartment in Avenel or in another country altogether. Working their culos off just to survive.

Franco stood frozen as he sucked on the Lemony Snicket.

The Frog meanwhile had plenty to croak about. "Fuckin illegals. Takin our jobs. *Our jobs.*" The Frog's lower jaw protruded as he watched the Mexicans roll onto his fuckin docks in his fuckin country in an American fuckin van escorted by American fuckin authorities. American authorities that closed the 20-foot barbed wire fence on him. *Him!* The kid that came up with nothing. Held his hand over his heart for every salute since kindergarten. Coached Little League. Community organizer for events year-round. Paid every last local, state, and federal tax dollar. Donated to troops in Iraq *and* Afghanistan. And now? The bombs were being dropped on him.

Franco looked past the fence. Past the laborers. To another person. Georgie Sachs, Jr. Aka Boy George. All of about 30. His baby face belied by a receding hairline that turned his forehead into a fivehead. The white whale was kept dry by an umbrella held by his bantam brown driver. They stood before some kind of stretch Mercedes Franco didn't know the name of.

The Frog rubbed his lucky 1955 D/S edition nickel. Thumbed over Thomas Jefferson like he was Tom Thumb. "And don't think it ends here. There's a domino effect. Everyone's wages. Our schools. Our healthcare. Taxes."

To Franco, the guys didn't look that different than the pictures he saw of the Newark project back in the '50s. The pictures of The Frog's one grandfather's side in the summer sun. In front of a brick slum. The Frog showed them to Franco once. He was always talkin about how they were real Americans who came here with nothing and thrived as a people. Integrated. Assimilated. His most recent rant had come over Tex-Mex at the hopping Tejada's.

Franco watched as Boy George waddled over to an escorted-in Escalade. Tinted on 22s. Franco had heard the stories from the old-timers. From back in the day when it was little Georgie's father's importing business. George Jr. would run around the docks in the summer. Gonzo would strain his body, thud down on one knee, find a dollar behind George Jr.'s ear. Miggy would look around the slip then slip little Georgie a Monopoly board that "bounced off a boat." The Mikes—black Mike White and white Mike Black—would swing Boy George by his arms and legs and pretend to throw him off the docks.

Well, Boy George was now all grown up. And he had bad news for his almost-retired buddies. Thanks to his shrewd vertical integration and multi-million-dollar investments in the area, he had full authority to operate his slip however he saw fit. (And being as that he had made so many millions off Mexicans in his restaurants and hotels, why not slip some over to his slip? But this part's just between you and Boy

George. Same for the part where George Jr., his father before, and their pocketed politicians all turned a blind eye as the "illegals" integrated. So keep it all under your hat if you don't mind. Boy George knows it's a lot. Hopefully you have a hat as big as Abe Lincoln's.)

The someone new Boy George was in business with stepped out of the back of the Cadillac. Like the Escalade, he was tall, dark, and handsome. Unlike the Escalade, he wasn't American made. Mr. TDH stood with his hands cupped at his crotch like a soccer player in wall formation. Cleated in alligator Guccis. Looking slick with his slicked-back hair. Put together in his slim-fit mocha suit. And his caramel tie broke the wardrobe tie with Franco's forestalled foreman. In fact, he was a step above the rung altogether. He spit commands in Spanish that lit a fire under his own foreign foreman who in turn got the Latino laborers going. Franco didn't know much about this mystery man. Except for one thing. He was some fuckin jefe.

The Frog turned to Franco. Not a word from his guy. Zip. Zero. Nada. "Hello? This ain't the news no more. This is your fuckin life."

Franco watched as the Mestizos got moving a mile a minute. As El Jefe and his foreman strategized. As the driver saw Boy George into the back of the stretch Mercedes. As his fellow longshoremen stood... *Locked out.*

The fucked-up situation busted Franco's brain so bad, he started having flashbacks. To those other battles he had as a boy on Bunns Lane. Playing chess with old Charles and his chestnut chessboard. Franco coulda swore he saw a king get escorted into the back of the Benz. A king who left someone with all of the moves of a queen in charge. A queen who hung back and strategized with a rook as they scattered their pawns about the front lines. Franco was hallucinating so bad...that next to him *stood a knight*. Was it dark or was it white? the Alice in Wonderland wondered. And that's when it dawned. Franco *too* had turned a pawn. You shoulda sawn. There were pawns all around. Just like the ones on old Charles's chess board. The ones first to get slayed in the fight. The ones that came in both colored and white.

When the pawn and the knight had to make way for the king's carriage, the pawn finally pawned up a response. "Fuckin Boy George. Like he unloaded all these boats all these years by himself." The pawn motioned to his fellow captureds. "Miggy shoulda never given him Monopoly. Shoulda given him cement shoes. And the Mikes shoulda tossed his ass in."

"We have to force Boy George's hand. Take away his options," said the knight. "Do something about these fuckin illegals."

Franco bit his lip back to reality. Toggled his creased face. Between the locked-out longshoremen and the Latinos laboring at breakneck pace. Toggled his creased face. Between a rock and a hard place.

The toad toed the line. "I'm sure all those guys over there are just great. Those guys who illegally entered our country and stole our jobs. But let me ask ya something. When I gave ya the ball. At the mound in our Little League championship game. Did ya lob any pitches in to the other team?"

"Nah."

"But I'm sure awl the kids on the other team were just great. Just a-okay," said The Frog with the appropriate hand gesture. "Life is a fuckin war. And it's time to pick a fuckin side."

Franco's toggling head landed on his fellow longshoremen. "What do you wanna do? Renegotiate? I'll take a pay cut," offered Franco the temp.

"Junior's bled us enough," said the foreman who made the salary of four men.

"You wanna picket? I'll be the first one here—"

"*Picket?* We got a better chance of playin the Pick-It." The Don grilled El Jefe across the way. "It's time we take the bull by the fuckin horns." The Don squared to Franco. "*KnowwhatImean?*"

Franco took a breath. Knew exactly what the fuck he meant. Meant he was asking Franco to get into some shit so crooked, he might never straighten out.

Franco gazed past the docks. Gazed at that fuckin hole in the sky. Where the Twin Towers once stood. Seven years later and *still* a hole there. But. Workers were in there prepping the foundation. Just like Franco rebuilding at the bottom of the MMA barrel. Ready to go sky high. So long as he could afford his next fight. Franco paid his team, his mortgage, and his child support like he was Ja Rule. Always on time. He turned to The Frog. "What do you want me to do?"

The Frog's jaw retracted like the roof of the Rogers Centre. "I'll meet you at your house tomorruh." The Frog stared at Franco. They were of the same stature. He smiled as he stuck a cig between his tobacco-stained teeth. Rapped as it flapped. "This nasty habit, huh? They start me on candy cigarettes when I'm six. Then tell me to cut it out when I'm 56. Thefuckoutofhere." He ran his pockets for a light. "Go ahead," said The Frog. With a friendly slap to Franco's face.

Franco hobbled in the wake of Benz taillights departing the docks.

Inside, Boy George was already on the phone dialing Dad. He told him all about how he was an excellent businessman that day. All about how he looked The Frog right in the eye, shook his hand, and thanked him for his service. And not only that. When he let The Frog know he was out of business with his crew and in business with the bargain basement one, Boy George didn't smile at all. Not even once. He even feigned disappointment as he shrugged and told The Frog his hands were tied. He was so proud, he hung up and popped a bottle of Dom Pérignon. Just a $500 bottle, though. It was only 9 am.

At least the knight left in a conundrum dark as night had found himself a light. A knight who, by rule, had the ability to make a first move himself. But why do that when you can push out a pawn? The knight lit his cig. Exhaled toxic air. Didn't dare leave his square.

Franco hobbled over to his blue beater. Precipitation always irritated the ankle. So he moved one step at time. Like one of them pawns on old Charles's chess board. Still. It was his cheek that really bothered him. The Frog's single slap somehow more irritating than all the pounding paws of Coach Nelly.

Franco was back to enjoying hands to his face later that day. His fancy footwork in the ring made the gym spin. A whirlwind of cinder blocks, broken clocks, abs full of rocks. Franco was whirling down to welterweight right on time. His turquoise tank soaked sapphire.

Boxing with Joey Yo. The only Puerto Rican Franco knew who went tanning. Half-Puerto Rican but still. His gelled-out curls hampered by headgear. The big man's only upper body coverage was the Puerto Rican and Italian flags—one etched on each shoulder. And TRUE JERSEY tatted across the Latino's lats. Franco's Boricua goomba would gleefully call himself a guido. He'd heard his old Italian uncles' diatribes about how it was derogatory. But they didn't get that it had become a culture. A badge of honor, even. Worn by everyone in guido nation from FBIs (full-blooded Italians) to Guindians (Guido Indians). They had taken the term and turned it on its head. Joey would say it was like what Cube and the rest of the crew did with the N in NWA.

Franco was light on his feet against the tan man. Had to be. Couldn't afford getting fitted with one of Joey's pipes. His homie was two bills and two percent body fat. Franco could have his way in MMA, but Yo knew how to throw. So comfortable, he gabbed as he jabbed. "Can't believe I lost that bet last night. Fuckin Coach K. Playin his white boys so much. They should call him Coach KKK."

Franco grinned—until Joey jabbed it away. "And the fuckin Cameron Crazies. They should come around here. Meet the Crazebey crazies."

Franco parried a flurry from Joey. Bounced back with a jab of his own. "That shoulda been your boxing name. The Keasbey Crazy."

"Fuck yo! You're right!" Joey went on the offensive. "Can't fuck with the Keasbey Crazy, son!"

The Bunns Lane Brawler met the Crazy's aggression as the two went toe to toe, blow for blow. Franco's favorite position. In the pocket. Trading rockets. Until the challenger blew up. Like when him and Joey were watching in fifth grade. When Mrs. V had to turn off the TV.

Joey cornered Franco.

Franco deked. Ducked. Uppercut.

"Oh shit. Barbosa better be ready!" Joey shook it off as Franco chased him around the ring. Feelin it.

Until a new challenger across the gym caught Franco's eye.

Julie. The straight-from-work manager ordered TJ to stay like a puppy in training. She then marched with her short hair and high heels over to the ring. Iced Franco out with her ice blue eyes.

"Oh shit. Sparring's over. Time for a real fight," said Joey as he hopped out of the ring. Added a departing "Wooo!" with the flair of Ric Flair.

Franco looked down to those frosted eyes. Goddamn did the last seven years harden his sweetheart. He didn't really wanna think about whose fault that was, so he cut to the chase. "What do ya want from me?"

"I got a call from Miss Lane."

"And that's my fault?" said Franco with a roll of his eyes as he rolled out of the ring.

"The apple doesn't fall too far."

"Right. Right. When he does good shit, he's your son. When he does bad shit, he's my son."

Franco watched as the little general crossed her arms. Napoleon in her pantsuit. The Emperor of TJ. She unfurled her arms and fired her weapon. A wagging finger that riddled Franco with insults. "He's your son when he spends his nights listening to that gangster rap garbage. Watching mafia movies. Hanging with hood rats. Doing who the hell knows what at school."

"What can I do for ya?"

"There's a storm coming."

When TJ turned two, Julie had finally gotten the chance to start taking college classes. Aced them all. Only the prospects for the 25-year-old mother from Local U weren't exactly the ones in the alternate universe she imagined. The alternate universe where she never met Franco and his wrong side of the track pack. The one where she went off to college and met the Brat Pack. Met boarding school kids like the one woman who actually cracked her company's executive board.

The energy company where 25-year-old Julie was a

customer service rep taking down ten bucks an hour. Listening to Jersey hotheads wonder why their goddamn bill was so high. *I know. Mine, too. Do you have a pool? Heaters can really run it up,* she'd say with a smile. And others wondering when they're gonna get their fuhkin powuh back. *No, I understand. You said you were a plumber? You know what it's like. When you get those disasters you work around the clock on. We've got our linemen double-shifted. Out there 24-7. We even brought some in from out of state. Sleeping in trailers we set up. I'll be here until midnight myself as a matter of fact. What's your number? I'll call you and let you know when our linemen are on the way.* Nine out of ten times, they called in as her sworn enemy and hung up as her old pal. Of course, one out of ten times even the Jewels couldn't calm em down. *Your company's a fuhkin joke. You're awl shit.* And her favorite. *They should drop a bomb on ya whole building.*

"Yeah, that would work wonders for the situation," Julie would joke with her right- and left-hand ladies. Alexis and Mercedes. As Julie did from the first time she took her seat and shook hands with them. "Oh look at my good fortune. I've always wanted a Lexus and a Mercedes." They'd looked out for each other ever since. Julie had Alex over for wine *(I've got pinaht noyer and pinaht griggeo)* whenever Alex was dumped by the local bros. She'd go to Mercedes' daughter's shows. *Better than Broadway!* guessed Julie as she showered Shanna Suggs with flowers and hugs. *Right, TJ?* And of course, Alex and Merce group hugging Julie at the church. Her mom in a hearse. Alex always offering double-date prospects to Julie. *This Friday?* Julie would say as she glanced at the most recent school picture pinned up at her desk. *I'm already taken.* Alex would catch her drift. *Handsome guy you've got there.* And just last week, Julie was scooped to that new high school program. By Merce. Horizons. Diverse.

The Lexus, the Jewels, and the Mercedes. Banking ten big ones an hour. Their riches found in each other. Right- and left-hand ladies in a sea full of them. Crammed into rows of desks like rats. Headsets strapped on like tagged tiger sharks. Doing the dirty work for the corner office crony. Part rat part tiger part shark. Julie's boss. Donald Harris. Or *Mr. Harris* as he required her to address him. Anything to hold his hegemony and his position in the good old boys' club. The one that carted him out from the Midwest to sit in on the Jersey subsidiary. And sit in he did. All goddamn day locked in his office in her hometown. With his radio on and the blinds down. (And don't even get Julie started on the corporate retreat. The allegations in Allegheny. Sex with his secretary. Twenty-seven and twenty-seven years younger.) Sitting there in his chair any time Julie brought an issue to his attention. Kicked back with his belly buttressing his BlackBerry. Like a Roman ruler with a bowl full of blackberries. *Well, what do YOU think we should do, Janie? That sounds good. Let's do that.* Then he'd cut her off when the thing on his belly started vibrating. Like he was radioactive. Then back to his radio and being inactive.

All to pay off the college debt from the distinguished school Julie went to. UCLA. University Closest to the Linden Area. And to maybe one day help Franco bail out of Bunns Lane once and for all. While the domestic plans may have stalled, Julie had since made it a rung up the corporate ladder. To Special Manager of Customer Affairs. Aka The Lady Who Gets Shit Done. Her reward was being called in for every storm no matter the time or day. And because of her grace under fire like she was *Grace Under Fire*, Julie had recently begun traveling. Who needs Hawaii when you can get carted off to the biggest crises along the Northeast Corridor? To be the final backstop for the biggest bitches and bastards calling into the company. The ones who were so clever, *they wanted to talk to the manager's manager!* On the bright side, Julie was now making a quarter the comp of Harris.

Franco's Julie. If only those complaining customers could see her eyes, they'd know everything would be okay. Unless those eyes were looking like they currently did before Franco. Cuz then there was a whole other storm to worry about.

The boxer's daughter and martial artist's ex had a toughness all her own. One that allowed her to work full-time, raise TJ, and put her mother to rest. Not to mention take on the debt forged by her late father.

Julie's father, Zaichek, was the son of Irish and Belarusian immigrants. His Belarusian mother had passed down her blonde hair and blue eyes. Gave him a look like he was straight outta Siberia. And gave him his name in the ring. The Belarusian Bulldog. A first-generation American who grew up on potatoes and borscht. And was built like a fuckin horse.

Zaichek's wife, Naomi, had been mulling for months what to name the baby in her belly. The baby she talked to all summer while The Bulldog was on the road. With two months to go, Naomi was down to two names. But if she named the baby Bathsheba (Betty for short), she'd be letting her Italian side down. And if she named her Sigismonda (Mandee for short), she'd be letting her Jewish side down. The 1970s seven-month pregnant mom was so stressed, she did what her doctor blessed. She was having a smoke when her water broke.

While Naomi was passed out from the emergency C-section, Zaichek had dashed in from the road. There was his nugget of a newborn. In the incubator with the blank card. Wailing. Flailing.

"By the way. We still need a name," said the nurse as she led the blue-eyed man with the busted nose and battered ears over.

"Eh what the hell were those names?" said Zaichek with a hand to his forehead. "Bethesda? Sigmund Freud?"

The nurse picked up the premature baby eager to get on with this crazy little thing called life. (Though if the baby knew then what she knew now, she'd still be holed up.) The nurse handed her over. "What was that? For a name?"

The blue-eyed man looked down. Was floored by the itty-bitty baby with the big eyes. Looking right at him. With the *same eyes* his mother had given him. The baby even *looked* like his mother. As if she had been reborn. His face lit up as he looked into those eyes. *"Yulie."*

"Julie?"

The man couldn't hear a word. He was in another dimension. Transported by those baby blues. To younger days. Standing there holding his baby girl. Nodding and smiling. The whole world around him could've crumbled for all he cared.

And crumble it did. The blond bomber had boxed his way to a brick box on Bucknell Ave. After growing up in an apartment, his only dream in life was to own a piece of God's green earth. The day he was to pay off the mortgage, he was in the morgue. They stuck him six feet under and stuck Julie's family with a $60,000 lien on the house. The guy who once slugged as hard as Babe Ruth had racked up big bills over his fight-induced Lou Gehrig's. Young Julie would sit at his bedside looking into his lost eyes. A Mrs. Robinson wondering where did he go? Her Joe DiMaggio. Now only talking the occasional nonsense. Like he was Yogi Berra. Looking nothing like he did in the picture of him, Julie, and Mickey on their mantel. And the $60,000 owed, after admin fees, totaled out to 61. Like he was Roger Maris. Dead before his time. Like he was Thurman Munson. And what does

Young Julie do? Starts the cycle all over again. The well-raised no-condom Catholic girl thought they could play her cycle. Instead, her beau hit right for it like he was Don Mattingly. The news of the home run that did Julie in came a couple days before she was to leave for Bucknell. Instead, she was sentenced to a life on Bucknell. But she wasn't gonna let it defeat her. Her boy would put his career first. Like he was Derek Jeter.

And now that Grandma was also gone and Julie was called out to a storm...

"I need you to take him," reported the manager.

Franco gnawed one of his gloves off. "You want the rest? I'm full," he said as he offered the glove to Julie. Her blue eyes only froze him out further. Franco dropped his gloves and the jokes as he mulled it over. The Frog was due to leap over to his house. And who knows what crooked shit he'd be into after that. More importantly, Franco had two-a-days for the next two weeks. All leading up to the biggest fight of his life. "Thought I was the problem. Now I'm the solution?"

"Do you have a better one?" Julie said as the bright lights of the boxing gym baked her blues. Blues weathering the stew of sweat, fungus, and mold swirling about. Franco always told her it was the easiest way to figure if you were a fighter. *Walk into a place like this, take one whiff of that, and you'll know.* Does it make you wanna run for hills? Or does it give you thrills?

And there Franco was, still breathing heavy from his roller coaster ride in the ring. Sucking it all in. Right at home. But there his son was. Looking for a home of his own. Franco looked once more into Julie's blues. Then waved T over. "A little notice woulda been nice," said the defeated fighter.

"I've had him for five years. You can handle five days," countered the victorious fighter, dropping her opponent again.

Julie put her hands on TJ's shoulders. "What are you?"

The little guy surrounded by a gym full of fighters could've melted to the mat with embarrassment.

"What are you?"

"Your heart and your soul," mumbled TJ.

Franco watched as Julie embraced TJ with a love that rivaled the fury she had for Franco. With a love that rivaled...the love she once had for Franco. When *he* was T's age.

"Take care of my boy."

"Aye aye captain," Franco said with a salute.

Captain Julie shook her head. Then shipped up to a Boston blizzard.

TRACK 5. FROGGER

AS THE FROG TURNED his Caddy onto Turner Street, his town turned around him. Back in '98, he knew all the right streets to maneuver his prior green machine onto. Knew all the right CDs to queue into his six-disc changer. Most often the Rolling Stones as he rolled in his throne. The Frog's bushy eyebrows would rise in the rearview as he admired his salt and pepper hair. The salt of wisdom. The pepper of youth. A handsome devil cranking "Sympathy for the Devil." A wise man who would stick to Green Street and its trickle of upkept colonials. Barron Ave where the block was lined with American flags on the Fourth of July. Hollywood Drive outfitted with Christmas, *Merry fuckin Christmas*, decorations in December. And in the spring, The Frog would crawl his classic Corvette down Main Street in the Saint Paddy's Day parade. In the summer, he'd arrange financing for the festivals at Demitri's and the Iberian. He even coordinated the Columbus Day Fair in the fall. And no matter the season, The Frog could drive and see the signs. The pizza slice atop Palermo's. The flag outside the Iberian. The diner lights of

Demitri's. The neon shamrock in the window of Tiffy's. Signs that it was his town.

Now? In '08? The jaded man in the jade Caddy couldn't even trust the signs. He cruised past Bobby's New York Deli. Fuh. Now owned by Habib from New Delhi. Past Sally's Cleaners. Heh. Sally from South Korea. The Frog had to hand it to em, though. One generation. Parents don't even know the language and their kids are acing the SAT. Buyin up the borough left and right. One more generation, they'll take the whole town. Hey, whatever gets those corporate fat cats a two-dollar tech division. Keep shipping em on in. Or shipping the jobs out. Whichever option inflates the stock options. Who gives a fuck about The Frog's nephew and his $100,000 college debt? Besides the financial fat cats getting fatter off that. At least his niece could always find work in this great nation's fastest-growing industry. "Adult entertainment." Hey, whatever sounds better on the way to the bank. So long as there's no Chapter 11, who cares about Chapter 69? Moral bankruptcy. And when The Frog banked a right, he couldn't believe what he saw on his left. The Message of the Week on the high school bulletin board. The American public high school. *El único constante es cambio.* The Frog stepped on the gas. Couldn't say adios fast enough.

He stopped at a red light outside Tiffy's. His old jukebox bar. Now such a shit show, they had a second sign out front. About no baggy clothes. No gang colors. Right on the door of his old haunt. Once home to wiseguys with 'staches and mullets. Now home to thugs with stashes and bullets.

Even St. Paddy's Day was suffering. Every year attendance was sinking to Cinco de Mayo. The summer festivals weren't as full either, were they? And the clusterfuck around Columbus Day. Holy Christ. There was a push in the district to ditch it for *Diwali* Day. Who the fuck was Diwali?

Did he discover America? No. He must be the one who introduced cricket. The Frog tried to voice his concern at the recent council meeting. About how some in town were utilizing the baseball fields, *baseball*, *America's pastime,* to play cricket. But all he got was crickets.

The signs were on the houses as well. The Frog had counted four foreclosures. And now a fifth on one of those old colonials. He shuddered over the rotted shutters. Shook his head over the manor with poor manners.

The housing crisis only worsened as he wheeled onto Bunns Lane. Where he saw the worst sign of all. *Housing Authority.* Why the fuck Franco insisted on living right up Woodbridge's rear, he had no idear.

The Frog's immigrant parents had loved the Newark neighborhood they grew up in. But year by year, apartment by apartment, their people left. And others moved in. By the time their own little guy was just a tadpole, they couldn't walk a block without getting clocked. So The Frog's family hopped farther south. By the time Newark was burning in the Long Hot Summer of 1967, The Frog's family had it made in the shade under their maple on Maple. Over on the good side of The Wood.

But right now, The Frog was looking at a block of apartments that reminded him of age 6. Where thugs slugged his father and mugged his mother. About six.

So the talking heads on TV that go home to their lofts and send their kids to lofty schools could try to sell The Frog Kumbaya all they wanted. The ones whose locals are good enough to clean their toilets but not good enough to go to school with. *Oh it's not them, it's the school.* What a joke. Swap the entire staff of whatever New York City high school you want with the entire staff from somewhere nice like Nutley. You'll get the exact same fuckin results. It was enough to make The Frog go nutly. *Gee I wonder what the problem is.* Let's flush 50 billion more federal tax dollars down the toilet trying to figure it out. Let's let the state stick us up for some more tax revenue reallocation to urban areas. No wonder why The Frog needed his harmless little side hustle. Sheesh.

But in the dusk of that March day, The Frog was actually feeling good. Feeling good about the corner hustler with the high hood and the low pants. Feeling good about the three toddlers being strolled along in a shopping cart. Feeling good about the burly Burberry mama with her new flip phone and food stamps. The one giving The Frog the stink eye as he walked by. Like he was her problem.

Normally, this would infuriate The Frog. Like that time The Frog put the news on Franco's ten-year-old TV. Took all of two minutes for the magic box to blow his top. *Excuses. Excuses. Excuses. Look at the NBA. Should whites hold an affirmative action march? An appropriation march? Over the hijacking of Doctor Naismith's game? No. Of course not. It is what it is. Meanwhile, they can appropriate out the ass. Like that group you listen to. The Wang Chung Clan. Guess that attitude makes me the bigot? Huh Franco? Cuz I'm asking that things be truly equal. Not in this day and age. Equality and justice is treating every minority group with kid gloves. And ragging on whites, men, and Christians all you want. They build the most successful countries in the world, and all they get is shit on for it. Look at the local papers. It's the district's fault, not their own fault, when their kids don't cut it. And then the one that does. Hops right into Harvard over the hard-luck valedictorian. Oh but you can't say nothin. Gotta sit there and clap. Oooh you better say not say nothin. While they make movies called* White Men Can't Jump. *Speakin of movies, do me a favor, Franco. That hit movie everyone's talkin about? Let me know when the sequel comes out.* No Country for Christian White Men. *And another thing. How the fuck did I even end up here? Defending Christian white men like I'm the fuckin*

68

Reverend Billy Graham? Sixteen in the '60s, I'm caddying at the country club. Sizzlin in the sun. Brownie, they called me. Can you believe that shit? I was a brown kid in a white town. Now I'm a white man in a brown town. And it's the same fuckin town! And I'm the bad guy either way! He's funny. The Man up there is funny.

And what does Franco give The Frog after all that? *Nobody's a group. Everybody's an individual.*

I give you a Rembrandt of a rant and all you got for me is two sentences? Sure, everybody's an individual, but we have to hear all about some groups' problems. We get some groups' perspectives all day every day. Not me, though. I say a peep, I'm a piece of shit. All I'm askin for is a fair shake. We're all sittin in the same soup. But that's not how it goes down when I gotta hire. Not how it goes down in our schools. Not how it goes down when you try to say somethin.

And what does Franco give him? Two more lousy fuckin sentences. *Was Rembrandt a writer? Or a painter?*

Boy, people really loved The Bunns Lane Brawler for his ground and pound. But The Frog? The Frog was most impressed by his deke and duck.

The Frog smirked. Normally, the mama now in her new Camry blasting that new song all over the radio—"SOS"— would make The Frog wanna call for one himself. It would usually make him wanna flee The Wood and pack. To somewhere playing Fleetwood Mac. Away from Rihanna and onto "Rhiannon." But on this day, all the white Christian man had for the hustler, the stroller, and the mad-dogging mama was a smile. All of them were pleasant reminders of what the man had to do. No excuses.

The Frog headed to Franco's door. Adjusted the object in his trench coat pocket. Something a little harder to dodge.

Sweat ran from Franco's forehead. Fell to his living room rug as he banged out push-ups. *"Forty-two. Forty-three. Forty-four..."* Didn't even hear the knock at the door.

TJ flew down the stairs. Peeped the peephole. Even at his advanced age, the man at the door put a pit in T's stomach. The skunk hair. The cavernous eyes. The protruding chin.

Franco hustled over. "Beat it," exhaled the exhausted fighter.

"Great Michael Jackson song."

"Just—"

"—beat it," sang TJ as he stammered up the stairs.

Franco reached for the door handle—noticed the TV on mute. Vintage Pac poppin off. Franco shut it off. Flung the remote across the room. What was he gonna do? Scoop The Frog to the acronym THUG LIFE? All he'd hear was "Thug Life."

The Frog stepped in. Saw T's sneaks disappear upstairs. "You playing Mr. Mom over here?"

"Somethin like that."

"How is the little tyke?"

"Good. Busy."

"Haven't seen him since he'd come over to ride his bike. Real nice at the park by my place. Before they paved it over with apartments."

"Right. Yeah. He's got homework." Franco motioned for The Frog to head on into the kitchen. "I'll make ya a drink."

The Frog glanced the TV as his Ferragamos click-clacked along the linoleum. Made their way into the kitchen. The Frog took a seat at the booth table against the back wall. Stretched his arms about.

Franco brought him a whiskey neat. Jameson. Had to be Jameson. The Catholic whiskey. Bushmills was proper for Protestants. Franco learned that a long time ago, serving The Frog in the basement casino over at Tiffy's. Franco cut himself a club soda rocks. Gave the illusion of a cocktail with his capo.

Franco sat under the lone light in the room. A 60-watt beneath a beige shade. The asymmetrical alignment of the booth table that Young Franco had banged in now caused him to sit illuminated while The Frog sat in the shadows.

The Frog began the interrogation. "You own this place, right?"

"For the time being."

"Paying your fight team?"

"Same."

"Last fight of your contract? They say this kid's unbeatable."

"Yeah, somethin like that." Franco sipped his carbonated cocktail.

"Gotta get back on the docks."

"That'd be nice."

"Ain't gonna just *happen.*"

Franco shrugged.

The Frog squeezed his folded hands. "Gotta make it happen."

"How's that?" said Franco as he sipped.

"Gotta get a hold of the honcho importing the illegals."

Soda gas rose in Franco's throat.

The Frog leaned forward into the lamp light. His head illuminated as he spoke of another's. "Twenty large for his fuckin head."

Franco's rocks glass rattled to rest on the table. He had been dodging the heavy-hitter shit ever since he got going with The Frog. Kept his distance by docking himself at the docks. By dropping off gangsta rolls then rolling to the mats. By cutting The Frog in on his fight earnings to get him invested in Franco the Fighter. All in all, it left Franco with a line of work he could live with. Makin a buck off gambling? Wasn't anything the state governments with their tracks and their lottos, the corporate casinos all across the country, and companies all over the World Wide Web weren't doing. They can all rake it in by the billions, sure. But the little guy himself can't make a few bucks off a few bets? Dafuckouttahere.

But now? Here The Frog was. Once again asking the temp to do the dirty work. Rake up rat shit? Fine. Mince through maggots? No problem. Drop into a junkyard and collect five yards? Okay. But *offing* someone? Franco considered saying he had a big fight. But he'd been telling The Frog that for ten years now. "I ain't a killer."

The Frog leaned his head in even farther. His deep-set eyes now illuminated. Hazel. "Nobody's a killer until they have to."

Nobody's a killer until they have to. The haunting phrase made itself a nice little home in Franco's head.

"You wanna pay your mortgage? Or bounce back across Bunns Lane?"

"I say no. Someone gonna take care of El Jefe anyway?"

"No. I'm just gonna let him take my turf." The Frog leaned back in the shadows. Sipped the Jameson as rich as his sarcasm.

"What's his story? This jefe," Franco said, flying through whatever the fuck the five stages of grief were.

"Name's Arturo. He's a fuckin crook. Rounds up a bunch of illegals. Puts together fake IDs for them. Contracts them out."

Franco sipped his soda. "He's got juice?"

"*We* got juice." The Frog reached in his trench coat pocket. Laid the Glock under the lamplight.

Franco glanced down the hall. *I could pop in—*

The Frog leaned in. Slid the .45 to Franco like he was at

the Little League mound giving him the game ball. Franco, taken by its weight, fumbled it to the floor.

The Frog hopped back. "Jesus Christ."

Franco picked the piece up. Handled it like a hot potato. For the hundred street fights Franco had in his life, he brought a gun to not one. "There a safety on this thing?"

The Frog grabbed the Glock from his goon. "Look. Right here. Safe as can be." The Frog slid it back over. Franco tucked it in his waist with the confidence of a turtle tucking his head in his shell.

"A middle man moseying the Mexicans in is into us for twenty large. Runs a trucking fleet outside AC. You pay him a visit. Find out how to get a hold of the honcho."

Franco sucked his soda down to the rocks. The fight game was growing by the minute. A win in a couple weeks and he'd easily have his biggest contract yet. Could walk away from this shit once and for all. Like he was supposed to seven years ago. Until those final ticks. When his ankle split. Then again. A loss in a couple weeks and shit was bleak. Locked out at the docks. Locked out of the fight game forever. What the fuck was The Frog always poppin off about after watching *Mad Money* with Jim Cramer? Diversity? Nah. Definitely not that. *Diversification.* That's it. Franco had been wishing lately, at 33, that he stepped up his responsibility. Not to mention that this Arturo was a gangster. A gangster that put Franco's fellow longshoremen out of work. A gangster that lives by the gun. So it's only fair if he dies by the gun. But. Could Franco *really* bring himself to pull the trigger?

He told The Frog he would.

TRACK 6. BUNNS PAIN

TJ WOKE UP in his old bedroom as he did five years before. Only now, when he sat up, he hit his head on the slanted ceiling. His Jeter poster behind him. His 1998 Dell set upon a flimsy formica desk. He looked out his wood-framed window. A sunny Sunday. One of those March days that made him think the good weather was finally there. Until he opened the window. Got whipped by the wind.

TJ spotted Dragon walking along in work boots. A brown-bagged lunch to boot. "Yo. Pickin up work at H———? Long walk," hollered T.

"More time to write my raps," said Dragon as he knocked on his noggin.

"More time to see what's goin on in the streets."

"Exact," said Dragon. Dragon, who rapped the first day of their freshman year,

> *I see all this pain*
> *This heartache desire*
> *Breathe it in*

> *Spit it out like fire*
> *Dragon here*
> *The situation is dire*

The two threw each other peace signs as Dragon dragged on.

TJ's eyes transferred to Franco—wrapping his run with a sprint down Bunns. "Eight am and you already got a run in?" TJ shouted.

Franco doubled over for a beat. Huffed and puffed by his barren garden. "And Muay Thai after I take you to school."

"It's Sunday."

"I know," said Franco as he harvested a dirt-bombed basketball.

Father and son shared smiles.

They made their way up the block. Past all the two-story cookie-cut brick projects with pitched roofs. Life-sized versions of the Monopoly hotels. Laid out in pairs in alternating east-west, north-south patterns to create quads in between. Quads of clotheslines. Coal grills. An H-head sneaking pills. As they walked the projects that projected people of all pigment, Franco said hey to McKay. Yo to Cho. Hola to Lola—aka Naval Officer Cruz. Visiting Mom after a one-year cruise.

The ball court was on the elevated end of the street. Flanked by a beige sound barrier that muffled Mack trucks tearing up the Turnpike. The Brown Monster. An expansive canvas for local artists. MENACE. DRAY. SCREWS.

And Franco's favorite. CROCK. With green block letters angled into points. The bottoms of the letters submerged in a pool of brown. "How about my man Crock?" said *Frahnc* as he tossed the rock. "Crocodile. From the swamps of Jersey."

TJ squared up to the netless rim backed by a rust-patched

backboard. The court was riddled with puddles from the wintry mix that made its way through the day before. Puddles that made it TJ's favorite time to play. When the court was clear, there'd be ten running full and another ten waiting, leaving little T left out. "If it meant Crocodile, it'd be spelled C-R-O-C," T noted as he bricked his first shot. "It means crock as in crock of shit." TJ rarely cursed around his parents. But he had to make the point. "He's melting away in a crock of shit." TJ drove and laid one up to get going.

Franco caught the ball under the basket. Recalled the time The Frog asked him what he thought *Gremlins* was about. *Like really fuckin about* as The Frog put it. Franco was holding Baby T at the time. Just like he was holding the ball right then. Young Franco said he figured it was about a guy who wasn't ready to be a parent. The Frog, meanwhile, focused on another aspect of the movie altogether: the Gremlins destroying the town. And came up with a far different answer. "Yeah, I dunno. Maybe art says more about the observer than anything." Franco fired the ball to T.

Father and son had one side to themselves. Two teen brothers had the other. Freddy with the fresh fade and fleet of foot. His older brother Lenny with more lank and less hair. TJ knew them from the block and the ball team. A soph and a senior. Both on varsity.

Franco warmed up with some Js.

Meanwhile, TJ watched Freddy fake the fadeaway, then run it to the rack for a flush. "Damn. I can't even get net."

"He's older," Franco fired as he fired a pass.

"One year," retorted T as he heaved another brick.

Franco chased down the rebound. "I never had those hops either." He fed TJ again.

TJ considered pointing out that Franco was a freshman way back in '89-'90. Before the AAU explosion. Before everyone wanted to be Like Mike. Before the internet intensified everything: nutrition plans, workout programs, year-round leagues. Ballin outta control. Back in 1990 Woodbridge, TJ imagined, you could wake up hungover, eat a bag of potato chips, pick up a basketball for the first time in nine months, and make the team. But TJ kept that all to himself. Had a hard time contradicting Dad. TJ instead doubled down and flung one with full focus. It rattled out of the unforgiving rim.

"Woulda went in indoors," Franco reassured T. "Besides. School's more important. You gotta do better in school," Franco said as he slid into territory Julie had asked him to cover. Or more accurately per the wording of her text, *told* him to cover.

Gotta do better in school. TJ laughed to himself over the ironic imperative from Dad. *Have to* do better in school would've been much more apropos.

Franco launched a fadeaway that nicked the far side of the rim and faded away. It was hard for him to tell TJ to do good in school, walk the line, go make somethin of himself. After all, Franco hadn't done any of those things. He didn't even have his own shit in order and he was gonna tell his kid how to go about it? Fuck, Franco's life was *never* in order. From the orphanage. To the foster family. To the teen pregnancy. To the up-and-down docks. To the street hustle. To the fits-and-starts fight career. To the failed marriage. In his 20s, he was sure his whole life would be sorted by now. Twenty-three and he was hoisting little T on his shoulders, hopping around on two good ankles, Franklins fallin out of his track pant pockets. Professional fighter knockin fools out in AC. And Young Julie. Ooh wee. Franco had the whole block clicking. *The whole town.* When the college grads from his high school soccer team were moving back to their basements, Franco was buying *them* beers. Throwing bangers in *his* basement. In the house that *he* bought.

But while Franco floundered, the grads left their basements one step at a time. Whack-ass internship. Step one. Emasculating assistant gig. Step two. Middling middle manager. Step three. Overworked worker bee. Step four. Worker bees that built new nests in bucolic Bridgewater. Breezy Bay Head. Cozy Cranford. Steps five, six, and seven. Off to suburban heaven. Anywhere but there. Outtie in their Audis. In their $50K cars bumping 50. With their Bose and their nose turned up. *Damn homie.* What the fuck happened to Franco? Nothing. Nathan. He was still in-town. Still on Bunns Lane. All in. His stacks pushed to the middle of the table. Trying to gut out a gut shot with only the river to come. The Return. To a top-ten fight.

As TJ ran after the failed fadeaway, it hit Franco as hard as the whipping wind. *Ten years since he last bumped "Sky's the Limit" in his basement.* He'd thought he'd made it *back then.* From ashy to classy like his boy Biggie. Back in his Michael Jordan year. But now in his Larry Bird year and still broke? Franco had love for everyone he'd kicked it with. From the projects to the penthouse. But what about him? While The Prince became a Playboy, he was a Penthouse. *Dirty dirty.* In the slums of Jersey Jersey. Despite working harder than anyone he knew. Organized his entire "post-college" career years around the fight game. Docked the dock hours. Intensified the training. Ditched drinking. Started *studying.* Taught himself how to use TJ's computer. Broke down video on every fighter he could find. Even started *reading.* Every MMA article he could get his hands on. Not only that. *Academic journals.* On everything from nutritional science to the sweet science. Studying video and reading into the wee hours. Miss Lane woulda lost her mind. There Franco was, studying studies from *Princeton*. Shit, he almost bought glasses and a pipe! Like *he* was Francis Freeman. Workin on bein a free man. Not owing nobody nathan. Like his old soccer teammate, Nathan. Workin at JP Nathan. Sellin mortgage-backed somethins worth nathan. Buyin up foreclosed houses like nathan. Gobblin up green like Joey Chestnut at Nathan's. College paid for his baby boy. Nathan.

All while Franco pushed his pony from Santa Fe to Portland, Maine. Fighting his way from a Brooklyn dungeon to an arena in London. Shit, even bein a father made him a better fighter. And vice versa. Focused. Motivated. Responsible. Sober. Where would Franco be without TJ and MMA? His whole adult life woulda been DOA. He woulda been fifty-fifty partners with The Frog by now. Forget The Bunns Lane Brawler. He'd be The Lizard. Even his side gigs with The Frog were all about allowing him to focus on Franco the Fighter. A decade-long 24-7 focus for the old teammate of Nathan. A focus that left him with exactly nathan.

And not only did Franco work harder than anyone he knew, he was pursuing his dreams. Wasn't that exactly what all the music, movies, and TV told him to do? *Motherfucker.* That's exactly what the inspiring words of "Sky's the Limit" ran out on. Motherfucker. It sure was, Biggie. The motherfucker for Franco being that one slip in the cage. Which led to that one slip with The Frog. To that one slip with his family. *Motherfu—*

Franco *had* to come correct in his upcoming fight.

But right then, he had to come correct as a father. He passed a rebound to his son who had already passed him. Better grades than Franco ever got. Higher IQ. Only half of Franco's crazy motherfucking DNA. The way it was before Julie dropped T off made a lot more sense all the sudden.

Franco could just keep his fuckin mouth shut and let her do all the talking. So he followed her lead. While Franco delivered passes, he shot stock messages from Mom. *All your grades count now. Miss Lane says you ain't tryin. You need an activity—gotta keep up with basketball.*

TJ sunk his shoulders despite sinking shots. It was all things he'd heard already. Only with worse grammar. TJ thought about explaining to Franco that he was too small to ball. That it wasn't rec league anymore back when the rim was so much higher relative to the pre-pubescent kids that all Franco had to do was teach little T to heave it better than the next boy. TJ thought about explaining that all they do in Lane's class is read books about kids in private school in the 1900s. *Early* 1900s. Yeah, TJ liked to read. But Will Hunting wasn't the only one with the wrong fuckin books. What did TJ's have anything to do with what was poppin in The Wood? Hanging with Franco was what would really get TJ ready for the real world. But TJ didn't explain any of that. He just gave Franco the yeah yeah so they could move on to more important things. Like is Dad mafia? Like why won't Mom let TJ wrestle? And most importantly, how the fuck does one fight?

The two got in a groove as T showed the right attitude toward the platitudes. T even started sharp-shooting from three. Worked his way around the world.

"Ho. Larry Bird."

"Ray Allen," said TJ low enough such that Freddy and Lenny couldn't hear. Them looking like Paul Pierce and Kevin Garnett. TJ looking like the Celts towel boy.

Franco came forward and challenged T. T crossed Franco up. But Franco caught up. Swatted T's shot. Sent the ball bouncing down Bunns Lane. "Come on. I gotta make it to Muay Thai anyway."

TJ ran down the ball. The work of CROCK caught his eye. Lenny meanwhile *ohhh'd* over Freddy flushing another one. TJ then looked down at his own ball. The graffiti wasn't the only writing on the wall.

Franco and TJ were walking the project side of the street when the lowrider rolled by. On the vinyl side of Bunns Lane. Chromed out from the 5-spoke spinners to the 26-inch twisted handlebars. Franco didn't even have to look up to the baby face above the North Face. Eddo. Fuck.

Eddo owed two Gs to The Frog. Two Gs The Frog pulled from the pay of the guy who vouched for Eddo. Franco.

"Motherfucker owes me two Gs," fired Franco, forgetting fatherly duties. "Ay! Eddo!"

The shout shook Eddo. Almost fell off his lowrider. "Yo Franco! What's good? Got your dinero next week no doubt!"

The answer to all Franco's problems pedaled away. The two Gs would be enough to float Franco until his fight night money came through. He could put icing Arturo on ice until after. And with a win? Put it on ice forever. "Hold the fuck up!"

Eddo fuckin stood and pedaled. His knit Raiders hat flapped in the wind. The West Coast wannabe ready to pump his way to the Pacific.

The Bunns Lane Brawler grabbed the ball from T. He gained ground with his first burst but lost ground as Eddo picked up a head of steam. Franco cocked the basketball back. Let it rip like Eli in the Super Bowl. Eddo played the receiving role of Tyree. Only he didn't catch the bomb that blew up his head. He flew off his bike like a character on *Jackass* as Franco ran up to jack his ass.

"Slaughterhouse furloughed me this week. That's all! I'll have your dinero next week no doubt!"

Franco cocked back for a trademark ground and pound.

"I got my daughter's christening. Don't hit me in the face, primo!"

Primo. Eddo was praying to God that Franco had Hispanic heritage. Like that would somehow earn him a break with The Brawler. Like they were long-lost fuckin cousins. A second ago, Eddo's tearin away like a race car. And now he's playin the race card.

"¡Qué pasa is you gotta pay!" Franco dealt a couple body blows to Eddo. But. Spared his fresh fuckin face. "You got fuckin money for spinners?" Franco then had to spare him altogether.

The block boomed with bass. An orange Challenger rolled by. Real slow. Tints cracked halfway. With that fucking song blasting. "Mi Calle" by Castro Y Gambino. TJ didn't have to know Spanish to know it was a badass beat as he stood across the street. Palms sweaty despite the winter weather. Word around Ill Co was that the orange Challenger was pushed by a CG-67 banger. The driver grilled Franco with his pierced eyebrow and backwards hat. And from TJ's point of view, his teardrop tattoo.

The gangsta's black eyes grilled Franco. *I fuckin see you.*

Franco's hazels shot right back. *Fuckin see you, too.*

Eddo let himself up. Dusted himself off. Hopped on his bike and pedaled away. La-dee-da. Like he was headed to a fuckin picnic at the park.

Franco called after him. "Next week. Plus the juice."

The orange Challenger power braked. Spun its tires for a good ten seconds. Then peeled outta there. Left Franco and TJ in a cloud of smoke.

Franco kept a tough face.

TJ wrinkled his. Didn't like the smell of it.

TRACK 7. RAY DAY

TJ WALKED TO his high school by way of Bunns Lane for the first time. Fuck, it was far from the high school. Almost in Amboy. Not that TJ was in a rush. Fuckin Ray. Another fuckin gray day. No weather at least. No wind. No wintry mix. Just still. A touch of humidity even. Made the 10 degrees feel like 20. What good fortune. Musta been the St. Paddy's Day luck of the Irish.

TJ continued along in his green hoodie and green vest for the occasion. The occasion that, according to Mom, was about two things. First and foremost, a celebration of Irish heritage and how Saint Patrick drove the snakes out of Ireland. But also a day of ironic mourning. To remember why God invented alcohol. To stop the Irish from takin over the world. Like her grandfather who had moved to America, served as a World War II medic, and built his own contracting business. Then watched it contract on the account of his contracted disease. The medic who self-medicated. His handsome son left not with a handed-down business but with a handed-down message: *Take care of business.* The handsome young man respected his father's ringside orders. And charged out with a nickname dedicated to his mother.

It was actually TJ's dad who loved the holiday unequivocally. In his younger years, he'd say it was cuza the car bombs. But back then, as it was now, he saw it as a day that brought together the town. With that slogan all around. *Everybody's Irish on St. Patrick's Day.* What a special day. That one day a year. When Franco knew what the fuck he was.

TJ yanked at his green vest as he walked. Puffy thing kept riding up. His hoodie was all tight, too. *And* the half-cut tag tickled his neck. Worth it, though. Couldn't be caught walkin around in size "Small." Instead, TJ was rocking size "Men's." *And* it was too tiny for anyone to want to take. Perfecto.

TJ trooped along like a Koopa Troopa past Pearl Street. Home to the hottest couple of ball courts in town. Even a couple tennis courts for the classy. Except for when they were locked up in the winter like they were now. Then their main function was to play host to steel-cage-style street fights where two kids would climb over and rumble. Whoever could beat the other badly enough to make time to climb out was the winner. And the play structure. How could such a monster structure from TJ's childhood now look so miniscule? Damn.

TJ's peregrinations pushed him past Town Hall. The mayor's office. It struck TJ that even the town wished it was back in the day. Back when the whole town had Friday night light fever. Back when Franco and Julie would take little T to every game. Back when the football team and its headbreaker Hector Herondo lined up at linebacker. When its assassin Anthony Akiro left chalk marks around receivers crossing the middle. When its O-Line elephant Aaron Vochuk made pancakes like he was Uncle Buck. When its baller Brandon

Sweet built a brand on the right sweep. When Ali Raja and the 4-3 D picked off passes like Ali Baba & the Forty Thieves. When Wyatt Irthe shotgunned any and all comers like he was Wyatt fuckin Earp. When The Sheriff and his men put teams in tombstones all the way to the town's last state title. Back in the day. Back when the blue-collar bangers on the bowling team, the *motherfuckin bowling team,* scored a turkey with three state titles in a row. Back when everyone in the hood was feelin good. Droppin some *Whadaya say now, WOOD!* The deep-voiced side-of-the-mouth battle cry that could be heard all around town. From basement bangers full of wasted creatures in Jordan sneakers to teachers n preachers in those Friday night bleachers. Back when the president, *Slick Willie himself,* slid into the halls of the high school to share his thoughts on National Kick Butts Day. (And to shore up some electoral votes in the process.) The visit all arranged by Woodbridge's All-American mayor on the rise. The handsome Irishman with the beautiful wife and kids. TJ was sure McGreevey, who had since then gained the governorship only to be outed in a national scandal and out of politics altogether, beckoned for back in the day. Then again. Maybe not. At least the love gov was living his truth. TJ, meanwhile, felt like a total fuckin phony. Hoodie like he was hard or some shit. Bench-warming on the ball team. A-student of stupid classes.

TJ continued to walk the boulevard of broken dreams. Past the middle school. He once saw a picture of the inaugural class. Ten cheery old chaps from 1910. Back when Proper was "proper." TJ wondered what they'd think of some of the kids out front on this cold winter morning, present company included. The baggy clothes. The beat-bopping Bose. The lack of backpacks. All a rueful reminder to TJ. He was halfway to Ray. Still, he carried on before he was late. Carried on hatin '08. Past Little League fields now so little. Wondering as he crossed his hood. What do you say now, Wood?

TJ made his way onto the frozen tundra out front of his high school. More diverse than ever. Now some kids were green. From the Irish kid and his green iris to the black quarterback and his girl Iris. But not Ray. Ray wore gray. A gift from T-gay. Must not have been enough because Ray's grill was still grilling him. Shit. TJ shoulda brought his Ouija board. So he could séance St. Patrick and have him bounce the boa constrictor before him. Like Ray's woken up the past few school days and said, *I feel like fucking up TJ today.* Or maybe he was chilling with Lenore the night before and she said something about TJ being cute or funny. Musta been that. Cuz she was also standing there with apologetic eyes. Some conspicuous space between her and Ray. The Big Pole. TJ liked to think it was cuz of the big bat he used to bat cleanup. Or cuz he was a quarter Polish. But that's as far as TJ would go. Didn't want to give Ray the satisfaction of another scenario. Ray who was standing there with the same salivating grin he had when he was in the batter's box. And the pitch being grooved to him today was TJ.

"What up little bitch."

"Nothin I'm good," responded TJ as if Ray had greeted him pleasantly. Considering Ray put a wrap on the rap this past Friday, TJ now chose flight instead of fight. He kept walking.

Ray mushed his head. "Faggot ass cut."

TJ thought about pointing out that gays had good fashion sense and that it was a compliment. But why get punted to another part of town? So, "Chill yo." Big mistake. Biiig mistake. Didn't TJ just learn in Lane's class that there were four types of sentences? And he chose a *command?* People *hate* commands. Thankfully, Ray was there to give him an enrichment lesson. "Don't tell me what to do, little bitch." Ah, Ray. Where would TJ be without him? In school. Relaxed. Ready to read and write.

Instead, Ray was pushing him away from school. A few feet. Then ten. Then ten more. Followed by a fall of five more. TJ turned to break his fall. Busted right through a Saran wrap sheet of ice. Into mud. CROCK come to life. Luckily, the stout gym teacher plopped in his lawn chair across campus was so curious about what was going on that he actually got up. It was enough to break things up.

As Lenore headed for the door, as Screws took a final puff of his P-Funk, as UN pulled in another pile of pesos, TJ pulled himself up. Mucked in mud as he slithered away. A garter snake driven by the glorious Saint Ray.

Franco's on-guard olive arms glistened with sweat as he darted around the ring. Looking like a tank in his hunter tank. A tank under attack. By Taz. The banger from Bangkok was half the size of Joey but twice as fast with twice as high hair—sprayed green for the holiday. The muy Thai Muay Thai terror threw a blizzard of knees and 'bows. Looking like a troll as he trolled Franco. A troll with lightning-fast limbs attached to a shredded torso. All tatted with Asian characters. Siamese if you please.

Franco had a hell of a jaw. Hardened over time boxing both on Bunns Lane and in the ring. But ten years into the fight game and a knee to the kidney still killed him. Same for elbow flexes to the solar plexus. Good motivation to fend them off.

Taz threw some kicks. "Actually you a cross between Pacquiao. And DiCaprio."

"Oh yeah? That's not bad—"

"The *look* of Pacquiao and the *hook* of DiCaprio." Taz swept the fool to the floor.

Fuckin Taz. Been breakin Franco's balls from jump street. From before Franco ever met him. Used to be Franco that held the Town Legend Belt. Back from when he was on a collection as a 19-year-old. The first three, the Joe Blows handed it over hassle-free. Even thanked *Frank* for coming by to pick it up. But the fourth. Cranky muhfucka barely put it forth. As Franco was walking out with Baby T in his car seat, the Joe Blow blew his top and beat feet. His haymaker was headed for the back of Franco's head when Franco reacted. The car seat swung around—Franco could still see the smile on Baby T's face—as the car seat coldcocked the dude upside his head. As the Joe Blow dropped, the latest town legend rose. The Baby Boomer.

While there were countless tales constantly bubbling up from the melting pot town of tough guys and gals, a lot of people had that as number one. Until the stick-up.

After decades of doing the dishes, saving up money, and taking English as a second language classes, Mr. and Mrs. Bidaya opened the Bamboo Bistro. Its slice of the Avenel strip mall was their slice of the American Dream. And their exotic dishes tasted like a dream. To them, anyway. When it came to the locals, it was the pad Thai that padded their pockets. Still, Mr. and Mrs. Bidaya couldn't be more grateful. They even had regulars who played the specials. The cops who copped the lunch special every Tuesday. The working parents who took the 2-for-1s to go on Thursday evenings. The retirees who sat every Saturday. There 4 pm on the dot for the early bird special. The Bidayas were blessed. They had something special.

So content about their place in the community, they left

the door unlocked after closing one night. Maybe many nights leading up to that night. But definitely that night. Mr. and Mrs. Bidaya were at the register when they registered two hooded hoods who rushed in and drew guns. Mr. Bidaya threw his hands up and said, "It's all yours." One walked around the counter. Booted Mrs. Bidaya's ass outta the way. When Mr. Bidaya began, "There is no need for—" his bucked teeth were bucked out. One hood bust out laughing like the bust-out teeth was Chris Rock's bust-out performance. The one where Rock was the first to take issue with guys like these.

Funny Money these two. While Funny laughed, Money stuffed his pockets. But as he ran the register on the counter, something else ran on the counter. Two little white-stained-brown sneakers. Owned by a diminutive dishwasher still in his apron and hair net. Funny wasn't finding shit so funny no more. He pointed with his finger on the trigger, *"Mothafucka—"*

The hair-netted dishwasher dropkicked the gun like he was a luchador. But it went off anyway. Mr. Bidaya rushed Mrs. Bidaya to the back as the dishwasher dropped Funny with one crack. Then charged for Money. But Money's begging for mercy made him stall. Money had taken a bullet to the balls.

The papers reported that the hoods were from Newark. Which was strike one in Franco's book. Making his birthplace look bad. No big deal. Just a first pitch to see what the pitcher had. Strike two was the kid on the cover of the paper that had even bigger hair than his best bro Joey Yo. And then strike three. The hundred-mile-an-hour heater that blew away Franco's best swing—his Baby Boomer. Local jokers come up with a *New York Post*-worthy headline for the shooting incident at the Thai restaurant. It went down in town lore as: The Bang Cock.

The incident had turned the whirlwind before Franco from Tanasith Bidaya into Taz. And now here he was, prankin *Frank* with this DiCaprio-Pacquiao shit. Franco scrambled to his feet. "You fucker." He countered with some kicks of his own. Tagged Taz in the head. Spiked his hair some more. Then moved in and muddled it up. When a kid walked in all muddied up. Shivering. Shook. Franco hurried to the side of the ring. "T. What the fuck happened?"

TJ looked up with his big browns. On the verge of tears. "I… Dad…" muttered the kid unkempt and all verklempt. "Teach me how to fight."

Franco slid the cawfee table outta the way. The living room's arsenic throw rug was now an MMA mat. "You sure about this?" asked Franco. Already fearing the fallout from Mom.

T, now in a clean white T, sat forward on the age-softened sectional. "No doubt."

Franco took a knee. "Your back's against the wall with this kid?"

TJ nodded.

Franco wiped away a lone tear that ran down T's face. Figured there were a hundred held back.

"He's on my ass all the time. Outside school. In class. On the internet."

"Cocksucker should be in none of your classes," Franco snapped back. He hated using a word *that* dirty. But not then. Felt good. TJ had had plenty of mothering. It was time for Franco to be a father. "Get up."

TJ hitched up his sagged jeans. Dad squared him up in a lefty fighting stance. It was so visceral. Especially after living with Mom and "Nanners" for so long. Mom's insistence on academics as she read a book or completed a crossword puzzle. Nanners' crocheting on her couch. *Plastic-coated.* Like it had to be ship-shape to ship to heaven. TJ now felt so alive, he half-busted a boner. Luckily, there wasn't much to see back then. The fresh-faced frosh, despite contrary reports to his crew, had not yet hit puberty.

Franco squared up in front of T. His lead right rested before T's face.

Damn. Dad had knuckles the size of T's knees.

"Sure this is how you wanna handle this?"

TJ had already pondered the question all weekend. A weekend that was an eternity in teen time. If he told on Ray, nothing would happen to Ray *and* TJ would get it twice as bad. If not outside the school, then everywhere else. The bathroom stalls. The town's malls. The basement of Persian Paul's. In fact, the question was so constantly on his conscience, TJ convinced himself that telling would lead to Ray beating him to death then claiming self-defense. "Yeah."

"Then you gotta deal with the heat," said the looming father, casting a shadow.

"I know," said the son, ready to step out of it.

"Throw a punch. But don't tell me when—"

TJ wound up and threw a left before Franco even finished his sentence. Still, the fighter caught it with ease. Talk about embarrassing. TJ threw his hardest punch and Dad nonchalant *catches* it with one hand. *Places it* down at T's side. Totally killed his boner.

"What's the shortest distance between two points?" asked the philosofighter.

"Teleporting," reported the pupil.

Father and son shared a grin over father's chagrin.

TJ then came correct. "A straight line."

"Zactly." Franco jabbed jabs on each side of T's head.

The fists flew by like fighter planes invading air space. "Quickest punch there is. Don't pull your arm back at all. Just straight out—boom." Franco snapped a few more. He leaned in for a body blow—T defended low. Franco's fist was already up top. "Misdirection," Franco informed as his knuckles took a nap on T's forehead.

TJ practiced jabs. Straight out. Snap. Snap. Snap.

"Put a little hop into it."

TJ did. Pop. Pop. Pop.

"Gimme some misdirection."

TJ jabbed but Franco's paws paused the punches. TJ faked the body blow, came back up top—

Franco defended. "Nice—"

TJ was already shooting on Franco's shins. Shimmied him into the shectional.

"Whoa! The fuck is that?" Franco said as he caught himself from falling.

"Misdirection," mimicked the son. With a smile bright as the sun.

Franco shook his head. Forgot how much of a kick he got out of his kid. "You're a step ahead of the game. Was just about to say that your best move with a bigger guy is to get him on the ground."

"Yeah, you already taught me that."

"Say what?"

"Back in the day. When I used to watch you train."

The fighter's fists fell to his sides. "You weren't, like, busy colorin or somethin? Playin Tetris on your Game Boy?"

"Tetris?"

"I dunno. Mario 10 or whatever."

"You're old," T jabbed.

But the punch only put a smile on his opponent's kisser. "Alright funny man. Let's take a blow." Franco put the coffee table back in position. The spring flower blossoming before his eyes had enough watering for one day. The spring flower that, the next day, was either gonna bloom. Or get snipped.

The blue Mustang groaned to a stop front and center of the school. The whip sheltering father and son from the whipping wind. Franco was dressed nicer than usual. Blue jeans and a short-sleeved collared polo. A little light for the cold weather but the petite polo was the perfect mix of professional and imposing. He knew the odds were that he'd be seeing Principal Mulligan soon enough and didn't wanna look like a bum. He was even clean-shaven and had his hair all set. The kid from Proper looked so proper, he had half a mind to apply ta Princeton. Maybe he'd ask Mulligan for his transcripts.

TJ didn't even care to brush his hair. Had the hood up on his black hoodie with the red W emblazoned on it. Along with track pants and sneaks. The fledgling fighter collected himself for a sec before running down to the cage.

"Till I Collapse" faded out. Franco had let TJ's boy Em do the talking on the way over. Starting with the military sound off that set the song off. The jump-off verses. And Slim's parting words. To not fall. To stand tall. All Franco had for T beyond that was a fist pound and a nod. And a stomach full of butterflies he barely kept in the conservatory.

TJ crossed the quad with pace. Found his hustle odd considering his odds. But as the winter wind whipped his face, he realized spring was only two days away. *It was all going to blow through.* One way or another. All TJ had to do was survive. And what luck, the teacher on-duty was one who actually took it seriously. His meticulous math teacher with the glasses and the dry classes. Mr. Lee.

TJ usually felt like a fraud wearing the Woodbridge Classic: the black hoodie with the red W and the hood thrown up. Didn't feel tough enough. It was the kind of thing someone like a Ray wore. But fuck that. Not today. It was T's town, too.

Ray spotted TJ crossing the quad. Sensed something was up. T-gay *never* wore the hood up. Little bitch had to have his spiky hair on full display all day every day. Ray took off "his" gray hoodie. Donned an XL T as big as T. Still, Ray's broad shoulders filled it out in full as it dangled about his waist. A human coat hanger ready to hang T. Ray stood stalwart in his steel-toed Timbos. A battleship ready to blow away the kamikaze headed right for him.

TJ's brave advance belied his inner monologue. *Think David and Goliath. Wait, how'd that go again? David slingshot Goliath in the head with a rock. How the fuck is that heroic? A slingshot back then was like having a gun! I don't have a gun! What do I got? Oh. Right. The teacher who can break up the fight. Fuck getting pounded to a pulp at Pearl Street. I gotta do this shit right here right now. Get my few moves in and get out. Stick and step. Nail then bail. Hit n quit. Wait, are those sex terms? Biggest moment of my life and that's what I'm thinking about. Ah fuck it—*

While TJ ran through those thoughts, he had run up on Ray. He cut through Dragon, Lenore, UN, Screws, and all of Ill Co like he was Moses parting the Red Sea. TJ's final steps were faster and faster but processed in his head slower and slower. With every last step he took, Ray got bigger. TJ threw his hands up and said, "Let's go!" Hoped only in his head did it sound like Frank the Tank tranq'd. "L e t' s g o o o o..." TJ, even after all the bullying, felt obligated to give Ray a fair fight. Fuckin power dynamics.

Ray put his hands up.

TJ telegraphed a left hook—Ray's head shook, *Fuckin*

rook—POP. Ray's smirk was burst open by a right jab from T. *It worked!* TJ was so delighted and dumbfounded, he laughed. Then it registered, as if on delay, what heads were yelling around him— *Fight! Lil nigga hit Ray!*

TJ followed it up with another fake, followed by shooting for Goliath's legs. The giant fell! TJ knew what was gonna happen next. He had seen *A Christmas Story.* He was gonna ground and pound the bully into oblivion. T teed off with his best Ralphie impersonation. But Ray's Timbo booted him in the abdo. Blasted his ass to the asphalt. Apparently, Ray had never seen *A Christmas Story.* The raging bull was more a fan of *Raging Bull.* While DeNiro was paid dinero, Ray came at T for free.

T checked Mr. Lee—busy redirecting a bus! Busting the driver's balls about rules and regulations. Fuck! T did some math of his own: It was him, Goliath, and no gun. TJ improvised a new move not covered with Dad. The backpedal. The backpedal overlaid with an apology. "Ray, my bad yo. It was an accident." *Accident? Good one, T!*

The towering teen before T uncorked a right like he was Tyson from *Punch-Out.* And Little Mac went down. Not in the traditional sense. TJ still had his wits about him. It was just that Ray hit so hard, TJ flat-out *fell* down. His left cheek split open.

Ray pounced. Told his own version of *A Christmas Story.* Once upon a time there was a right hook. Then a left hook. Then another right. Then another left. Then another right. Then another left. (Ray wasn't the best storyteller.)

One benefit to being small was that TJ covered up well. He shrunk into his shell. While he got beat to hell. But like Rocky, he didn't hear no bell. So T cracked back. His punches packed. With just enough to disrupt. He pulled himself up.

T and Ray squared up bloody face to bloody face. Fist to fist. Breath to breath. About to go again when faculty descended.

Principal Mulligan himself twisted TJ's arm behind his back. Hauled the mauled kid in. But TJ scooped up a commemorative keepsake on his way. A hoodie. Gray.

Franco held a needle and suture over the stove flame. "How ya feelin?"

TJ sat on the stool before Dad. Rubbing alcohol stung the gash below his left eye. His head pulsated. His stomach panged. "Good." TJ's grin gave way to a wince as a needle dashed across his gash. Dragging a suture to limit the scar in T's future. "Tell your mother I took you to the ER."

"Why not just use Mom's insurance?"

Franco prepped the next suture. "Between the deductible and the wait at the ER...forgetaboutit. And besides, *I* can take care of you." Still, Julie was eventually gonna find out about the suspension one way or another. Three days for a first-time offender. The standard policy Franco had already been familiarized with as a 14-year-old himself. System never made sense to Franco. Do something bad at school and they give you a vacation. Not to mention get you behind on your work and set you up for more failure. "Fuckin Mulligan."

Franco's scowl turned to a grin as he sewed the second stitch. TJ wanted to know what was so funny. Franco told him forgetaboutit. But TJ insisted. After the millionth "don't tell your mother" warning, Franco was off...

"When we were freshman, me and Joey Yo bookied bets. Mulligan finds out about it. Calls us in his office. Then he calls my foster father, who's twisted, of course. And Mulligan calls him. Right on speaker phone wit this smug face. Like nothin could make his day more than embarrassin a fuckin freshman kid. And I'm waitin for my father to go off any second. *You're in the fuckin principal's office, what the fuck, you're no good.* So Mulligan says to him, 'Do you know that your son has been bookie'ing bets for March Madness?' And my father goes, 'Yeah. I got Duke!' I swear ta God me and Joey laughed so hard, we fell out of our chairs."

TJ was laughing so hard, he almost did the same. Was so wrapped up in the tale that Franco got two more stitches done.

As Franco wrapped the last few, he wrapped the story. "Then my father goes, 'And he's only layin six!' Mulligan's face was beet red. He didn't know what to say. And my old man goes, *Who you got?* Me and Joey had to hold onto each other. Hold our mouths shut. So Mulligan just hangs up the phone. And Joey has the juice to say to him, 'You hear that, Mr. Mulligan? We're only layin six. You want in?'"

Franco and T were laughing so hard, Franco was wiping away tears. Delirious like he was watching Eddie Murphy's *Delirious.* So spun, he had a blurry vision of Julie through his tear-soaked eyes. Like a desert mirage in the heat wave on the horizon. Franco grabbed his kitchen rag, wiped away his tears. But the mirage remained."I work around the clock for four days. I get one day. Before heading to another mess altogether. And this is how I have to spend it?" With every rhetorical question, Julie stepped forward. *"Suspended?"* Her heels landed on the linoleum tile. One by one. Like a pissed-off pirate's peg leg. *"Homemade stitches? Modeling your lousy teenage behavior?"* Captain Julie rolled up on the taller deckhand like TJ rolling up on Ray. Only this time, the little one instilled fear in her foe.

Franco absorbed her opening barrage. Came back with a dodge. "You say somethin about me bein a model?"

Julie shook her head. Franco's funnies had flamed out. "It's sad that you don't know what modeling means. You're a thirtysomething father. You, of all people, should appreciate the importance of that."

TJ, the recurring ref of their ring bouts, registered a potential low blow. He'd keep an eye on it. Fight on.

Franco fired back. "Did you know TJ was being bullied?"

"No." Julie supported herself with a hand on the counter. Franco had landed his counter.

She fired back. "There are other ways to deal with it. Now he's gonna miss the rest of the school week." Julie moved in for a closer look at her son's stitched-up cheek. "And now I don't have a leg to stand on with Miss Lane and getting him into Future Problem Solvers."

Franco waved off her inspection of T's cheek. "Maybe it's time he manned up and took care of things like that himself. Instead of having his mother call the school all the time."

Oh no he just didn't. TJ leaned so far back in his stool, he again almost fell off.

"Right. Okay. I'm out of the equation for four days and look where we're at." Julie motioned to TJ's stitches.

T fingered the stitches on his fileted face. "They feel pretty good."

Julie cut the flame on the stove. "Get your stuff. I'm taking you home."

"You're done with?—" Franco and T said at the same exact time.

"You owe me a Coke—" Franco and T again said at the same exact time.

Having *again* said the same thing at the exact same time, T rushed in with another, "You owe me a Coke!" a second ahead of sire.

"Ohh!" Franco crowed in defeat.

"I'm not done in the field. I have to head right back out. Thank you two very much. I'll have my neighbors keep an eye on him."

TJ tagged into the ring that was now WWE wild. "Keep an eye on me? Who? That Peeping Tom across the street?"

Franco tacked on two cents. "Come on, Julie. You can't leave a 14-year-old kid home alone."

Julie hit the tag-teamers with their own words. "Well, TJ can man up and take care of things himself!" Double clothesline.

Franco and TJ lay on the canvas. Out cold. The victorious Julie had no time for a gloating strut around the ring. She hustled around the arena, collected TJ's things.

TJ might as well have returned to the role of ref and slapped Franco's kitchen table. *One. Two. Thre*—

"Hold up." Franco threw Julie off the pin like The Rock stonewalling Stone Cold. If only Jerry Lawler was there. "Let him man up then. T. Where you wanna stay?"

TJ stood at the entryway between Franco, focused in the kitchen, and Julie, livid in the living room. Between a tough guy trying to sew up much more than T's eye. And a storm manager who had sheltered TJ from day one. Between a deckhand on the *HMS TJ*. And the captain of the ship.

"I think... I wanna stay with Dad."

The captain stood near the front door with her arms crossed. Paced from bow to stern and gave a stern warning. "You've got one more chance."

Franco responded with a line from "One More Chance." Told Julie he had that good love. She didn't know?

TJ bit his fist. Took everything he had to hold in a laugh.

"I'm not kidding. One more. Take care of my boy."

The deckhand could've just given the captain another aye aye. But he had bigger ambitions. *"He's my boy, too."*

The captain steeled her steel-blue eyes on the insubordinate. Then did an about face. Laid a hand on her baby's face. Got a sense of the patchwork the deckhand had done. Then got a sense of something much more sinister. She sensed a mutiny about.

TRACK 8. YOGI

NOBODY'S A KILLER until they have to. The line ran through Franco's head as he showered off another early-morning mat session with Coach Nelly. The line steaming him worse than the shower. He had docked the Dock Thing for four days. The Frog wouldn't stand a fifth.

Franco shut the shower to lather himself with soap, the shoulder-wide stall leaving no room to otherwise evade the agua. Meanwhile, a second line haunted his head. One back from Lane's class no less. The Frog was once the only guy Franco could trust. And now he was asking Franco to do dirt no amount of soap would ever wash off. Whether Franco got away with it or not, the act would effectively kill him and all he stood for. It was Wednesday, March 19. Four days since The Frog stuck him with the murderous plan. Like Brutus sticking Caesar. *Beware the Ides of March.*

But paying his own way was also what Franco stood for. With the Eddo fail, the dock lockout, and the killer he'd face in the cage the following Saturday, Franco needed an umbrella for possible thundershowers ahead. He ran through

The Frog's plan as he dressed in front of his dresser. *Head down Atlantic City. Guy's name is Yogi. Runs a trucking outfit that's an outfit for something else. Human traffic. He's in bed with Arturo. Tell him he's got two choices. He can pay the twenty large he owes us thanks to his bets on the Nets. Or he can give us Arturo.*

TJ was at his flea-market desk. Wanting to flee the assignment Lane pressed. A presentation. A prompt: *Our high school is one of diverse influences. Describe a cultural movement in the United States that has helped weave the fabric of the nation as we know it today.*

TJ had seen versions of this prompt before. To him, it was code for: write about Abraham Lincoln or Martin Luther King. Not that he didn't have love for them. But by the third presentation in a row delivered by freshmen without one millionth the speaking ability of either man, even old Abe would tip his hat down and take a nap. Worse, T was gonna be with the last group of presenters. On his first day back from suspension. Which, on the bright side, wouldn't be until after the weekend.

So T skated on the assignment as he surfed the Web. Spaced on MySpace. Then popped onto that new Facebook joint popping off. Where all of Ill Co was popping off. Obsessed with yet another new kind of thing. An image. *A still shot of TJ popping Ray!* Even TJ had to laugh over how high he had to punch. Jumping to jab. So affixed on the punch, TJ didn't even notice the photoshopping at first. The jeans around T's crotch hung down to the ground. He read the captions. Across the top: LITTLE MAN. Across the bottom: BIG BALLS. TJ did an internet search and figured out that this thing was called a me-me. And this one was all about him-him.

All of Ill Co weighed in with comments...

> UN: littel mack!
> Screws: crunk
> Dragon: Five-foot ferocious!
> Lenore: Wow (*Neutral as fuck*, TJ thought.)

And on and on as TJ scrolled comments from kids across the school. TJ ate them up like Pac-Man eating pellets. Even reached a Power Pellet—

> Ray: respek

Pac-T kept reading. Gulped ghosts until the Power Pellet's time expired—

> Ray: i did endup woopin his ass doe

Still, Pac-T was satisfied. He may not have topped it all off with eating the cherry, but he had beaten the board. And now? It was time for some next-level shit. TJ turned off his monitor. Turned for the door.

Franco turned the tuner in his groaning car in need of a tune-up. Kanye's "Stronger" was killin it on Hot 97. Franco was wishin it was '97. Sure, this new kid could spit game. Mad game. Maybe even be the face of the new generation on Bill Simmons's Mount Rapmore one day. If you wanted to go beyond founding fathers. Franco didn't even have that part down. Could barely calculate a consensus on the gangsta rap era alone. Figured it was probably Dre. Biggie. Pac. Jay-Z. If you were okay with icin out the Ices. And Franco would personally give a nod to Nas. If he ruled the world. Or would he give the last spot to the last great gangsta rapper? Yeah, he was 50/50. He'd give it to Nas. Or 50.

Franco figured that's why he wasn't feeling this new cat. This new cat that T probably had on the slimmest of lists. With Slim. It's just, he wasn't... *Street*, Franco concluded as the Stang protruded onto Green Street.

Franco flipped the station. Looking for that Jersey Haitian. A '90s rap refugee. In search of a Fugee. But Power 105 was popping more of the day's top hip-hop. And 100.— was so thick, it was playing Robin Thicke. The whole thing made Franco *th*ick. Rap had gone mainstream. Corporate. Materialistic. As cumulus accumulated above, he flipped through all the New York stations. Still, he couldn't find any playing songs from the only recent album he liked. Nas's *Hip Hop is Dead.*

As his pony galloped onto the Parkway South, Franco wondered if it was him who went south. While rap rose up from the projects to the penthouse, Franco was still living on Bunns Lane. Living like it was still Nineteen Naughty Three. Still tryin to keep his head up like he had a pact with '93 Pac. Meanwhile, Curtis Jackson was giving the gat up. Turning fifty cents into fifty million while Franco was checking in with a .45 and forty-five cents in checking. Ready to chump someone off for chump change. Damn. The chump had to change. *Had to win that next fight.* And the sooner he took care of the day's business, the sooner he could get back to focusing on the fight. Franco stepped on the gas, passed on the right. Almost ran over a dead fawn. Its shoulders shimmied out past the shoulder. Marshall Mathers on the mind of the Mustang's rider as he passed the blood splat. Wondered where the parents were at.

But as the Mustang stole away from The Steel Cage,

106

Franco felt more and more at ease. Free on the freeway, he put in an old CD. Bruce's *Live* album. The right choice for sure as he ripped down the shore.

The Mustang steamrolled the rolling hills of the Parkway. Forest lining both sides. As Franco passed the PNC Bank Arts Center, he reminisced about when it was The Garden State Arts Center. The place where him and Joey saw George Thorogood back in high school. When the inebriated underagers outdid the Bad to the Bone headliner and got kicked out for fighting.

Ten more miles south, the sun shone into the Stang. Warmed Franco's forearms and foretold of spring. The blue bomber had an extra spark as it dashed past Asbury Park. Past Bricktown toll booths. Past signs for Seaside Heights. All while its driver dreamed of Julie. Still in love with a Jersey girl as he listened to "Jersey Girl."

The Mustang funneled from four lanes near Woodbridge to three lanes near the Arts Center then to two lanes as it tore through mile markers 70-something, 60-something, and 50-something. The monotonous mile markers that told you one-tenth at a time exactly how far you were from Cape May. The southern tip of Jersey. The northern end of the Parkway atop Jersey clocked in at mile 174. Woodbridge at mile 129. Franco's personal fave, Seaside Heights, illed at 82.

Below Exit 82, South Jersey might as well have been the South. The barren pines of the Pine Barrens haunted the highway. The area's population apocalyptic. Just a scattering of Phillies phans too phar phrom New York. The demographic divide further accentuated by the Southern accents. South Jersey, after all, dipped below the Mason-Dixon. Dead west was Virginia. As was West Virginia. And Cape May, if you may, was farther south than Bullittsville, Kentucky. The Confederate Monument at Finns Point the finishing touch of the only Union state to make the unpopular choice. Of never giving Lincoln the popular vote.

The Mustang made it out of the 70-60-50-something markers. Franco looked forward to the 40s. The Parkway miles, not the drinks. (Although he had liked those, too. Back in the day. Drinking 40 ounces to freedom listening to *40oz. to Freedom.*) Emerging from the sticks of Jersey was a marshland of saltwater tributaries cutting through swaths of brush. A marshland that, hundreds of years ago, musta been what the Woodbridge-to-Newark stretch looked like. While Franco's stomping grounds developed into an interconnected organism of bridges, factories, and oil tanks—all with a sheen of rust that suggested it had risen right from the muck—the 40s were rather undeveloped. Franco envied the allure of the boater casting his lure. Envied the headphoned boy on the bridge who bobbed as he watched his bobber. Envied the couple just sittin on a dock of Great Bay.

As Franco was just wastin time idealizing their lives, the skyline had snuck up on him. Always his cue to play "Atlantic City." This day was no different. Although the song took on a much different meaning this go-around. The song used to be a pump-it-till-the-speakers-popped gambling anthem for Young Franco and Joey. Back when the 19-year-olds, back in 1994, would floor it to the shore.

Inside the T——, they'd get drunk on Jack n Coke as they blackjacked n joked. A desperate city more than happy to let the kids sitty. A wise move as the two often left without their loot.

They'd play "Atlantic City" once more with the skyline in their rearview. Not so loud the second go-around. It turned into a soothing song as they'd (only half-jokingly) sing to each other. The 6 am sun would continue the soothing. Along with another couple. Just sittin on a dock of Great Bay.

Then there were the one-day getaways with Julie. After thirty days of diapers. Thirty days of middle of the night needs. Thirty days of Julie nursing a baby in one arm and reading a school book in the other. Thirty days of Franco down the docks only to come home to a two-year-old so temperamental. Praying he'd only temporarily gone mental. Thirty days of saving up a lil down payment for their own piece of pavement. In the meantime living with Julie's mother. Thirty days of paying the old lady rent, listening to her vent, wondering where their lives went. Thirty days of watching their friends do whatever the fuck they wanted. Living rent-free with Mom and D. Bullshit jobs easy as ABC. Then Franco and Julie's one day. To get faded with fake IDs. To do some rooftop drinkin n smokin in Hoboken. Franco would suck a cigar and sip an old fashioned as if he were Hoboken's hometown hero himself. Their one day to meddle through the Meadowlands and scalp some Devils nose bleeds. Then watch The Polish Hammer make someone's nose bleed. Their one night to go clubbing at Hunka Bunka. Nights of X n white hot sex. Their one day to go to Monmouth track and bet on some ponies. Then mosh at the Stone Pony. Or to try some grapes off the vine in Vineland. When Franco would whine all the way to the winery. *It looks like a refinery! We coulda stayed in Woodbridge.* Then he'd have a few glasses. Slow his nerves to molasses. All along these stops, the two would get glassy-eyed only to miss their baby's eyes. The big browns that seemed to have a light on behind them. Thirty days of looking forward to leaving him. Then spending their one day bereaving him. The way he'd raise his armpit, inviting you in for a tickle. Only to shut it and giggle. The way Julie tried to teach him for months to say "Mama." Yet his first word was "Dada." The way he was handsomer than Franco and smarter than Julie. The way that for all their bitching and moaning

109

and all of *his* bitching and moaning, he was Julie's "sweetest pea she ever did see." And Franco's "main man." Toddler T would respond to Franco's sentiment by pointing to his own chest then to Franco's. To his own. Then to Franco's. To his own. Then to Franco's.

Of all those one-day getaways, AC was Franco and Julie's favorite. They'd bomb on the Expressway. To the bomb city across the bay. Franco would track the casino skyline from left to right. The towering Taj showboating next to the Showboat. Then the Sands sticking out of the sand. The casino run ceasing around Caesar's. With the last stop The Trop. All as Franco crooned Bruce's classic tune.

Franco would treat Julie to strip steaks off the strip. In a cash-only hole in the wall only a goodfella could find. Then they'd stroll the boardwalk. Pop in the Taj and let the dice flow. Like they were Ashanti and Fat Joe. And when the night was done. Hit the hot tub like Pun. Sip champagne bubbles. And forget all their troubles.

The morning hangover was exacerbated by having to get back for baby boy. Franco would get up first. Make Julie a *cup a cawfee*. Watch her sit up and sip. The cold lines from "Atlantic City" at the tip of his lips.

Then there were the AC trips Franco enjoyed even more. The fledgling fighter's first fights. When he rolled with both Js. One rolling Js. The other helping him smoke them. Franco meanwhile clean as a whistle. Ready for the ref's whistle.

Franco so thoroughly mopped up the first few amateurs that the hotel staff had to mop up after each one. Franco took one of his main lessons from the streets—*get the guy on the ground*—and turned it into a signature ground-and-pound strategy. Not that he didn't have any struggles. The first Jiu-Jitsu opponent he faced had attempted so many guillotines, Franco was sure he was French. But Franco persisted and bought Jiu-Jitsu lessons of his own with the $500 purse. Crushed Julie's dream of a Louis Vuitton purse. Yet another Frenchman who tried to put Franco in a guillotine. (BTW it was a December fight and it was less than the $600 required for an employer to file a 1099 on an independent contractor. So keep it on the DL if you don't mind.)

Franco was not only earning money but also a rep. He was a fan favorite in AC. A Jersey boy who fought like the state. Scrappy. Relentless. Carried his pride no matter the opinion outside.

It was around those early fights in AC that Joey Yo, high on vodka and Vicodin (the latter prescribed to Franco for post-fight injuries and promptly passed to Joey), came up with the nickname. *The Bunns Lane Brawler, yo!* It was perfect. It repped where Franco was from and how he fought. It also took the negative stereotype around town—"BLB" for Bunns Lane Boy—and spun it into something positive. And to top it all off, the nickname was kinda funny. A play on the clownish wrestler, the Brooklyn Brawler. Only Franco wasn't fooling around. He promoted Joey Yo from boxing coach slash corner man to boxing coach slash corner man slash hype man. Kordell Stewart had nothing on Joey. "The Bunns Lane Brawler" was soon added to the flyers for all of Franco's fights. Fights Franco couldn't wait to get to. Pedal to the floor in his Air Max as he pumped "Atlantic City" to the max. Singing those opening lines about a rumble. As he got ready to rumble.

Those fight trips were the only trips where Franco still saw the optimism of "Atlantic City" on the way home. As the tune played, he'd dream of turning it all around. He'd dream of dissolving his debts to The Man and absolving his allegiance to The Frog. He'd dream of a future as a big-time fighter and a first-class father. Taking the lyrics to heart as the casino skyline lingered in his rearview.

It was only on this latest trip for The Frog that Franco realized how bleak the song was. And here Franco was living the bleakest lines of all. About a guy out of work. About to do dirt. Even worse, Franco realized that those other lines, the ones he had put so much hope in, were... *What was that word Lane loved to use? Fuck. Shoulda paid more attention in school. Oh wait. The word Robin Williams uses in* Good Will Hunting. *Yeah, that's it...* Ironical. The realization hit Franco between the eyes like a pop from The Prince.

Franco turned off the tune. Turned off the Expressway well before AC. He double-checked the directions The Frog wrote on the back of a White Castle napkin. Franco was in the right spot. In industrial outskirts. Just like the ones he was always eager to get away from on trips to AC. Only this time he was far from the skyline. On the other side of town. Atlantic Shitty.

The Mustang popped along a potholed road like a militia mustang on cobblestone. Its rider concerned about the fort up ahead. An industrial garage bolstered by a fleet of eighteen-wheelers. A Confederate stronghold fixin to hold the Mason-Dixon. Franco a visiting Yankee. And not the kind he dreamed of as a boy. A Yankee who now dreamed of turning his pony around, tucking in both their tails, and heading home. But his general wouldn't grant a pardon. So Franco parked his pony. And marched on in to Confederate quarters.

Franco sat in the Southern general's office. Nothing he hadn't seen up the docks. The grease-smudged phone. The files and paperwork. Flypaper that didn't work. Shelves of tools. A cracked window that let in the cold. Airing out the mold.

Two Cane Corsos barked and jumped at the door.

Till their master heeled them to the floor.

The giant then had to lower himself just to enter the room. The archway his archnemesis. Yogi. The bear. The biiig bear. Forget Joey Yo. This guy was Big Show big. Like Franco could rear naked choke him for three weeks to no avail big. So big, Franco stood up to greet him...then tried to stand up again. Franco shook Yogi's ham hock of a hand like he was shaking hands with a gloved Lou Gehrig. Guy made a babe out of Babe Ruth. The .45 sacked in Franco's sacrum suddenly felt good.

The two men sat across from each other. "Fighter?" asked Franco as he nodded to Yogi's oversized knuckles.

Yogi nodded. His overgrown hair shook.

"Heavyweigh—" began Franco.

"Super heavyweight," croaked the man from deep within his belly.

"I fight—"

"You're not here to discuss fighting."

"You owe twenty large," said Franco without flinching.

"I doubled down on the Flyers. Left it on The Frog's voicemail."

Franco shifted in his seat. The Frog had left that part out. Assuming it was true. Franco put the probability at 80 percent. Still. "We don't take voicemail bets," informed Franco.

"That's not how The Frog worked it with me."

"You have an out. Just give us Arturo."

Yogi stroked his black beard like he was Blackbeard. Pondered the plank for the Yank. "Sure. Soon as you serve me some frog legs."

Point taken. Why the fuck did Franco think it would be so fuckin easy to come down here and get Yogi to give up *his* guy? Oh right. Cuz The Frog told him it would. *But bring the gun just in case.* When Franco had asked The Frog if this Yogi guy would be trouble, The Frog turned on the charm. *Have you ever met a guy that gave you trouble? Huh, tough guy?* Then gave Franco one of those friendly slaps to the face. Franco couldn't think of a guy that gave him trouble at the time of The Frog's rhetorical retort. He could suddenly think of two.

"All due respect—" Franco began.

Yogi belly laughed. "You boys and your sayings. You can say anything as long as you put 'All due respect' in front of it, right?" Yogi stood up. Ready to give Boo-Boo a boo-boo. "All due respect, I'm not paying you. All due respect, I'm not gonna give you Arturo. All due respect, I'm gonna give *you* to Arturo." Yogi yanked the Yank from his seat. "In the back of a meat truck."

Franco tore away—his t-shirt tore away. He crashed to the floor. His gun slid to the door. Franco went for it—Yogi blasted him with a knee to the diaphragm. As if he had Franco's weakness diagrammed. Franco plowed into a shelf. The big man attacked like a hammerhead—until Franco took a hammer to his head.

The big man went down. Right on top of Franco. Half-conscious and fully focused on choking Franco out. There was a reason the fight game had weight classes. Franco had enough trouble tangling with Bobby Brazil. This guy was the *size* of Brazil. Franco wondered if that would be his last thought on Earth as Yogi choked him out.

Yogi crushed Franco's windpipe with a single paw. His other pawed for the gun on the gum-stained tile. The bear then proved himself homo sapien after all as his able appendages wrapped around the handle of the gun. His index fingered the trigger. He pressed the gun to Franco's forehead. BLAM!

Franco figured the shot deafened his ears in his final

millisecond moments. He didn't hear a loud bang. Just a thud. Followed by another thud. Yogi had keeled over. *What the fuck?* Franco thought he was in *The Twilight Zone.* Thought that he was dead and all that science fiction shit turned out to be true. Different dimensions and all that. His new existence was so warped that T stood over him. Holding a shovel. As if T had just dug his dad out of a grave and into a new life.

Because he did. Back on Bunns Lane a couple hours before, when little T decided that he was ready for the big time, he had snuck into Franco's trunk. Tucked a sock into the socket. Latch atchually. Then hatched out of it and waddled over to the office window. Like a baby bird perusing for his parent. Like in that Dr. Seuss book Franco would read to toddler T.

Teen T's heart raced a hundred miles an hour. Half nervous, half excited as he rambled bits and pieces of the backstory to the flustered Franco.

"What the fuck!" choked Franco.

TJ shrugged with the shovel. "Well, the hammer didn't get it done." T looked down at Yogi. Looked at his shovel. At Yogi. At his shovel. T put the back of his hand under Yogi's nose. "Don't worry. He's not dead."

"What the fuck!" Only this time it wasn't Franco. It was a trucker in a trucker hat. And aviator sunglasses. Ready to kick the Yanks' asses.

"Come on!" TJ ran to the window.

Franco tucked the gun and tucked through the window. The two ran off like Romeo and Juliet avoiding the wrath of the Montagues. Or was it the Capulets? Franco made a note to ask T later.

The Yankees ran for their pony parked outside the Southern stronghold. Under direct attack launched by the two Cane Corsos that had launched out the window behind them.

Franco and T hopped in their horse. Rolled up their windows as the barking dogs' snouts snipped at them.

The Stang's tires spun and spit gravel for a second that felt like forever.

The Northern pony reversed out. Then charged forward. Into an ambush. The truckers had flocked to a pickup hitched up on oversized tires. A gun-racked mudder manned by a mudderfucker passing out rifles like he was Robert E Lee.

Franco yanked hard on the reins of his pony, skidded it into an about face. The horse finally regained a grip of the gravel. Charged away as shots unraveled. CRACK. CRACK. CRACK.

"Get the fuck down!" Franco shouted as he shoved T into the door well. The rear windshield was then blown away as the Stang blew away.

The following adrenaline-filled fifteen minutes felt like fifteen seconds. Until Franco finally felt safe enough to whip his pony off the road and whip his son's ass. Franco yanked the door open. Yanked T out. "How fuckin stupid are you!"

"I saved your life! You could've died!"

"*You* coulda died!"

"Relax, alright? I'm ready for this shit."

Franco, toe to toe with T, was caught off guard by the comment. "Dafuck..." Franco wrinkled his face. T's comment was a round-one hook that had woken him up. He gathered himself. Crouched down. Let his guard down. Eye to eye with T. "You think I taught you to fight to be tough with these?" Franco motioned to his fists. "I taught you to fight to be tough up here." Franco motioned to his head. "You wanna be a real tough guy? That's where it's really hard to be tough."

Visions ran through the young Yankee's head. Visions of another Yankee. The mentally toughest person he knew. Number two. Jeter. His flip throw. His stadium dive. His game-winning World Series home run at 12:03 in the morning. In front of the home crowd in mourning. Doing his part, Mr. November, to heal the events of September. Because nothing, not even 9/11, was gonna hold New York back. And TJ suddenly felt like nothing was gonna hold him back either. Franco had just countered with a hook that woke TJ up as well. "I got it."

Franco looked into his son's eyes. He'd concede, in part, that the high noon sun might explain it. But he could also see that the mysterious light inside was on. The one that lingered somewhere behind his boy's big browns. The one he'd see emerging from the infant's eyes when he rocked him to sleep. The one he'd see on the Seaside boardwalk as the rides lit up the night something special. The one he'd see when he taught the tyke to ride his bike. The one he'd see when his boy slapped a hit then slapped Dad five at first. The one Franco hadn't seen in years. But there they were once again. On the side of the Garden State Parkway. Next to a shot-out Mustang. His boy's eyes amber against amber waves of marsh. New Jersey the Beautiful.

Franco threw another hook. It swung past T's head and pulled him in for a hug. Franco's new vantage point: his vanished rear windshield. "Now let's get dafuckouttahere."

The beastie boys broke north as families of deer came forth. They lined the hills in droves as Franco and T drove. The temp suddenly sat damn near 60. March was looking like it was gonna be in like a lion and out like a lamb after all. And after all the lion and lamb had been through, they were still divided on tunes. The lamb wanted to hear some of that Wu-Tang. But the lion, feeling as part of the earth, felt like putting his ear to the street. He spun the FM dial. To his surprise, it turned out to be 100.— that had him jumping. Almost out of his seat. "Oh shit! Little Steffanie! Girl's been cuttin this up in

117

North Jersey." Franco turned it all the way up.

TJ wrinkled his face. *What the fuck is this?*

"I seen her up in a club in Clifton. Little girl. Big voice. Biiig voice. Lit the piano on fire. Lit the *place* on fire."

TJ couldn't believe his ears as Franco popped the pop beat.

"I asked a guy who she was. Thought it was her manager. Turns out it was her father. A Jersey Joe named Joe. Made it big. Hopped over the Hudson. Anyway. I'm tellin you. Do not fuck with this girl."

"Dad. Eff with means the opposite now. *Do not eff with her* would now mean, *don't listen to her.* You should be telling me that I *should* eff with her."

"*Fuck with* means somethin nice now? That don't make no fuckin sense."

Father and son laughed.

Franco cranked the song all the way as the Mustang cranked into overdrive.

TJ shook his head. Of all the artists they could've ridden home to—Pac, Biggie, The Wu just to name a few—TJ definitely did not have his money on Lady Gaga.

Franco bobbed his head. "She could be, like, the latest part of the whole Italian Jersey thing."

"The mafia?"

"No!" Franco shook his head as the Mustang shook a car on the left. "The Italian Jersey *music* thing. Goes all the way back to Sinatra."

TJ wrinkled his face. Then. "What about us? Are we Italian?"

"Yeah. Your mother's mother. Jewish-Italian."

"No but...what about...you? What are you?"

Franco revved the Mustang into the red. He had given the kid the juice to take on Ray. And now the kid was comin after him.

The old pony roared through the rolling hills of the Garden State. The sun overhead. Trees budding green as the pony galloped past the Veterans' Memorial. The arena's circular edge was decked with Star-Spangled Banners billowing in the wind. Like it was a birthday cake for Uncle Sam himself. While Franco had finally found the answer himself. The one he'd be searching for his whole life. "I ain't nothin...if I ain't American."

As the Mustang's gears turned, so too were the ones in TJ's head. Franco had given him some food for thought for his presentation. And he couldn't wait to get home to feast on it.

It was a day so eventful, father and son would almost forget about the trooper who pulled them over for the rear windshield. Franco had kept his hands at ten and two. As one was supposed to do. Then told the trooper the truth. "I'm real sorry, officer. But...we were attacked by a bear."

TRACK 9. DON'T CALL IT A COMEBACK

TJ WAS HALF-ASLEEP as the third presenter in a row linked Lincoln to a beard, being tall, and a log cabin. Shit TJ knew since Lincoln logs. Then Lane called his name. Gave TJ one of her patented glasses-at-the-end-of-her-nose stares. "Your turn."

TJ got out of his desk with his index cards in tow. Walked up the aisle like it was death row. He looked out at his fellow inmates. UN sneaking a T9 text. Ray carving his desk. (DRAY.) Poor Lenore next to the boor. Not the prince she pictured when she was four. And the rest of the first-period class. Tired as fuck and feeling like ass. School would start at ten. If it was up to them.

"What if I told you that someone from the very same streets you walk on, the ones you walked on *this morning* to get here, made it out with music?" TJ cold opened in the cold room.

T's fellow inmates sat up.

"Let me ask you something else first. What do you think of when you think of Italians? *Jersey* Italians."

The inmates threw out answers faster than hands.

"Mafia."

"Guidos."

"Big T. Tony Sopranooo," responded Ray with a hand over his mouth.

"What if I told you that there was another Jersey Italian thing? One much bigger than the mob. One that has lifted countless souls from the soles of their boots. All around the world from here to Beirut."

The inmates at attention, T went on to explain what Franco tried to figure the day before. "The real Italian Jersey thing has been to make music to move the world. With real deal Italian—" TJ looked out at his eclectic cohort. "Real deal *immigrant*—" T looked at Dragon. "Real deal *American* ideals. Hustle. Heart. Heads on straight."

T's comrades leaned in.

"It all started back in Hoboken. A hundred years ago when a bunch of mostly brown and totally broke immigrants moved in. It became a dock town of tough guys and gals who stared at the Empire State Building with even bigger dreams. One of them was Frank Sinatra. Now you gotta—have to—understand that this guy was Jay-Z and Timberlake back when Woodbridge was timber n lake." T punctuated his punch line with a playful smile.

The gen pop gently snickered.

"You know how if you go to a Yankee game, they always play 'New York, New York' at the end? That's Frank Sinatra. I mean, this guy coming up was just a hobo from Hoboken. But he went on to inspire people around the world. To this day. From Billy Joel's 'New York State of Mind' to Nas's 'NY State of Mind' to Biggie lyrics, you can trace it all back to the Chairman of the Board."[4]

TJ looked to Lane. Couldn't get a read on her furrowed brow. Was she intrigued? Or could she not believe her goddamn ears? Lincoln ending the slavery nightmare. MLK having a dream. And now Lane's listening to TJ spout off about some hood from Hoboken? Was the Future Problem Solver wannabe creating a Current Problem? What the fuck was he thinking? Then. He remembered. He was thinkin, maybe the old lady loved the guy. He was thinkin, his inmates had him covered on King n Lincoln.

So on T went. "You know those *Jersey Boys* ads that are all over the place right now?"

UN slouched in his chair. "No son, no. Don't even go there with those corny—"

TJ pointed back at UN. Like he was at the podium of the UN. "Yes son! Yes!"

The other delegates delighted in T's response.

"I know you probably see them as some corny boy band from Bernardsville or something. But these guys were straight outta—out of—the projects. *Newark* projects. Yeah, you see the glitz and glam of the Jersey Boys on the commercials. But what you don't see is how they came up. How Tommy DeVito, who needed a few bucks to get going, went to prison for a heist in an alley. How Francesco Castelluccio had to change his name to Frankie Valli. Something more vanilla for the vanilla audience."

The Jersey boys and girls as diverse as UN delegates sat up in their seats.

After T sprang Springsteen on them, *You know, the guy we all danced to at homecoming. Living our Glory Days,* he moved on to the main event.

"Who's Snoop's main man?"

---

[4] And a year later, Jay-Z would be in an Empire State of Mind.

"Dre!" offered a now engaged UN.

"Who's Biggie's?"

"Diddy," said Lenore. Giddy.

"No doubt. Who's Richie's?"

"Like, Little Richard?" asked a little student named Richard.

"Nooo," said T with feigned offense. "Richie from Woodbridge. Richie who balled on the ball team and walked the very same streets you beat feet on this morning."

The Jersey boys and girls gave curious looks. *Who?*

"His main man was little Johnny Francis. Little Johnny who sailed over from Sayreville on the Driscoll, like we've all done a million times, and picked up Richie Sambora. Right off the streets of Woodbridge. Two working-class kids livin on a prayer who were gonna make it out dead or alive."

Ray shook his head. "Oh I feel ya, son. I feel ya."

The overweight UN weighed in, "He's talkin about—"

"Shut the fuck up and let him finish!" roared Ray. The big cat then purred to the teacher like a pussy cat. "Sorry Miss Lane."

Lane sat stone cold. Motioned for T to finish.

T wrapped up and from that day on everyone in the class, from the homies to the crass, had mad respect for Bon Jovi. And mad respect for T. Ray stood up and slow-clapped. Followed by them all clapping.

T's eyes changed lanes to Lane. Her stare longer than ever. Glasses at the end of a nose as long as Pinocchio's. "You were supposed to start with the name of the presentation."

"Oh. It's called Stereo Types."

"One word or two?" interrogated Lane with an eyebrow raised.

"Two." T threw up two fingers across his chest. In the

form of a peace sign.

The phone call came after school. TJ picked up the off-white phone from the kitchen wall on Bunns. It was Mom. Droppin a bomb. She had just gotten a call from Miss Lane. Apparently, TJ's presentation had hit Lane like *Anchorman* had hit T. So different, the observer wasn't sure what to make of it. Only to realize hours later he/she loved it. In Lane's case, she said it was because it was *thoroughly original and exquisitely crafted*. TJ's presentation. Not *Anchorman*. (Although Lane did appreciate *Anchorman* as well for both its politically incorrect 1970s setting and positive feminist message.) And not only did Lane love it, Julie's boy, *her boy* as Julie kept calling TJ, had an open invite to join Future Problem Solvers.

TJ stood stunned in the kitchen on Bunns. "That's...great."

"My boy. I'm so proud of you." Julie then told TJ she had to get back, but the call had been a nice shelter from the storm. Mom. Always killin with Dylan.

But when TJ hung up the off-white phone, something was off. *Her boy.* As she said over and over. But as Lane said, *Exquisitely crafted and thoroughly original. Exquisitely crafted.* Yeah, TJ had honed that presentation all night like he was high school Julie circa 1990. But. It was based on something Franco had said as they tore through the streets of Jersey. *Her boy.* A more accurate tale would be the one T learned about in *A Bronx Tale.* A line from C occurred to T. About how he was getting two educations. One from school. And one from the street. That way, he'd be twice as smart. TJ looked in the living room mirror. Big eyes like Mom's. *Exquisitely crafted.* A chiseled chin like Dad's. *And thoroughly original.*

TJ looked out the front window to the projects across the

way. A smile lit up his face as four five-year-olds ran in a race. And it wasn't just that sight that caused him delight. The son of The Brawler had come up with his own nickname. The Brain from Bunns Lane.

TJ waited by the front window for hours. Like he was five years old all over again. When he used to wait for Daddy to dock his car after a shift at the docks. TJ, now damn near 15, was once again excited to tell Daddy all about his day.

Franco parked the pony and unsaddled. On his cell phone. He bobbed back and forth on his brown grass.

TJ came running out. "Dad! Dad—"

Franco halted T with a hand. Spoke into the cell. "Are you fuckin kiddin me?" Franco paced back and forth so many times he coulda mowed his little lawn by now. "Gimme an hour." Franco flipped the phone shut.

"Dad. You're not gonna believe—"

"Not now." Franco again threw his hand up. Hopped back in the Stang. "I'll be home…" Franco couldn't finish his sentence. Couldn't think straight. Like that time Julie dropped the D-word on him. He couldn't process anything T said. He had to cruise and clear his head.

Franco took the Turnpike North debating a call, *what to do*, on the call that just came through. Like he was sitting at a Borgata blackjack table. The rider ran through his life's hands. He figured his birth was a 16. Not the best of hands, his own mother letting him out of her hands. But considering the alternative of not existing at all, he'd take it. The Dealer then dealt him a childhood full of busts. Foster parent after foster parent in it for the rent. His last mother moving on to a better place. Leaving Franco with the old man and his unshaven face. Lost in space. Little Franco always belting out

"Happy Birthday" as he wondered what it was like to be the kid behind the cake. The hosting parents taking a host of pictures. Franco always on the outskirts. Halfway in the frame. Smiling to conceal his shame. Meanwhile, his own *birthdayyys* was as bad as Biggie's. "Dad" too busy drinking Tanqueray to acknowledge the day. Had money for booze but not for shoes. While little Franco wore Adidas sandals in winter. Walked through slosh that soaked his socks. Little Franco would wonder if he should leave The Table altogether. The cold shoe leaving him cold and without shoes. But there were the intermittent wins that kept him hanging in. Getting seated next to Joey Cano in kindergarten. Twenties for the kids who would be friends past their 20s. And more 20s, two jacks Franco would figure, as the new jacks got bigger. From balling on Bunns to chasing buns. And Franco's favorite. Cooling at the Cano's. Where Joey's Puerto Rican papá and Mediterranean mamma would make pasteles n lasagna. Where the fami(g)lias on both sides would converge on little Joey's birthday and argue over which was better. Which side had more pride. More who fought n died. More blondes that dyed. But little Franco had another vantage point from atop the pool's slide. He saw below the surface as he slid toward the pool's surface. He saw two similar sides. Full of love and laughter. Matching arms to see who was tanner. Those intermittent 20s from The Dealer that had Franco concluding, *That's what he must be.* Puerto Rican-Italian. Or at least what he wished he was. Wished, in the middle of one of Joey's joyous parties, that for once he would be the star. That the stars would align and Joey's tío or tía or zio or zia would reveal himself or herzelf as Franco's long-lost parent. The intermittent 20s that would finally come around after a recurring run of busts. The 20s that would look so good all the way around the horn. Until The Dealer dug up a

21 and sentenced Franco back to his hell of a home.

The Mustang droned past Turnpike oil tanks. Its driver half there, half at The Table handing out his life's hands. A song emerged from the radio deep within the recesses of the rider's brain. All these years later and the man was still slayed by Manfred Mann. Could still hear that ditty. "Do Wah Diddy Diddy." And remember when he first saw Julie. Damn, so pretty pretty.

The first day of Franco's freshman year. (He loved how whenever he referred to his freshman year, more upwardly mobile mopes would ask, *Which college?* Ha. They musta read a million books and they couldn't even read the walking talking one right before them.) September. Easily the most underrated chronology on the calendar. With its warm weather and clear skies. School kids with hopeful eyes. And of course. The month that Franco met Julie. The stunner who needed no stunners. Walking along with her little backpack and her little back packin. Her blue orbs floating along as if God had pulled two pieces of September sky and stuck one in each eye. Then yanked a sheath of October night and laid it atop the fair lady. Blessed her with skin as fresh as November rain. The Goddess decked Franco like a December wind. At first sight, he had fallen. For the Female of Fall.

Young Franco hurried over and improvised. Asked her where the gym was. They were right next to it. Stupid. Wanted to hit himself in the head. *Well, where you goin?* Followed by, *Oh yeah, me too! I was...just jokin about the gym.* Jokin? What a joke. Nothing funny there. Swore ta God he'd kick his own ass if he kept it up. She hit the halls and he kept up. Made chit chat about this and that. Then the freshman tried to shock her. Told her he made varsity soccer. She hid her interest along with books at her locker. Then brought the courter to her home court. She asked if he was doing any clubs. Young Franco shrugged, "Just teen nights at Hunka Bunka." As his joke sat for a beat, his hopeful hazels searched her blues for clues. Like he was that nerd from *Blue's Clues*. The little lady bust out laughing. So surprised by her own outburst that she covered her mouth. Young Franco smiled back. Looking like a million bucks back then. His full head of hair in its heyday. His pre-fighting fresh face. Charming grin upon his chiseled chin.

Franco would joke for years that it took Julie ten times longer to fall in love. Franco in five seconds. Julie in five minutes. Julie would then always correct him and let him know that's actually sixty times longer. *Yeah but sixty times longer don't sound as good.* And on and on they'd argue. Till Franco would concede a loss to gain a kiss.

And on that first day of freshman year, Franco followed Julie right into class. Stared at her eyes as they stared at the board. For once in class, he wasn't bored. He looked on, impressed as she summoned the answers from summer reading. It wasn't until the end of class that the literature-loving teacher remembered to attend to attendance. It wasn't until then that everybody raised his or her hand. Save for the hood in the hoodie. Doting on the goody-goody. It wasn't even Franco's class. (Though for the rest of his life, he would casually mention how he was once in Honors English.) Franco missed his next class, too, as he was sent off to the office. His first high school period ever...and Miss Lane had brought the pain.

Still, Franco had booked meeting Julie as a blackjack. After fourteen years of cold shoes, The Dealer had finally bestowed him an unbeatable hand. Sure, The Dealer was also showing an ace. But Young Franco didn't need insurance. His head, his heart, and his other part gave full assurance. And for years, he felt great about his blackjack while The Dealer tended to other hands. But sure enough, The Dealer too turned over a blackjack in the early aughts when Julie said they oughta divorce. Best Franco could do was chalk it all up as a push as Julie pushed out of their marriage and took T across town. Franco had let them all down.

The Mustang groaned past Newark Airport. Planes full of people coming and going, living lives all over the planet. While the Newark-born boy once again boomeranged back to Newark. A trip that had become all too familiar as a part of The Frog's familia. The Frog and his offer to cut Young Franco in all the way. With both the docks and the accompanying extracurriculars. The Dealer was offering Young Franco an alluring 11. A no-brainer double down. But Young Franco thought twice. Wasn't feeling it. Instead, he hit. Wanted to take the temperature of being a temp. All the years since and all Franco had to show for them was a four from The Dealer. Sitting at 15 total with The Frog. Hit? Stand? Surrender?

Franco pulled the Mustang off the Pike and into downtown. His mind refocused on the more important hand at hand. The hand that caused Franco to dock his Stang not at the docks but in front of The Vault. America Bank's new arena. Home to pro sports. Events of all sorts. Like Franco's upcoming fight. Franco put a quarter in the quarter-hour meter. That's all he'd need. To lean against the hood of his Stang, stare at The Vault, and figure if he was up for the heist.

When he had gotten the call back on Bunns, Lama had let Franco know the news. The Prince's dance partner for the main event had suffered a torn tendon.

Fuckin Lama. Franco asked if she was kidding. She who, upon taking the inked agreements from Franco at her office in '01, said, "You do understand that you owe me 10 percent of everything, yes? Fight earnings. Promotional earnings.

Dock earnings." Franco's speckled hazels grilled her singular blue-meets-gray-meets-green Middle Eastern eyes. Whatever the color, it was as solid as her expression. The 26-year-old fighter stood up and had his arms going like he was Joey Yo—talkin about how he had to feed his family with the dock money and what the hell's that money gotta do with her—before Lama finally bust out laughing. "I'm kidding. I don't want your dock money. In fact, let's beat The Prince and you won't have to worry about it either." Franco sat back in her guest chair. Padded. Leather. Arm rests. Franco in his prime and primed for big things. Man was that chair comfortable. And the view out the tenth story of the Jersey City office. Fuckin A. The Statue of Liberty. Right there. Franco had half a mind to reach out the window and give Lady Liberty a fuckin high five. His other half a mind wanted to pick up Lama's fifty-button phone and call in for a straight-edge shave. Yeah, just sit back and stare just past Lady Liberty. To those two behemoths rising so high, Franco couldn't even see their tops. Yeah. Get that straight edge and calm his nerves over his new manager. His manager who, after just the first episode of that hot HBO show about Hollywood, would go on to earn a new nickname around the fight game. Lama Drama. But on that day in '01, it was all good for the kid from The Wood. Franco sat back in that padded leather chair. Twenty-six and sittin on top of the world. Soakin in those towers sun-kissed. Feelin as juicy as Sunkist. About to get paid. Blow up like—

Boom. Seven years. Seven fuckin years. The first year rehabbing. The physical therapy in the mornings. The docks despite doc's warnings. The second year getting back to fighting shape. Franco reassembled his team like it was an *Ocean's Eleven* prequel. *Franco's Five*. Wait. Nah. More like the Wu's *36 Chambers* "Intermission." Cuz Franco was on a mission. Fuck a career-ending injury. It was only intermission.

His comeback sent him back to regional fights in his third year. He wasn't a new jack no more, but the Jersey boy walked like a man and fought like a man in front of hollering crowds happy to have him back in AC. Franco was once again believing in the city's song as the Stang sailed away with each win. Didn't last long, though. He won three in a row. And was back in The Show.

In the fourth and fifth years, the 30-year-old with the reattached ankle was to serve as a warm-up for new fighters. And he was for the first two. But the next two. *They* turned out to be warm-ups for *him*. If he could take a third in a row, Lama could parlay it into a three-fight contender contract.

In that final match of the fifth year, Franco was chompin at the bit. Gnawin in Nawlins. Up against Shui Ming. Out of rural Beijing. Ming was a cagey veteran known for studying his opponents to the T. And it was no different for the father of T. Ming went after Franco's reattached ankle like a Goonie on the hunt for One-Eyed Willie. But The Bunns Lane Brawler was looking like his old self as he clocked Ming all over the cage. Then cornered him in a vertex, dropped him with a suplex, and put the crowd's cheers at an apex.

In the land of Johnny B Goode, Franco be so good that he knocked Ming down late in the second. Went in for the kill. But Ming got saved by the ding.

No sweat, thought the fighter who barely broke a sweat. Franco would finish him in the third. Bury him like he was Chuck Berry. Buryin a guitar riff. Franco strutted to his corner, looking like a lean machine way down in New Orleans. The soulful crowd so-full of love for the Jersey fighter. Kid was bomb. Like Marty McFly at the prom. When he rocked out to "Johnny B. Goode." Yeah, Franco be feelin good. As fly as McFly. Like he was back in his prime. Like he and his team had flown DeLoreans down to New Orleans.

Franco's fight team rubbed him down, talked him up, and wished him luck. But all he heard was Chuck. Singin about Johnny B Goode. Risin from the hood. How he came so far. And became a star.

The bell rang for round three. The ten thousand in attendance cheered for Franco like he was born on the bayou. Cuz he was. The northern bayou. The fuckin swamps of Jersey.

Franco came out swinging. Franco's relentlessness swept the crowd right off its feet. Till Shui Ming swept Franco off his. Ming tied Franco up with the skill of Brazil. They sat interlocked like they were on a seesaw as the momentum seesawed.

Ming applied an Achilles lock.

"Roll it! Roll it!" barked Brazil.

Franco rolled to his side. Shoved Shui's controlling knee out of position. Then shooed Shui with a kick.

Brazil raised his fist. Roared, *"Yes!"* His fighter was at his best.

Save for the now-aggravated fuckin ankle. Franco hobbled around the cage. Clocking the clock for the first time in his life. Begging it to tick down to the decision he'd take handily. All he had to do was keep shooing Shui.

Shui shot and shot to no avail. Then shot his load on one last shot. Franco backed up the bad ankle. But Shui clamped onto the good one. Franco shifted his weight to the bad one and went down. While Shui had used psychology reverse, Franco had Nelly and rolled a reverse. Then used a Brazil move to take the purse. Franco finished Ming with a rear naked choke. His Jiu-Jitsu no longer a joke.

The Nawlins crowd hooted and hollered over the gutsy performance. But while the ref raised Franco's arm, he could barely put down his foot.

The next day, Joey and Nelly had to help Franco hop through the hotel parking lot. Brazil and Taz hustled ahead and grabbed the car doors. They opened sideways. Same way they always did. No DeLoreans down in New Orleans.

Year six of the comeback. Sure, Franco's new three-fight contract was for The Show minimum but still. They'd be fights against actual contenders. A ladder to the top. A ladder Franco was game to climb. One win at a time.

Franco figured the first in Denver to be right up his alley. A Chechen bruiser named Umar Basayev. But as the bell rang for round one, Franco's tweaked ankle was ailing. He lumbered around the cage in round one like he was in the championship rounds of a barn burner. Worse, Basayev was the same height as Franco but bigger. They had both weighed in at 170 the day before. Franco's rehydrated, re-fed 180-pound fight night weight was usually an advantage. Even 185 now in Franco's advanced years if he was bein honest. Yet Basayev was even bigger. *And* the hothead had the exact same style as Franco. Came right at him. Rather than go to the ground with a bad ankle, Franco went toe to toe, blow for blow with Basayev. The bum-rushing Russian was a walking contradiction. Twenty-five yet bald like he was 35. Twenty-five yet acne like he was 15. Though Franco split both the guy's eyes, it was Basayev who took the split decision. As Basayev's hand shot up, Franco looked down to his ailing ankle. The Brawler shook his head. He'd *never* been outbrawled. Still. The Denver crowd tipped their hats to Franco. Battered like he was in a car crash and still standing. So impressive was the loss (although Franco would beg to differ—a loss was a fuckin loss) that The Bull, the fight commentator who conducted the post-fight interviews, wanted a word with Franco.

Joey helped Franco across the cage. Past Basayev and his boorish camp. "Fuckin steroid fuck. Could kill someone with that edge. Fucker should be in jail," jeered Joey.

The battered Franco leaned on Joey and leaned into The Bull's mic amid cheers for the tortured martial artist. "Nah nah. Thank yous. I didn't get it done. Next time. Thank yous." Franco made a fighter's fist then hopped past the hopped-up Basayev, busy celebrating with his fight team. All of them chanting in Chechen as Basayev raised his homeland's flag.

Joey made a fist behind the flamboyant fighter. "Should crack him in his bacne..."

Franco's arm around his bro tightened. "Let's get dafuckouttahere."

Yo begrudgingly let it go. Threw an arm around his bro. Helped him hobble away.

Franco and his fight team hopped in the Stang the next day. Two time zones from home with only two fights left. The fivesome sat in silence all day.

The driver tried to forget the decision in Denver. Flipped his CD case to John Denver. The driver's face as rocked as the Rockies. As puffed and blue as the partly cloudy skies above. And as fuckin hot as the helio ahead. He just wanted ta listen ta country. As he drove through his country. On a stretch of God's Country. But that fuckin Basayev big as a fuckin country. Like he was Bryant Reeves Big Country. On substances dirty as a cunt tree. The two sluggin in the trenches like soldiers in a foreign country. The winner raising the flag of his country. The loser feelin like a man *without* a country. While his ex single-mommed across the country. Like she was the star of *North Country*. While Franco lost and let em all down. From Julie n T. To God and Country.

Hours after the sun dipped below the surrounding mountains, the pony continued its ride through the valley of the shadow of death. The driver with the same name as Julio flipped through CDs—anything but Coolio. As Colorado ran to Nebraska, as dusk turned to dark, as his guys shut their eyes, the rider continued to turn the page. Finally ceased on Seger. "Turn the Page." The driver stuck in his rolling cage. Commiserating with the song. As his engine groaned along. How many times? How many times had Franco looked in that rearview from left to right? Coach Nelson. Husband. Father. Pillar of the community. The 40-year-old *AD*. Stuffed in Franco's horse carriage like it was 40 AD. Taz sittin bitch even though he could bitch out all of Woodbridge. Spiked-out hair hitting the roof. Style cramped along with his legs. Brazil's bald dome bobbing against the bantam rear window. Another 40-year-old. With an academy full of 4-year-olds. Yet there he was, miles away as his mile-long legs pushed up against Joey Yo's seat. Joey Yo. Two bills and sittin shotgun in the crowded car like he was the captain of a clown car. Co-captain. With good ole Franco. And the whole team in tow. For another loss in The Show.

Franco checked the Mustang's headlight setting. Already set to bright despite their dimness. The pony's eyes had gone south slowly but surely over the years. Franco peered into the desolate road ahead. Like Columbus looking out at the Atlantic. Wondering if there was a New World he'd ever arrive at. Or was Franco's Earth...flat?

The setback made Franco's second fight of the three-fight set a make-or-break. Against the tenth-ranked fighter, Thiago Alves. A win against a top-ten contender and The Show would have to follow it up with another. A loss and the third fight of his contract would be a rumble at the bottom of the barrel. A nobody on his way out. Making scraps for one last scrap.

To avoid that scenario, Franco would have to take down Thiago, a Jiu-Jitsu technician, in Tulsa. A fighter straight outta Brazil and backed by a well-heeled team. In matching warmups of yellow and green. Franco had leaned on Bobby Brazil a lot leading up to the fight. They rolled on the mats so much, they might as well have rolled down Main Street. Still, Jiu-Jitsu wasn't The Bunns Lane Brawler's strong point. Jiu-Jitsu was meant for the long and strong. He was compact and jacked. His heft and tight tendons that helped him pack an extra punch and score an extra takedown were the same ones that hampered him in Jiu-Jitsu. With its need to stretch. To slip. To grip. To tweak.

So there Franco was in SE Hinton's hometown. Feeling like an outsider. A Pony Boy who rode in on his pony ready to sock a soc. A soc well-backed and fighting from his back. A Venus flytrap begging The Bunns Lane Brawler to come on in. But Franco, thanks to the extra work with Brazil and the lesson learned in his pop at The Prince, avoided the homerun ground and pound. Just patiently waited like his boy 50. Danced around the flytrap and picked it off trichome by trichome for tri rounds. Nothing fancy. Nothing flashy. No bells. No whistles. No bullshit. Franco emerged unscathed yet found the fight one of his most brutal due to its test of technique and patience.

As Franco, his outsiders, and their pony galloped across the map, their careers had gotten back on it. Still, Joey was all shifty in shotgun. "Man that was some fuckin fight. Fuckin slow burn. I'm still all stressed out about it," said Joey as he filled the carcass of a Phillies. "The fuckin...Ulsa in Tulsa."

137

"What's that?" Franco said with an edge.

"I'll cut it out when we start camp," said Joey, blunt, as he rolled his blunt.

"Not that. *The Ulsa in Tulsa*. Like, as in *ulcer?*"

"Yeah. It's a fuckin joke."

"Like you're from fuckin Boston?"

In the backseat, Nelly, Taz, and Brazil shared looks.

"Here we go," sighed Brazil.

"Ding. Ding. Ding." declared Taz with three taps of his finger.

"I don't know—it rhymes," said Joey with his hands out. "And what's your beef with Boston? Like *Good Will Hunting* ain't your favorite movie."

Franco cracked his neck as the Stang cracked a hundred. "I got love for Boston, but...their fuckin World Serieses all the sudden. Their fuckin Super Bowls. Their fuckin million movies. Where are *we* at?"

"The Godfathers. Your no-goods in *Goodfellas*. *A Bronx Tale*," noted Nelly.

"When you factor in music. It's game over. Biggie. Jay. Nas. Shit, I could go on till we get home," boasted Brazil.

Franco looked out at the passing plains alongside the single-lane highway. "All good. No doubt. But... Where's *Jersey* at?"

"New York New Jersey. So what?" said Joey as he sparked his blunt. "We live right across the river from the Wu. You could take a canoe to the Wu!"

"The Fugees are Jersey," fed Brazil to the starved fighter. "Redman and Naughty. First rap hit ever was the Sugar Hill Gang."

"Iced Tea," teased Taz. "Dee one you look like."

"Ever heard of Bon Jovi? The Boss?" noted Nelly.

"Don't be sleepin on Whitney Houston," reminded

Brazil.

"Damn right. Greatest National Anthem of all time. Belted out by a black woman," noted Nelly. "Unimaginable when it was keyed by Francis Scott Key."

"Never forget that night. Watching in the barracks with my brothers," reminisced Brazil. "I was deployed the next day."

"Fuckin back in the day, son!" waxed Joey.

"Exactly. I'm talkin recently. Where's Jersey at recently?" clarified Franco.

"G-Men are lookin good," replied Joey. "They're Jersey ta me."

"Dee *Sopranos* just ended," tallied Taz.

"Yeah. *The Sopranos* was good," replied the driver, eager to pass a car he was stuck behind. "Then it all went black." It was a green Cadillac.

Joey puffed. "Damn homie. All I said was the Ulsa in Tulsa. Now you're givin me a whole other one." Joey exhaled. "How bout I put an r at the end of it? Like a real Jersey Joe. Straight outta Newark. The Ulser in Tulser. Like your nigga The Fr—"

"Why you gotta bring him up!"

"Dee truck! Dee truck!" yelled Taz like he was Tattoo. About to get tattooed.

Franco cut the wheel—the Stang cut away from the Mack. And back. Behind that fuckin Cadillac.

"I don't know what to tell ya, Franco," adjourned Joey with his hands out. "You wanna call it *da fuhkin Ulsuh in Tulsuhhh?*"

"Why you gotta say it like you got an eighty IQ?"

"Nigga whateva," puffed Joey.

"Enough with the niggas already. Nigga," spit Brazil.

"You don't think Puerto Ricans got African blood? Shit.

139

Same for my Sicilian side. You ever see *True Romance?*"

"Man you ain't no nigga. You a guido."

Nelly looked out at the passing farmland. "I have to say. Growing up in the '70s, I never thought I'd hear two guys arguing over who's a bigger N-word." '

The band of brothers cracked up.

"True Romance? Don't *Boyz N The Hood* cover it all in like the first five minutes?" floated Franco.

"What do they say?" inquired Joey. The blunt hanging from his mouth like a professor's pipe.

"I don't remember. Haven't seen it in like twenty years."

Joey looked to the back. "Can you believe this fuckin guy? He knows exactly what the fuck it says. But nah, ole Franco's gotta be all cryptic n shit. Gotta make me go huntin for this fuckin movie. Like I'm Davy Crockett. Anyone got a coonskin cap I can borrow? So I can go find this fuckin movie? Is it on HBO On Demand? One of the eight million other on demands? Is it on TBS this Tuesday night? Do I gotta fuckin circle my calendar? Do I gotta go to fuckin ShopRite and rummage through the old movie rack like I'm a fuckin bum? Do I gotta rent it from the box out front? Barter my old baseball cards at the fuckin flea market? Anybody interested in Donruss? Walk all over the mall like I'm Where's Waldo? Bang on the door of Blockbuster? My breath all foggin up the glass. 'Hello? Are you guys just closed? Or shut the fuck down forever?' Do I gotta send away for the shit? Do I gotta write Santa? *Dear Santa, my fuckin friend Franco is all pretendin like he don't remember the first five fuckin minutes of* Boyz N The Hood. *So if you could stuff it in my stocking...* Any of you guys back there got a copy I could borrow? I don't even need the whole DVD. Just a piece of it. That has the first five fuckin minutes. All becuza the Austin Powers International Man of Mystery over here. The fuckin X-Man Xavier

McDaniel over here. Fuckin Rey Mysterio over here. *The Da Vinci Code* over here." Joey took his biggest puff yet. "That's it..." Joey exhaled. "That's what Franco is! I just figured it out. He's fuckin Austin Powers, Xavier McDaniel, Rey Mysterio, and the *Da Vinci Code* all rolled into one. Everything those guys are, that's what he is. I did it! After all these years, I fuckin did it. *I* cracked Franco's Da Vinci code. Like I'm Tom Hanks!" exclaimed Joey as he smacked the driver's shoulder.

The Stang shimmied.

Joey took a final puff of his finished Phillies. "Oh and how the fuck could I forget? Jersey's got that MTV *True Life.* The guido episode in Seaside. *Cheese balls!*"

Franco's left hand was on the wheel like he was throwin a left cross. His eyes on the St. Louis skyline ahead. But at that distance, coulda been anywhere. Atlantic City. "No offense, Joey. But you're better than that."

"Don't be fuckin with guido nation."

"I'm not. I'm just sayin. There's a lot more to you. To Seaside. To fuckin Jersey—"

"Just cuz you're too good to go clubbin anymore—"

"Dafuck! I'm tryina give you a compliment—"

"By disrespecting guido nation!"

And back and forth they went. Like Pony Boy and Darry. Going back and forth in the hot-boxed car like they were back in their boxing ring.

By the time they were passing St. Louis, Nelly got out. Ready to live in the Lou like he was Nelly. Taz said he'd join him. Wanted to see if his hair would fit under the arch. And Brazil? He was ready to catch a bus to Brazil.

Franco and Joey sat in the car.

"Ah fuck it. I know you got nothin but love, brotha." Franco put a fist out.

"Same." Joey met the fist bump. "Now. How we gonna

get these three back in the car?"

Franco was already putting in a CD. He turned the volume all the way up.

Joey got rolling. Like he was Kelly Rowland.

Franco came around the car. Pointed at Nelly, Taz, and Brazil. Helped Joey sing their way outta the dilemma as they belted out "Dilemma." Joey Yo threw an arm around his best bro. Franco. They hit the high note together. Down since day one no matter the weather. Two birds of a feather. While the other three flocked. Formed a flying V. To head north. To New Jersey.

"Come on, Nelly. I'll get ya up to speed on Nelly." Franco slapped his coach's back.

"Thanks."

"Least I could do," said Franco more to himself as they headed back to their pony.

The Stang rocketed along the open road. The five teammates feeling as fresh as the Fab Five. Even Nelly sang along to Nelly. "Ride Wit Me." How it must be for the money. Franco glanced his best friends crowded in the car. All of them singing as they sailed past St. Louis. Nah Nelly. It wasn't the money. Franco dropped it into overdrive. The pony blazed through the dirty dirty. Musta hit a hunid thirty thirty.

Now Lama Drama had hit another gear altogether. No bullshittin. The Syrian was serious. The Prince's dance partner, one Umar Basayev, had put on so much Herculean heft that his Achilles couldn't handle it. It had torn earlier that day. The Achilles. Damn. Franco actually felt bad for the poor guy. Maybe he'd visit him in the hospital. Bring him some food. Nothing crazy. Just desserts.

The Show needed a replacement. Fast. Someone in the same weight class. Someone already in the area. Ready to go. Someone who'd be a draw in Jersey. Someone who had a history with The Prince.

To which Franco replied, "Barbosa don't have a history wit The Prince."

To which Lama replied, "I'm not talking about Barbosa. I'm talking about YOU!"

The revelation unraveled him. Franco almost fell out of his Mustang in his driveway on Bunns. His heart raced so fast, he was sure the good news would instantly turn to shit on account of a heart attack. Franco was so flustered, *he started advocating for Barbosa.* "Why not Barbosa? He's number four."

If only Lama could've reached through the phone and clamped her manicured mauve nails around her client's neck. "Barbosa's a super fight! Not a last-minute sub! They can market a Pay-Per-View for a month. Plus he has his whole career ahead of him. He's not gonna walk into the longest finishing streak of all time on five days' notice," sighed Lama. "You on the other hand. Let's be honest."

Franco was shaking off the shock as he asked if she was fuckin with him. As TJ was trying to talk to him.

"Look. I floated this thing to the powers that be and they said yes. You don't think they're making other calls? Brainstorming other ideas? We've got one hour."

The hour was almost up. Franco leaned on his Stang in downtown Newark. Casing The Vault. It was a tough call. The Dealer had just dealt him a 10. Franco's favorite hand. A double down where no card coming was too big. But. A double down was unwise against an ace. And that's exactly what The Dealer was showing with The Prince.

The conventional wisdom would be for Franco to stick

with his original fight. What he needed first and foremost was a W. He felt he had a solid 18 against the up-and-coming Barbosa. Franco had been training for him for months. With The Prince and only five days' notice, there may be things he may not notice. Meanwhile, the well-heeled Prince could gather all of Franco's weaknesses in the week.

Franco leaned against the hood of his Stang. The hospital he was born in right behind him as he watched all walks of life walk the streets of Jersey. The pretty little lady in scrubs. The municipal worker scrubbing graffiti. The businessman selling on his cell phone. Never slacking in slacks. One white. One brown. One black. Which was which? Who could keep track? A daycare teacher with ten of all shades in tow. Even a towhead. Franco smiled. Baby T was a bit of a blond bomber, wasn't he? But his hair had gone dark little by little like the day unfolding before Franco. Now as dark as the shades on the old lady crossing the crosswalk with the help of a cop. Getting passed by school teens in uniform, their focus on ascension uniform. Even faster yet was the runner checking her vitals as she zipped through the downtown once again vital.

Franco turned to the hospital behind him. He always knew he was born in the gutter. It struck him then that it was the one he was standing in. Last he looked, as a teen about T's age, the hospital was a sad sack of bricks in the broken heart of Brick City. Now? Renovated. As was the whole downtown. Franco nodded. Feelin it. The Dealer's Plan suddenly made sense. As the sun set on the city, the prodigal son had returned.

Franco hopped in the Stang. He blazed down Broad Street like a bully as the Devils warmed up for the Broad Street Bullies. There was no time to waste. The Cinderella Man had to prepare for The Prince. He kept his glass slipper on the gas. Excited about his life's new arc. Like he was Noah with his new ark. As the Mustang roared. Straight outta Newark.

TRACK 10. (W)RAPPED UP

FRANCO MADE IT HOME hours later after an emergency session with Brazil. Flew up his flight of stairs in five strides. "Ay T! Sorry I couldn't talk before!" He knocked on T's door, but there was no answer. He opened the featherweight door. It danced on the hinge. No T. His stomach tinged. That fuckin commercial ran through his head. *It's 10 pm. Do you know where your children are?* The manic Monday continued as Franco searched from unfinished basement to patio pavement.

Franco sat at the computer in T's room. Clicked the mouse. Clicked the white f squared off by a blue background. MyFace or some shit. After a couple inadvertent clicks, the first asking Franco to share his feelings with the world, the second asking him to message Kronic Karl, Franco found what he was looking for. A message about a motel party. The thread ran out on an exchange between Screws and T...

     Screws: Pickin up liq then u
     T: Better be bumpin Naughty!

Franco stared. Stewed. T's line a reference to the run of flea bag motels on Route 1. From Woodbridge to Rahway to Linden to Elizabeth. Motels Young Franco would tell you were made famous by Naughty by Nature's "OPP" video. Now, as he investigated his son, he had fully inched toward infamous. Franco flung the mouse against the wall and stormed out, ready to crush another one. *A freshman and already getting fucked up? On a school night? Who the fuck does that?* Franco nixed his usual passing glance in the bathroom mirror.

The Stang stalked through the tough little towns one by one. It mauled past Woodbridge Mall. Peaced past Rahway Prison. Landed in Linden. Screeched to a stop. In the K—— Motel lot. Stinking like pot. As music popped. Franco scanned the row of outdoor doors. Stopped on the room with the bass boom. Room 112. Franco shook his head. Shoulda known. The room number made notorious. By a rhyme from The Notorious.

A hand snatched two Natty Lights. From a bathtub full of ice. The handy man had to get back to the kid rappin nice. He stepped over passed-out Luke. At the toilet full of puke. Unlike Vader, he was not Luke's father. So, he continued *fah*ther. Turned into the main room, turnt.

Screws handed UN a Natty. In exchange for a fatty. While Dragon dragged on his turntable. On the room's lone table. Bumped a backbeat from behind Ill Co's backs. Lenore bobbed her head. In a bomber jacket she maybe. Borrowed from a baby. Ray next to her in a vest. Vibing with all the rest. As the kid rapped in jest.

TJ. The pint-sized king of the court atop the king-sized bed. A tenth of tequila to his head. The other tenth still bottled—a makeshift mic he throttled. His hands and feet darting in concert. Slaying the impromptu concert. Ill Coers smiling, bouncing, clapping. Emcee T rapping. Flippin em out with the flippant riff as they smoked their spliffs—

> *"Ding ding ding*
> *English class is over*
> *I beheaded Homer*
> *Cut Shakespeare with a spear*
> *Hemmed Hemingway's mouth shut*
> *Then jumped for joy*
> *When I jacked James Joyce*
> *Threw 'bows on John Knowles*
> *And his fiancée*
> *Cuz the only Knowles I wanna knowles*
> *Is Beyoncé!*
> *And F Scott Fitzgerald?*
> *Man, EFF Scott Fitzgerald!*
> *I gatted him AND Gatsby*
> *Then wheeled in a cannon*
> *Blew away the whole canon—"*

T had the place jumping as homies howled.

Between a solo cup sip and a blunt hit, Ray added, "Fuck that nigga Homer!"

T even got a look from Lenore. One he'd never seen before...

> *"I'm goin insaney*
> *Run me a kite*
> *And save me, Hosseini*
> *I wanna read under a Friday night light*
> *Diaz for días*

Talkin bout tíos n tías
Then build a glass castle
Out of Angela's Ashes
Next to a wishing well
Wishin Simmons n Gladwell—"

Everyone enjoyed it save for the OG at the door. The OG who barged through the crazed coeds and snatched the irreverent reverend. The father grabbed Minister T by the baggy T. Like he was Mr. T.

Ray was about to raise up.

Till UN piped up. "That's his pops, yo!"

TJ added, despite being wrangled away, "He can kick everyone's ass in this room!" TJ's posse couldn't hardly wait, to crack up over the line from *Can't Hardly Wait*.

But as TJ dipped, so did the mood. Dragon breathed fire into a new beat, tried to cheer up the brood.

The Mustang groaned down Route 1, as tired as the towns it toured. As tired as the talking to Franco had just given T. About the drinking. In a scumbag motel on a school night. With kids who are gonna end up in the prison they just passed.

Now it was TJ's turn. Finally had the chance to tell Dad about his day. About how he aced English class. Put Lane on her ass. Gave a presentation. That was his greatest creation. "It's like, it was the biggest moment of my life or somethin. Like I was...talented or somethin."

Franco was as silent as the streetlit strip ahead.

"Never mind," T concluded.

Franco read the sign as the pony moseyed past: *Woodbridge Township Welcomes You. Established 1669.* Then ponied up a response. "My first fight. There were only a couple weight classes back then. Had to take on a guy 20 pounds heavier. It was a big roll of the dice. Had no idea which way it was gonna go. Turns out, I steamroll him. Me, your mother, and Joey, we're poppin bottles in the club. It was only a matter of time until I was world champ." Franco shook his head. "Ten years later. I'm still on the grind."

Franco pulled the reins of the pony as it rolled up to a red light. "One victory ain't shit. One little story and all the sudden you're the greatest of all time? Ya know what Shakespeare was doin on weeknights while you're busy gettin wasted in motels?"

"Being dead?"

"Writing. And while you're busy clowning...writing some more."

TJ pressed four fingers to his forehead. Pressed the important information into his inebriated brain.

"And don't think it's all stupid shit, either. I wish I woulda read all that shit in high school. Important life lessons in there."

"Like what?"

Franco flipped his phone open, checked a TEXT: *Yo franco wuts good. Got ur doe. Meet u out bak the slawterhouse?* Franco thumbed back: *Two min.* Then turned his attention back to T. "Like I always remember in *The Odyssey* or *Iliad* somethin about a boat in the night and mermaids singin and the boat crashin into rocks. That was some deep shit."

T nodded. "Probably gangster as hell back in 800 BC."

"Exact," said Franco as he turned the Stang toward the town's outskirts. "Ya know, I even read the first few chapters of *Catcher in the Rye?*"

"Yeah?"

"Thought it was gonna be about baseball," shrugged

Franco.

TJ laughed.

"Then your mother told me the title meant somethin about a guy catchin kids from fallin off a cliff—" Franco's words fell off a cliff. He tilted his head as he got a weird feeling. The book suddenly sounded appealing. "Anyway. Your mother knows all that shit. Around when we split up, I overheard her say to herself, '*Tis better to have loved and lost then to have never loved at all.*' And I was like, damn, why didn't I read more Shakespeare?"

"Uh pretty sure that's not Shakespeare," chimed T.

"See? This is my problem," Franco said as he steered the Stang into a gravel lot. "All that school stuff. Keeps ya from gettin street stupid." He continued off T's look. "When ya think you're so fuckin street smart, you start gettin stupid."

T nodded. "Word."

"Sit right here. I'll be back in five minutes. Don't move."

Franco stepped into the darkness. On the edge of town. Made for the rusted-out slaughterhouse with the pitched tin roof that allowed for aeration. Got entrenched in the carnal stench. One he was used to. He'd done this pickup a million times before. Midnight Monday night. A little later if the final football game of the week was still in the balance. Eddo would toss him the dough at the back door. Say no more. But with the beef on Bunns Lane, Franco was a little more on edge than usual. He picked up to a trot through the gravel lot. Scuttled through a puddle. And carried right on along. With the most street stupid move of his entire life.

Franco reached the back door. Sniffed. The Q-Tip fan found the smell more vivrant than usual. He heard squeals. Sniffed again. Franco would've taken the usual rotten smell. Of pig carcasses resting in peace. Over squealing pigs not long for one piece. The slaughterhouse was mid-kill. An operation in overdrive. As was Franco. It had been a long day. A full day as a father, a fighter, and, now, a foot soldier. Worse. The manic Monday didn't have shit on the Tuesday he was two minutes into.

"Yo Franco! What's good? Money's on the break table!" yelled Eddo as he held extra-large electrified forceps. "Gotta keep these uppity fuckers in line." Eddo applied the forceps to a pig's neck. Nuked it into a seizure.

Franco hung a turn, beelined for the break table. Past inverted pigs with slit throats. Their blood conveying as they hung from a conveyor belt. Others on deck. Impatiently waiting their turn.

Franco grabbed the envelope. Turned and bumped into the boss. Mr. Tall, Dark, and Handsome himself. *El Jefe.* Arturo. Looking like a don as he donned white slacks. Not a drop of blood on them despite his place being bathed in it. He crossed his arms. The sleeves of his blue button-down with the white cuffs were already rolled up. Franco was just the latest business matter El Jefe had to tend to. Last but certainly not least. El Jefe stood there looking like Gordon Gekko. Franco like a punk in Ecko.

El Jefe motioned to Franco's envelope. "Go ahead. It's yours."

Franco's hazels hitched up to meet the 100 percent pure Colombian café eyes of his enemy. "All good." Franco back-pocketed the envelope. Bulled around Arturo.

But Arturo's long legs slinked back two steps. Nixed the Texas two-step. "Of course. There's another matter we need to discuss," informed Arturo with his hands behind his back. "The one of you trying to fucking kill me."

Franco clocked the place. Eddo standing there with the Frankenstein forceps. His coworker slitting throats with a look of indifference as to which type of mammal. The cholo strutting in with the piece in his waist and ready to waste Franco. Franco recognized this challenger. He drove an orange Challenger.

Arturo turned to his vato with the teardrop tattoo. "¿Dondé esta..." El Jefe's voice trailed off to a whisper. After a brief back and forth, El Jefe sent the banger hustling along. Like a coach sending a player in for his big shot. El Entrenador then trained his attention on his otro jugador. "Eduardo. Take a break. Join us."

Eddo, suddenly hard as fuck, strutted over to the gathering like he was Tupac cutting through a courtroom. "Am I gonna need these?" said Eddo of his electrified forceps.

El Jefe shrugged, *perhaps*. Refocused on Franco. "Please. Join me in my office." El Jefe motioned, *after you*.

Franco entered the glass encasement. Gave himself worse odds than any trip into the cage.

El Jefe folded his legs under his desk. Folded his hands on it. "Do you think you're the only one with your ear to the street?"

His guest declined to answer.

El Jefe clarified, "You and *la rana.*"

Franco again stonewalled the (extremely) southern Stonewall Jackson.

"*¿Qué eres tú?*" asked Arturo from behind his tidy steel desk.

Franco tried to settle into his ergo-something chair. "My Spanish ain't so good."

Arturo leaned forward. "What. Are. You."

Franco pondered all the ways he could answer as Eddo and the returning CG-67 banger breathed over each of his shoulders. Course Franco could've went with how he wasn't nothin if he wasn't American. But that line was for T. Fuck this guy before him. Franco searched his brain for some elusive answer that might get him out of this jam. But all that played in his fuckin head was that fuckin Frank Sinatra song. That one his old man would blast out of their project apartment as he got blasted. Dancing around with his goddamn *martini*. Straight vodka in a rocks glass. Getting rocked off his ass. Singin that tongue-twisting line from "That's Life." Fumbling around and fucking it all up like he was Professor Lambeau. Only to rewind the tape and butcher it all over again.

Arturo slammed his hand down on his stainless-steel table. WHAP. "What! Are! You!"

Franco responded to the chairman of the board like he was the Chairman of the Board. "I been a puncher, a pawn, a player, a playa, a prince, and a fool."

"So you're Italiano, Sinatra?"

Franco shrugged, the fuck knows.

"What kind of man doesn't know his heritage?"

"A bastard," interjected Eddo. Piping in with color commentary like he was John fuckin Madden.

Arturo leaned back. "Look at you. This is America. You could be anything you want to be. And you chose to work for the fucking Frog?" Arturo flung a fleet of folders off his desk. "*¡Una rana babosa!*"

Arturo clasped his hands, collected himself. "But. It is not your fault. Bastardito."

Franco clenched his jaw. Cracked his neck. Figured if he could climb over the desk and at least choke this fucker out before getting fed to the pigs.

El Jefe carried on with charisma. "You see, Franco. Sure, you can go online and see that Woodbridge is fifty-odd percent white. Then you walk around town with your own two eyes. And you see blancos with blanco hair. Pouring out of the retirement homes. Limping out of their houses to hop buses to Atlantic City. Then you walk around the schoolyards. And it's a bit browner. The Frog? The mafia? *La cosa nostra?* Dead. Muerto." El Jefe stared Franco dead in the eye. *"Hay una cosa nuestra."* Arturo motioned to himself, Eddo, and the CG. "This is our town now."

"It's a lot of people's town," fumed Franco.

El Jefe opened his arms. "And today is your lucky day. You have an opportunity to join the right team. You think the director of marketing at Facebook is any more talented than the one at MySpace? He—or *she*—" Arturo noted with a raised finger, "is just on the right team. That is all."

"I ain't much for suits," said Franco.

"Of course not. Big fighter. Word on the street is, you might fight The Prince."

"The street is fuckin Twitter now?" shot Franco.

"It's like Bob Dylan once said—"

"Said the diplomat—" raised Franco.

"Mm. Okay. Guess we could go on all night, you and I," concluded Arturo as he leaned back. "But time is money." He straightened his posture. "So. Will you. Be fighting. The Prince?"

"Haven't decided yet," bluffed Franco.

"Well." Arturo stood up. About as tall as Abe Lincoln. "I've decided. You *are* going to take the fight. It *will* have a Vegas line. And you *are* going to take a fall."

Franco never had the prestige of a college degree. Of being a full-fledged longshoreman. Of calling himself a full-time fighter. So he had come over the years to value the only things in this world he did have. The same things Scarface had. His word and his balls. Franco stood up. Looked up at Arturo. "Why don't you try stickin your head up your ass—"

Eddo and the CG clenched their weapons. But El Jefe

only calmed. Reclined in his chair. "Oh, you're Scarface now? Next, you're going to be telling me about how all you have is your balls and your word."

Franco did everything he could to keep his shoulders from slouching. If his own don had half the intelligence of the jefe before him, he wouldn't even be in this situation to begin with. "Ya know. Everything you're saying. It's startin to make a lot of sense."

Arturo and his bangers shared pleased nods.

"Between us," began Franco as he shared conspiratorial looks with the three gangsters triangulated around him, "I know a good part of town the three of you should get into."

"Oh. And where's that?" said a most interested El Jefe. He and his guys leaned in for a closer listen.

Franco let them in on the secret. "Rahway fuckin Prison."

Eddo and the CG-67 raised up—

But El Jefe belly laughed. "That is a good one." He patted his desk. "Scarface would be proud." He laughed some more. Wiped a tear from his eye. "But. While you and Al Pacino are both un-fucking-sure if you're Italian or Latino," said El Jefe as he motioned to the throat slitter out on the floor, "there is one big difference between you and Scarface."

Franco waited for it like a patriot waiting to be hanged.

"Scarface didn't have a son."

Franco darted to the glass. His eyes darted to the conveyor belt in motion. To the third of the three little piggies strung up by his hind legs.

"Dad!"

Even for a fighter, the adrenaline that rocketed through Franco's body was otherworldly. Franco's brain told him to skip the formality of trying to overtake the three gangsters with guns and gadgets, but his body turned to turbo mode as he tore a path toward T. Best he remembered, he head-butted the CG, decked Eddo, then convulsed into a seizure.

Franco came to with electrified forceps around his neck. Held by El Jefe himself.

"I'll do it. I'll fuckin do it," fired Franco.

"Like you told The Frog you'd kill me?"

"I fuckin mean it. I'll throw the fight. *Just get him* the *fuck down.*"

El Jefe motioned for his butcher across the way to let the third little piggy go.

The fighter meanwhile slapped the concrete slab he lay on. For the first time in his life, Franco had tapped out.

TRACK 11. CORRECTIONS

FRANCO AND TJ stood at the edge of the Sewaren dock. The overnight chill in full effect. They leaned on the low iron gate. Its bars black as the night. Hoodies up as the hoods stared across the river. In the light of day, they could see the Staten Island apartments across the way. Wonder which few were home to the Wu. Not tonight. Nothing but darkness. Save for the red lights that surrounded them. Red lights that ran along the refinery to their right. Red lights planted on the plant to their left. Red lights anchored atop oil tanks across the Arthur Kill. Red lights bestowed upon buoys. And the singular red light that lingered. Way down. The antenna of the Empire State Building. Dimmed to a dot at this distance. A singular red light that Franco and T stared at gazey. Like Gatsby tracking Daisy.

Franco shook his head. Seven years since 9/11. And still. A fuckin hole where the Twin Towers once stood. Franco freed the first of six Bud Heavys from its plastic noose. Ready to trade in his six-pack for a six-pack.

"Thought you didn't drink in training," stated the

uninformed son.

Franco waved him off. Chugged his first brew. Squeezed the can till it coughed carbonated foam. Flung it at the trash. Cracked another. All in on getting trashed. "You understand now? Why your mother left me?" Franco finished the second. Sentenced it to the same fate as the first. Clang. Franco opened the third. "I'm no good."

TJ took his eyes off the remote red light. Looked at his dad. Breaking bad. "The Challenger rolled up. You told me to stay in the car. *I* got out. *I* followed them. With no fuck—no plan whatsoever."

Franco downshifted to sipping. "I wanna tell you how stupid you are for doing that. But. It'd be bullshit. I'm the stupid one. Teenage son and I'm running around the like the teenage one. Hustling pickups. Chasing dreams. Only lookin out for A number one."

TJ pressed on his temples, his body a hungover temple. "Mom *took* me away from you."

Franco cracked his fourth Buddy. Was running out of friends real fast. "Course she did. One week and look what I done to you. Scarred for life." Franco motioned to T's stitched cheek then to the great beyond. "Inside and out."

"Bullsh—"

A tugboat belted out a honk.

"See? Even the tugboat ain't buyin it," Franco noted.

"Or. It's calling you out on yours," retorted T.

"You'll understand when you're older." Franco waved the kid off. Sipped. "I thought my old man was halfway decent once, too."

T tore his hood down. "I'd fight Ray all over again. Got me props *and* my head on proper for that presentation."

Franco shook his head as the beer went to it.

TJ looked to the little waves lapping against the bulkheads

below. "As for Yogi and back there, it's on me. I'm some kind of real adventurous idiot sometimes." TJ shook his head. "And to be honest, I kinda like having these gangsta stories to tell."

Franco shot T a look.

TJ put his hands up. "No more. Got plenty."

Franco shifted into fifth beer. "You think it's all fun and games now." Franco sipped. "These memories'll come back to haunt you." Franco sipped some more. "And if you don't believe me, ask Bruce Springsteen."

While TJ pondered what the fuck that meant—

The words to "The River" flowed through Franco's head like a river as he looked out at the river. The teen pregnancy. The shotgun wedding. The backbreaking job. If omniscience was God. Then Springsteen was Franco's.

Franco put the pedal to the metal mouth of his final friend. Then fingered the corner of his right eye. The nick. Of all Franco's scars. From the slice across his right ankle that he'd looked down at a million times. To the divot on his shin from an opposing player's cleat. To the one etched in his inner thigh by a fence as he fled a Rottweiler. To the one on his stomach post-spleen rupture. To the one across his left shoulder when the fucker brought a knife. To the one dripping from his lip, it having been split open so many times. To the ones under each eye. Of all of them. It was the nick. At the corner of his right eye. That he'd get removed if God allowed one. The nick from the day after The Slip. When Julie told him she was taking T to her mother's. *What, for like, the day?* asked Franco. *For like, the rest of his life,* informed Julie. For all the killers he'd been in a cage with, it was the first time Franco went into shock. The ensuing argument was a blur. He could barely make sense of his own words let alone Julie's. All he knew as he stood in front of the door was that he was ready to filibuster like he was a congressman. Lobbying against whatever the lobby paid him to be against. No. Like he was Abe Lincoln. Trying to keep their union together. No. Julie was Abe Lincoln. Making her own emancipation proclamation. On and on the argument went in circles just as confusing. The girl who aced English and Spanish resorted to a language the fighter before the door would understand a little better. She socked him in the eye socket. The engagement rock he bought with his last buck found a new setting. In the corner of his eye.

Franco rubbed the nick. And sipped. And rubbed. But there was no erasing the reminder of the marriage he killed. No erasing his very own teardrop tattoo.

While the beer and bad memories mounted in Franco, TJ had mounted a defense. "Memories? I got memories from right here. From this spot alone."

Franco paused his sip of number six. "Back in the day?"

"Back in the day." TJ turned his attention away from the Arthur Kill and onto the docks. "On one of those summer Saturdays when this place is full of guys fishing. I'd go around and come back and tell you, 'That guy's fishing for fluke. And that guy's fishing for porgies. And that guy's fishing for snapper.' And on and on I'd go. Then you'd wave me off. Sum it up in a single sentence. 'Ah we're all fishin for the same thing. Power.' It's like, it blew my mind. Like I could feel my brain wrinkle. Look past the bullsh— Look deeper. I do that to this day."

Franco took a small sip from his sixth. "Wasn't that like two sentences?"

T, the up-and-coming attorney, moved right along to exhibit two. "And my intimidating-ass coach from the one year I played Pop Warner. Coach Butch. That I never wanted to see again cuz I sucked so bad. He was fishing right there.

Right. There. I never woulda went up to him in a million years. But you made me. Made me shake his hand. Look him in the eye. Ask him how he's doing. I must've manned up a million times since then."

Franco stared down into the mouth of his half-empty can. Or was it half full? "A million? I thought you were supposed to be good at math."

"Come on. You got much better jokes than that." T looked across the river. "Like the time you warned me I'd die if I tried to swim to Staten Island. I said, 'Cuz of the distance?' You said, 'Nah.' I said, 'Cuz of the current?' You said, 'Nah. Cuza the toxic waste.'"

Franco laughed mid-sip of his final Bud. All thanks to his best bud. His main man.

Attorney T drove his point home. "I mean, people go around all the time joking about Jersey pollution and all that. But you, like, crafted that joke just so. I find myself doing the same. Like all the times. From jokes to rhymes."

"I see what you did there," said Franco as he again stared into the mouth of his half-empty-or-full can. "Then I had to go and fuck it all up."

"About that," TJ sighed. The night's deepening chill made his breath visible. He'd never asked. But fuck it. If they were having it out, they were having it out. "Was it...just that one slip?"

That one slip. The Slip. The Slip being Julie away for a night in The City with Alexis and Mercedes. TJ was dropped off at his grandmother's. All while The Frog brought the house to Franco's house. The coffee table was replaced by a craps table. A portable poker cloth was now the dining room tablecloth. The kitchen table was converted to a blackjack table as Franco was dealing like he was Black Jack McDowell. And that's when trouble came knocking. The Frog and four silicone knockers. He escorted the escorts upstairs despite Franco's stares. One worked Mom and Dad's room, while the other one took the room of the 10-year-old boy. The 10-year-old boy as curious as George. The one who had convinced his grandma to drop him back home in a desperate bid to stay with Dad. As it turned out, the move was exactly what separated him from Dad. Mom wasn't hearing that Franco had no idea there'd be girls. Wasn't hearing that TJ ran out as soon as the woman went in his room. Wasn't hearing that Franco got TJ out of the house altogether.

"That thing was my fault, too!" exclaimed TJ with his arms out.

Franco shook his head. "Your mother put up with a lot. Couldn't go off to college. Home with you while I ran around Woodbridge with The Frog. An inebriated idiot comin and goin as I pleased like I was Henry fuckin Hill. Ran around all of Jersey with Joey Yo. Late night runs to AC thinkin we were as money as Mikey n Trent. Ran around all of the USA with MMA. Makin about as much money as an '80s wrestler doing high school bills. Barely paying the bills. While your mother's juggling a job, a household, and an education. She put up with it all. Until it affected you. Then that was it." Franco ran an index finger across his throat.

Franco sucked in the Jersey smog like he was trying to suck in the whole situation. Take it all back. Impossible. He exhaled. "I know you think that in the Story of Your Life, Mom's the bad guy and I'm the good guy." Franco crushed the half-empty-or-full debate as he crushed number six. "But it's the exact opposite. Everything she's ever done. Ever. Has been for you." Franco tilted the can farther. Took down every last drop. "I can't say the same." He crushed the can. Chucked it at the trash. Clang. Couldn't even get that right. Franco put his hands in his hoodie. Headed to the trash.

Cleaned up his cans. Headed to his horse.

TJ stared at that distant red dot. His brain busy making some of its biggest wrinkles yet. "Dad." TJ hustled over. "Hold up."

Franco opened the door to his Stang. "Don't worry. I've driven these streets a million times."

"Not that."

Franco crossed his arms on the roof of his car.

TJ tried to do the same but came up short. Carried on anyway. "Last summer. Mom was reading this book called *The Corrections*. Have you heard of it?"

"I hearda the Department of Corrections."

The two couldn't help but grin. Humor their savior from the grim.

"It had a boy on the cover, so I started reading it. At first, I was like what is this boring-ass book about an old couple in the Midwest? And their three kids who are, like, college-educated and living in big cities and stuff. But I kept reading, cuz I don't know, it was just...good writing or something. And I kept wondering, who's the good guy? Who's the bad guy? And I kept changing my mind. Like, oh, the mom's the good guy, then she says or does something shitty. Same for the dad. And the son. And the daughter. And the other son. It's like, the realest shit I ever read. No heroes. No villains. Just people. Really complicated, messed-up people."

"Huh," said Franco. His brain the one now adding a wrinkle.

"I think what's important is..." TJ shook his head in search of the right word. "Intent." TJ looked down, felt like a real dork using the fancy word in front of Dad.

"Nah. I get ya."

"I think you always had good intentions," said son. "And it's all gonna make sense. When you knock The Prince senseless."

Franco took a breath of the frozen Jersey air. "About that," he said with an exhale that could deflate Earth. He nodded for T to hop in the pony.

Franco turned the key. The pony wheezed and kicked. He turned it again. She wheezed and kicked. And wheezed and kicked. He tried again. But she just couldn't get her legs under herself. After 10 years and 200,000 miles all across America, Franco's pony only had one trip left. To the glue factory.

Across town out on Route 1, another pony had plenty of kick. Its driver having had plenty of liq. He ran a red light and ran his whole carriage around a telephone pole. A pole that protruded into the exact spot a passenger had sat earlier that night. Until his father found said passenger in a motel and dragged him into another mess entirely. At least the kid would live to tell about that one, though. The driver, meanwhile, was laid up in the hospital. His skull split so badly, the repair procedure included tightening in some literal screws. To go along with the driver's figurative loose ones.

TRACK 12. WARNINGS

FRANCO WALKED THE TRACKS as his head ran Biggie's track. Franco ready to die as Biggie spit from *Ready to Die*. "Suicidal Thoughts." Biggie waxin about burnin in hell. And how he'd fit right in. Maybe Franco would see him soon.

Franco shook his head as he forged ahead. A forest of trees on each side. Towering over him. Whispering in the wind. Franco finally ready to do what Julie had done five years before. What she would've *always* done. Put their boy first no matter the fallout.

Franco tracked the full moon above. The Man looked down with particular pity. Maybe it was too little, too late. Franco pulled up the hood on his black hoodie from high school. The one with the torn collar and lost strings. The one that fell over the gat needling his back. Franco shook his head over the realization that he had learned more about religion from rap songs than from CCD. Shit, he didn't even know what CCD stood for. But he knew those lines. From "Suicidal Thoughts." About why be a misfit in heaven? When you could do street shit in hell 24-7. About how square shit is whack. How he'd rather wear black. If eternal empathy was God. Then Biggie was Franco's.

Even if Franco remained on Earth past evening, he wasn't long for the world. Once he cut ties with The Frog and dumped the upcoming fight, he'd be livin on a prayer like his boy Bon Jovi. Needing a Hail Mary like his pal Pac. And Franco was well aware of how Pac ended up as the bell from "Hail Mary" tolled in his head. Fuck. Shoulda picked Pac. Franco shook his head. Coulda had a spot reserved at Thugz Mansion. Instead, he was gonna be burnin in hell with his boy Biggie. Fuckin Franco. Couldn't even get his God right.

The man in black crossed Rahway Ave without even looking. His eyes on his flip phone. On a TEXT from Joey Yo: *All systems go*. Almost got cracked by a hauling Mack. It never even saw the phantom in black.

Franco stalked through the first of two church grounds older than America. Two-stepped over tombstones over 200 years old. Winged skulls etched atop them. Death's-heads. The Man on the Moon peeked through the trees, went out of his way to shed a little extra light on them. Franco looked them all in the eye. Had to find Thomas Nelson the First. Partly to pay respect. Partly to rub the tombstone in hope that some of that charmed First Family of Woodbridge aura would rub off on him. Help him avoid being rubbed out. Franco ran his hand over The Third's tomb. Coach Nelson's great-great-great-great-great-grandfather who was so great-great-great, he died in the Revolution after being a revered reverend. Franco then reached the tombstone of Nelly the First. Took a knee. Crossed himself. Then crossed out of the church.

The changing season's weather whipped swirling winds. An empty Budweiser can rolled toward Franco. Then rolled away before he got the chance to kick it. The Man tracked

Franco through budding branches. Had to keep a spotlight on the star of the play. Probably a tragedy, Franco figured as he walked through another patch of ancient tombstones. *Nobody's a killer until they have to.* The Frog turned out be Nostrafuckindamus. Cuz now Franco had to. He marched past tilted tombstones stuck into the ground like midget surfboards. One riddled with Redcoat bullets. Fired from a Brown Bess musket. Back when the colonists said fuck it. Franco had similar feelings as he continued toward the ass end of the church.

A rat ran one way and a skunk scurried the other as The Frog stood still. Hands entrenched in his trench coat pockets. Standing under an emergency exit light casting a red tint.

As Franco headed for The Frog, he took one last glance back. Peeped the lot of the sub shack. Made out the old-ass Explorer in the back. He then rolled up with his black hoodie up. A Grim Reaper. That pulled a heater. Held it in his hand as he laid out his plan. "I'ma tell you this once. And once only. *I'm out.* When my boy almost gets killed, I'm out. And before you go threatenin me or anyone in my family, let me make somethin real clear." Franco put the .45 to The Frog's forehead. "I *will* kill you."

The Frog stood as still as a pipid on a lily pad. Clenched his underbite. Hazel to hazel with Franco. The Man on the Moon illuminating Franco's. The exit light tinting The Frog's.

Franco mashed the gun into The Frog's chest. "Take your fuckin gun." A Hamiltonian gesture to defuse the latest Jersey duel. Franco Hamilton then did an about face. Didn't get more than a pace—

"You're a mangy fuckin mutt, you know that?" croaked Amphibian Burr.

Franco turned.

"I tried to give you a family. A community. A career."

Amphibian Burr cocked the gun. "But you're shit. A Bunns Lane bastard. Bunns Lane bred. And you're gonna be Bunns Lane dead—"

Only the Hamilton of Hoodbridge had learned from his history. He nodded to Burr's midsection. An infrared dot danced on The Frog's chest. Like it was bopping to an old 45. Back in 1965. The dot then nae nae'd up his neck. Cha-cha'd around his chin. Macarena'd up his mug. Settled on his forehead and did a little ditty. Like it was Diddy. Dancing to Paperboy's "Ditty."

Hoodbridge Hamilton laid it out. "You fuck with me? Now or tomorrow or any time. I've already paid someone to fuck with you." Franco stepped over—snatched the fuckin gun back from The Frog. Pressed it in his fuckin face. In the nook between cheek and nose. "I *will* widow your poor wife. Leave her with nobody. You sick fuck. Sucking me in as a surrogate son." Franco wrapped his index finger around the trigger. Ready to waste the father figure.

"I wasn't gonna shoot you," croaked The Frog. His front limbs raised.

Franco pressed the gun harder into the old man's face. Then harder yet. Then. "You're already dead." Franco dropped the gun.

The .45 fell to The Frog's feet. He'd never admit it, but a shiver ran down his spine. Burr.

The changing season's winds blew Franco one way and The Frog the other.

The Frog turned and shared some parting thoughts. Like he was Andy fuckin Rooney. "When The Show chews you up and spits you out. Just like the fat cats in this country are doing to the rest of us. Then maybe you'll see." The Frog raised his voice as the two continued to part. "You got nothin. Not even God!" Nothing from Franco. Of course not. "It's written right on our money, ya know!"

Franco turned to The Frog without breaking stride. "I got plenty of God. But I got the back of your nickel, too."

The Frog peeled his trench coat aside, pulled out his lucky 1955 nickel. Turned it to tails. *E PLURIBUS UNUM.* Whatever the fuck that meant. Maybe he'd look it up on Diwali Day. He continued on his way.

The Frog was Catholic, but he couldn't agree more with the Protestant church he walked away from. Its white tower rose from its white chapel. A middle finger unfurled from a fist. Flipping off the flipped town. But the farther the Rolling Stones fan got from his Street Fightin Man, the closer he got to his 19th Nervous Breakdown. The Frog stalked the ave as rabid as Mick Jagger stabbed with a dagger. Fuckin car was in the shop. And worse. Those tones. From the Rolling Stones. They rolled in his head like stones. The man hearing "Get Off of My Cloud" coulda swore he smelled something. The man walked his town looking for the smell like it was Laci Peterson. Was it the creek below the bridge? Nope, it was high tide. Was it the homeboys crowding outside Krauszer's? Smoking Newports with ankle long shorts. Or the Ricans running their kids in from their Accord at this insane hour? Or the Asian with his two hands on the fire hydrant? Doing squats like the ave was a 24 Hour fuckin Fitness. Or. Was it the white trash taking out the trash? Barefoot and braless. Fuckin A. All the good ones got away. Didn't they.

The Frog took a big whiff of his whole town right then and wished to the smog-hidden heavens that he too had caught the first white flight to Tinton Falls. Wished that he too had left his brick town for Bricktown. So mad he didn't move to Howell, he could howl. The Man on the Moon dared him to have at it. The ready to howl honcho was suddenly certain *his hair was overgrowing. Its dye dying in an instant.*

And those fuckin tones! From the Rolling Stones! They rolled in his head like stones! He wanted to say goodbye to "Ruby Tuesday." Wanted "Wild Horses" to drag him away. Wondered why "You Can't Always Get What You Want." The daggered Jagger staggered. Past the refinery. Maybe that was the smell. Past the dumpsters of the apartments that departed his park. Maybe that was the smell. Past the reeds of the marsh. Just them. He hoped.

The mad man caught a second wind as he wound onto his block. Against his chest, the Glock. His heart of stone as he heard "Heart of Stone." He prayed to God to give him shelter as he heard "Gimme Shelter." He jumped like Jack Flash as he heard "Jumpin' Jack Flash." He dashed down the middle of his road. Closed in on his red door. At the end of his cul-de-sac. Hearing. "Paint it Black."

The Frog flew into his bathroom. Phew. His hair was still ship shape. He looked down at his 1955 nickel. In his hand the whole way. He thumbed the five-cent piece that reminded him of five-cent candies. Five-and-dimes. Five years old. His good old nickel from the good old days. He looked down at the man on heads. His very own TJ.

Yet the man with the dark hair with the white streak was still unsettled as he stood before his bathroom mirror. The putrid smell remained.

The swirling wind had wound Franco another way. Rap and religion still on his mind. Only Pac's ominous "Hail Mary" had hailed to "Only God Can Judge Me." Franco's steps matched the upbeat beat.

Then Franco's roll slowed as he caught up with his bro. Good ole Joey Yo. Franco gave his Boricua goomba a handshake-hug aside his old-ass Explorer.

"You like that shit? How I put the dot on his forehead?" asked Joey as he poked his finger to his own forehead. "I knew that would piss him off."

Franco grinned. "His chin protruded past Port Reading."

"Shit, he had a chin to China!"

Franco and Joey Yo lit up with laughter.

Joey Yo pulled a flask from his hoodie pocket. "Goddamn that was nerve-wracking, though." Joey sipped. "I *woulda* blasted his ass."

Franco shook his head, gave Joey Yo a fist bump. "No doubt, brotha. No doubt."

"It's fuckin...*warm* all the sudden," noted Joey.

Franco pulled his hood down. The Man on the Moon teased sparkles out of the boy with kaleidoscope eyes. "Look at this. Out on the backstreets past midnight. With the warm weather n all," floated the Beatles fan.

"Like when we used to sneak out," Joey added.

"*I* didn't have to sneak."

"These warm nights after being caged up for six months. Had to hop out a window."

"Had to step over my stepdad."

The best friends had a hearty laugh.

"You ready to roll?" Joey made for the Explorer.

Franco sucked in the warm wind. After months of rain, snow, and hail. "Fuck it. Wanna walk?"

Joey sucked in some warm wind himself. "Fuck yeah, I wanna walk. We can egg Stan Macha's house like it's Mischief Night."

"Pop into Matt Pinto's pool."

"Bang on Bethany Devers' back door."

"Jump on Jamie Tran's trampoline."

"Throw a banger in your basement."

"Oh, shit."

"The good old days, son!"

The good old boys who looked nothing like good old boys laughed like they did as little boys. They beat feet and slapped backs down Barron Ave like they were entering intermediate all over again.

"It's funny. Senior year. '93," began Franco as they slowed to a stroll. "And we were already listenin to the Wu talk about the good old days." Franco carried on with a hop in his step. Feeling loose. The ankle warmed up from the weather and the walk.

"Huh?"

"Ya know. That one slow track on *36 Chambers.*"

"Oh yeah yeah yeah. The one with the old soul singer. What's her name?"

"I don't know," shrugged Franco. "I thought it was Raekwon's mom."

A laugh burst out of Yo. He threw an arm around his bro. "Oh I know. 'Can It Be All So Simple.'"

"Right. Like, was it really better back in the day? Or do we just remember it that way?" wondered Franco as they walked past their old school.

Across town, a man was such a wreck, he put on a record. Poured himself a Jameson at his portable bar. Slouched into his shag couch. Slipped out of his trench coat. Listened to the soul singer singin about the good old days.

As the 45 spun in the man's temple, he put a .45 to his temple. He looked to his walls of framed photos. His first day of first grade with the missing tooth and the tin lunch box. Eighteen in a tank top with muscled arms. Leaning on his muscle car. His wedding picture. Him and his wife looking right into the camera. All eyes and smiles. Eager for the adventure ahead. *Of course it was better back then.* The man cocked the hammer back. The Glock ready to strike midnight.

The man's shaking hand managed a drink of the Jameson as he looked to framed photos from down the docks. To the young man with both hands raised from the bow of a behemoth. *So much fuckin better.*

The man's index finger pressed firm against the trigger. As he saw himself holding a most beautiful figure. His baby niece. Wrapped in fleece. Being squeezed by her godfather. The godfather who had a charming chin. When it donned a grin. *This world has gone to shit! SHIT!* The man eyed a team photo from his Little League coaching days. Boy, did he teach those boys. Standing tall beside them. Arms behind his back. A soldier of his community. Tears ran down the man's eyes. As the lady on the record waxed about the good old days. He squeezed the handle of the Glock. *It's all shit!* He clenched his eyes for the final goodbye. *I'M SHIT!—*

Wait. What was that? What the soul singer just said. We just forget the pain of the past? Only remember the good? The man opened his flooded eyes. Looked to the record. The soul singer was singing right to him. He put the gun down. He'd have to play the song back. Figure the meaning of the track.

The man had a few more sips as he re-played the Pips. He looked in his parlor mirror. Saw the tracks of his tears. Which reminded him of "Tracks of My Tears." Ooh, now that was a song. Back when they knew how to make music. The man readied some more records. He was gonna have himself a little going away party.

The man lit a cigarette and ran "Tracks of My Tears." Had a little smoke as he listened to Smokey. The man then let the cig linger on his portable bar. Was moved to groove about his parlor. He wiped away his tears. Saw the full moon through a space in the blinds. The man looked up at The Man. Sipped his whiskey neat. He had to admit. The Man was pretty neat.

"Marie! Come have a drink with me!"

The man parted the blinds of his bi-level. The Man invited himself in. Illuminated the parlor from red to pink. "You gotta see the moon, Marie! It's a beautiful fuckin moon!" He gazed up at The Man. "He's watchin over us! Just like when we were kids!"

Marie hurried out in curlers. Her tight robe restricting her frantic stride. "WHAT!" she shrieked. "It's the same fuckin moon!"

"You don't understand, Marie! Smokey's on. Dance with me!" The man swayed his hips and snapped his fingers. Like he was a member of Smokey's Miracles. After all, he was alive. It was a fuckin miracle.

"What is going on with you?" asked Marie.

"Smoke! The good kind!" The man smothered the lit cigarette into his portable bar.

"Your bar top—"

"I'll fuckin fix it tomorrow. Take me five minutes." The Miracle opened his arms. Snapped his fingers. Swayed his hips. "Dance with me, Marie!"

Marie shook her curlered head. "I need something slower. How about...'Time Is on My Side'?"

"Are you kiddin me, Marie!" dealt the dancing man.

"But you love the Roll—"

"That's the last fuckin song on Earth I wanna hear!" The dancing man circled. Wooed his woman. "I need something, Marie. Something with more...*soul*," said the man with a fist to his chest. "I got it," he noted with a raised finger. He grooved over to his 45s. Like it was 1965.

The man dropped the needle on a new song. Dropped all his worries. Took his lady in his arms. Husband and wife had eyes and smiles as big as the ones in their wedding photo. They danced like it was that day. When they danced to the same song with glee. "Stand by Me." The Man cast a spotlight just like the one they had that day. They danced surrounded by their framed photos. Surrounded by their friends and family. Just like they did that day. Back in the day. Marie rest her head on the man she married. Like it was the day they married.

The man shuffled his feet. Looked to The Man. Took a big inhale. Then. "You smell nice, Marie."

The wife was so cozy on her man's shoulder that she almost shut her eyes. Almost. "What's that on the cawfee table? Is that a *pistol* in my *parlor?*" shrieked Marie.

The man snapped out of his bliss. Looked to the Glock. "Ah that? That's nothin. I'm gonna throw it in the Sewaren sea tomorrow."

Marie looked up at him. "Hon. Are you okay?"

The man looked into his wife's eyes. "I haven't felt this good since we last danced to this song."

The look in Marie's man's eyes was more serious than the pistol in her parlor. She lay her head on his shoulder.

The man looked over Marie's shoulder. To the 45s sprawled about his bar. To the jacket of the first record he spun that night. To the beautiful lady on the cover of it. Gladys Knight had saved the Dark Knight.

And Ben E King had him feeling like a king.

The Man on the Moon made his way into Franco's open window. Franco had sucked the summer wind till it left him for dead in his bed. Then something else blew in. Something mystic that tiptoed over and tapped him on the shoulder. Gave him a message. A premonition personified.

Hours later, Franco sprang from bed. Went over and looked out the open window. The premonition was nowhere to be seen. Still. He soaked in the pink dawn of the new day. Then ran out the door.

A Bunns Lane Boy belted, "Yo Franco! Whoop that pretty boy's ass!"

Franco stopped in his tracks. Nodded. Then hurried over to Amboy Ave. Street numbers ran upward as other numbers ran up in his head. Ten years prior, Franco had put ten Gs down on his hundred-fifty-grand house. After a decade of chopping at the tree that was his mortgage, Franco now had half a hundred in his house. His "pension" from the fight game could be cashed out for fifteen. Ditto for the one from the docks. Eighty Gs. Twenty shy of the hundred Arturo stood to win by betting The Prince.

Franco ran along Rahway Ave. Toward Joey Yo's. The sprawling two-story compound with the stone façade that was the mansion of Young Joey's dreams. Franco flew up the stairs. Could hear rap blasting as he rapped on the door. Of Unit 204.

Joey swung the door open mid-workout, mid-sweat, mid-sentence— "No, I'm not gonna lower the fuckin music. Do I ask you to shut your daughter's goddamn piano off—"

"How do ya shut a piano off?"

Joey welcomed Franco in with a "Shut the fuck up."

Franco moseyed over to the kitchen table packed with packages of protein powder. Stacked with videos of stacked guys. Franco perused *Pumping Iron*. An old fav from back in the day. "Hey, uh, remember that time in seventh grade when I lent you twenty bucks for firecrackers?"

"Are you fuckin serious?" said Joey, still jacked from

getting jacked. "Let me go get my fuckin wallet." Joey beat feet past equipment from various fads. A thigh master. A stair master. All to delay meeting his Master.

Franco slowed Yo's roll. "I'm not here for that twenty. I'm here for another twenty. Large."

"You been juicin me since seventh grade?"

"What? No. Forget the fuckin twenty for firecrackers. I was just tryin to break the ice. Before I asked you to break the fuckin bank."

Franco and Joey sat at the black kitchen table like an amicable Pac and Biggie. Circa '93. TuFranc went on to explain how he was tryina make a dollar. But only had eighty cents. "What I'm saying is, if I can guarantee Arturo a hundred myself, I'm off the hook for the fall."

Joey stood up in grand Italian fashion. Or was it grand Puerto Rican fashion? And didn't he have quiet cousins on both sides who would never grandstand like he was now? With his hands on his hips. Pacing. Hands flailing. "First you ask me to whack a mob boss. Now you want twenty large to double-cross another? I'm tryin ta become a teacher!" Seven years since Franco's fall from grace forestalled Joey's chance to launch a training career. Five years since the internet erased his family's travel agency. And Joey was still seeking his life's agency. "You know what it took me to save up twenty Gs? Double-shifting at the warehouse. Clubbing once a week. Once!" Joey motioned down the hall. "Not to mention a roommate I caught jerkin off. In *my* room!"

TuFranc stood. Hands clasped before him like a Salvation Army officer grateful for any donation. "I know. Look. Think of it as a bet. If I win...big return on our investment."

Joey put his hands on his hips. Caught his breath. Grabbed a plastic bag from his kitchen counter. "Then we make it a fair fight." Joey tossed the bag on the table in front of Franco. Full of glass bottles so little yet full of liquids so powerful. Magic potion. "I picked em up off Herc soon as you texted me you were fightin The Prince." Joey put his hands up. "Just to keep it fair is all. We don't let it go down like Denver."

Franco sank into a chair. "I could get tagged."

"Cuz they went after baseball? That's only cuz the racist fucks couldn't stand Barry Bonds and his big fuckin head. Oh yeah it was all good when Mark McGwire was hittin em past Pluto. Fuckin best thing since Babe Ruth. And look at Lance Armstrong. Allegations out the ass awl these years. And he's a national hero. They ain't testin anybody in MMA either. The Prince ain't just a mixed martial artist. He's a fuckin mixology artist! Holed up in a Saudi embassy that time the British Olympic team tried to test him. Tell me that fucker ain't on the sauce. The dressing, the gravy, *and* the sauce. EPO for endurance. Amphetamines for energy. And this stuff to get buff. Fucker's got five more pounds of muscle since your last tussle."

Franco eyed the magic potion. The answer to all his problems. From fuckin Herc. Franco shook his head, wouldn't have it. His mind inclined to realness over magic. "I ain't never been finished. Never."

"Yeah, but there's these things called decisions."

"Championship fights are five rounds. The Prince has never gone past three."

"Neither have you!" Joey pulled on his puffed hair. "Because you've never been *in* a championship fight! While The Prince has been in plenty. Knockin niggas out in no time!"

Franco stood up. "I take him the distance. Further than he's ever been. Way out in the fuckin ocean. Where his fuckin dinghy, his fuckin life vest, his fuckin flare gun are all miles behind. Back at shore. Just me and him in the deep blue sea. And I drown his ass." Franco's metaphor lingered so heavily, it seemed to cloud out everything else in the room. Leaving just him and Joey. Then—

"Did you think that shit up before you got here?"

"Mighta popped in my head on the way over."

"Ya know, you already fought this guy once. Before all his added staff and added stuff and added experience. And even before all that... He kinda broke your ankle."

Franco took a breath. Looked out Joey's window to their town. To passing trucks. A kid with Chucks. Givin a bum a few bucks. "I'm gonna admit somethin to you right now that I haven't even admitted to myself." Franco looked back to Joey. "*I* slipped up. *I* broke my ankle. But that's how we learn around here, ain't it? The hard way."

"Right. Right. What you don't learn at first, you do it twice. Forget Eric Church. You're fuckin Billy Joel, son!"

Franco was in no mood for Joe's joelking. "Listen. Do you got twenty Gs for me? Or do I gotta go rob a fuckin bank?"

The Notorious JOE again tried to lighten the load. Of Franco asking for the mother lode. "I feel like Biggie, son. You stickin me for my paper. My homie who used to smoke blunts with me..."

"If I win. We smoke a fatty," sold Franco.

"If you lose, we smoke mad fatties. In your old apartment we move back into together."

"Least we'll get that college dorm experience we never had."

Joey was already over at his 50 Disc changer. He ran track five of disc six.

The beat dropped. The beeper beeped. The Notorious rapped.

The two homeboys bobbed their heads. Listened to
Biggie spit verses full of curses. They strutted around the
room. Rapped along. Loud enough for all nine hundred
neighbors to hear. Then Joey inquired so loud about what
one was gonna do "WHEN BIG FRANCO COMES FOR
YOU!"...it was as if The Prince himself could hear the
Warning.

The final days leading up to the fight were a blur. Franco's
body went through all the normal motions. He danced
around the ring with Joey and Taz. Rolled around the mats
with Nelly and Brazil. Ran around Woodbridge with he,
himself, and I. Franco even went ho hum through the
abnormal motion of handing El Jefe a duffel full of dough.
Franco's whole life in a handbag. Dropped it off like a UPS
driver dropping off a package.

Franco also went ho hum through the abnormal motion
of attending his first presser. He sat in front of the mic.
Hunched over. Arms crossed. A sea of reporters and flashing
cameras before him. Didn't even flinch when The Prince said
he was *fifteen and Franco*. Said how he was gonna finish
Franco. *Again*. *But before the final bell, I reckon*. How he was
gonna *do the lad dirty*. *Right in Dirty Jersey*. Franco then said all
the right things in the conference room of the new hotel in
Newark. About how he was glad to get a second shot. About
how he just wanted to win one for Jersey and his fans across
the country. About how he was gonna just focus on his game
plan and tune everything else out. While the first two
sentiments were true. The last was a lie.

For every dream, there's a nightmare. Franco was having
one the whole week. Wondering if The Dealer had set him up
for the ultimate bust. It wasn't enough for Franco to privately

lose it all like every other degenerate who doubled down to his last dollar. No. Franco was gonna go belly up before millions on Pay-Per-View. His ankle hurt more than he'd admit, didn't it? He was lucky his last opponent didn't attack it, wasn't he? The Prince's camp had Franco's whole fight game decoded down to the last deke, didn't they? Franco was trying to beat Super Mario Brothers straight-up. The Prince had Game Genie. And those fuckin six Bud Heavys Franco had? Sluggin a six-pack while The Prince took six shots below the back. Franco years past his peak physical age while The Prince had just arrived at his. His physique, his staff, his experience all exponentially improved. And while The Prince was peaking, Franco was puttering. Wheezing and kicking like his old pony. The entire state of Jersey would be watching as his faded headlights found their way to the cage. All his fans across America would be cheering while his brake pads chirped to a stop. All to watch the Porsche Prince blow away the old pony. Right in front of TJ. There to witness once and for all that Mom was right. As Franco, too, was turned into glue.

TRACK 13. WOODBRIDGE

AFTER PRESSING DAD, T was able to attend the presser. Got a bad vibe as he watched from the back. Was depressed the whole way back. They didn't say anything to each other. Didn't even sit together on the NJ Transit train. They sat opposite the aisle. So they could both sit at a window and stare out at their stomping grounds. Listen to the conductor run off the stops. His voice crackling over the static feedbacking from the speaker. *"Welcome to Newark Penn Station. Next stops. Elizabeth, Linden, Rahway, Woodbridge."* The North Jersey Coast Line. Ha. Sure, the train coasted to the coast after the Amboys, but there wasn't any sand or sea in sight for this rough stretch of ride. Just mud and murky water hiding murked mobsters. And of course, the towns. Those tough little towns. Newark's industrial outskirts with its brick factories that almost brushed the train as it tracked past. Some closed down. Their broken windows a window to broken dreams. Some in operation. TJ peeked through the windows cranked out a quarter way. Wings of a bird debating flight. The horde of seamstresses inside debating the same thing. Then onto Elizabeth and all its asphalt. Exhausted immigrants wonderin if it's they own ass fault. Standing at the dilapidated platform trying to catch a lift to the America of their dreams. Unlikely they found it when the train linked them to Linden. With its little houses and big block letters tagged onto the wooden fences facing the tracks.

Out the other window, Franco caught the work of CROCK. On the outskirts of Rahway with its one-story garages, warehouses, industrial shops. A commercial zone where no one shops. Then past the junkyard and into Woodbridge. TJ leaned in. The forest was a little denser all the sudden. The lots a little bigger. The train station revamped and overlooking the petite park. Kids playing on the play structure. Next to the ball courts and tennis courts whose locks were now sprung for spring. A park that wouldn't blow your hair back. But it got the job done, didn't it? TJ left the train with a hop in his step. Then halted.

G-Dub was passed out against the brick wall. Franco took out his wallet. Sawed off a sawbuck. Almost put the ten bucks in G-Dub's Dunkin' Donuts cup. But. That color toffee non-coffee. Franco instead tucked the Hamilton inside the chest pocket of G-Dub's jacket. Even better—no one would jack it.

Franco and T walked home. Still didn't say a word. Save for when a new Mustang moseyed down Main. "Nice," muttered Franco. When they got home, T went right to his room. Told Franco he had something important to work on.

The next morning was the morning before the fight. Friday. A school day. So T went on his way.

Franco meanwhile started the morning the same way he did the day before every local fight. With his run around Woodbridge. He usually looked forward to his burrow through the nine boroughs. But his mind was a mess as he threw on his sweats. Of the million Rocky quotes, he only heard one. Over and over. About how you gotta be a real moron to be a fighter. About how you're just about guaranteed to be a bum. Franco could already see it as he hobbled down his stairs. The cover of the Sunday *Star-Ledger*: THE BUNNS LANE BUM.

Franco stepped out the door. Almost stepped on the Discman. "What the fuck?" Franco picked it up, turned to put it back inside. He always ran without music. No music in the cage, so none for his run around The Steel Cage. Had to have his mind ready for war. Like fellow Jersey boy Memph Bleek. But there was that piece of paper tucked under the Discman:

Dad. I know you usually don't run with music. But,

And goddamn if T didn't know his dad—

You gotta get your mind ready for war.

Franco strapped the Discman on his upper arm like an astronaut affixing his space suit. Only with more difficulty.

Franco then did his traditional trot across the street like he was Andy Pettitte taking the bump. He ran up the project side of Bunns Lane. Pressed play as he passed his old apartment. Anthemic rock rocked his ears. "Born in the USA." Franco shook his head over the genius mix of downtrodden lyrics hidden inside uplifting music. Fooled the president himself back in '84. Franco picked up the pace. He reached a double-lane highway and got a double dose of The Boss. "Born To Run" as Franco ran onto Highway 9.

A mall-bound bus of black folks breezed past. One dude threw two signs to Franco. An E with one hand. East Coast for sure. And a W with the other. Maybe showing Franco love from coast to coast. Or maybe the W was for *Woodbridge*. Which, to Franco, covered even more ground. Franco sent a fighter's fist back. Pondered the ambition of the rider as the disc played "Ambitionz Az a Ridah."

Franco hauled into Hopelawn. Past the bowling alley where a couple of blue-collar Bettys were just leaving their league match.

"Ay Franco. You gonna mash His Majesty or what?"

"Yeah, what's it gonna be, Bunns Lane Brawler?"

Franco only had a shrug for the two ladies rollin outta the bowlin alley with the biggest balls in town. Just two more reminders of how big a bust The Dealer had set him up for. Franco reeled off Route 9 past an old-timer reeling in nothing but bait from the creek that ran past Lou Creekmur's. The Hall of Fame NFL lineman who was famous for playing through dislocated limbs and other ER-worthy injuries. All back when the NFL was so young, he had made more money in the offseason as a trucking manager. The Brawler could relate. Save for that one part. Where Creekmur went on to become a champion.

Franco pushed past a park as the Discman dished out "If I Can't." He took a pass from one of the hooping Hispanics. Dropped a trey and put them all in a panic. Even 50 woulda scored it a 50. Too bad tomorrow was gonna be ten million times harder.

Franco cruised into Keasbey. Aka Crazebee. Past a mami pushing a baby.

"You that fighter, aintchyou?"

Shit. Too many people knew him already. Wait till tomorrow. Franco definitely wasn't ready for Freddie as the Discman rocked "We Will Rock You."

Franco ran along the Raritan. Puerto Rican Perth Amboy

perched to the east. White-as-the-South South Amboy to the south. Franco in between. Jogging past smashed 40s. Then out to Highway 440. Past a billboard promoting the fight. For a split second, Franco thought it was him on the left. With the nifty nose. The almond eyes atop chipper cheeks. The glowing skin that gave way to spikes scurrying this way and that. But no. That was The Prince. Franco was the fighter on the right. Looking just like The Prince. After ten licks with the ugly stick. Franco always thought he was halfway handsome. But The Prince was world-class handsome. Internationally approved while Franco was barely over the hump in his haggard hometown. The billboard an advertisement for Franco's delusion. What he thought he looked like versus what he actually looked like. Mario Lopez versus Mario Fauxpez. Could the same be true of Franco's athletic ability that was the bedrock of his foray into the fight game? Him and his three-sport athlete talk. He managed to pass on the court by passing to superior players. The five-niner who ran himself rail thin in soccer n ball all winter n fall. Then sprung into baseball season as a 160-pounder who ripped singles and beat out bunts while it was the big boys who banged him in. And the soccer team that he bragged about being varsity as a freshman? Buncha working-class kids foolin with fútbol in a town obsessed with football. Pre-1994 World Cup, pre-Alexi Lalas, pre-Tab Ramos snacking on Snickers. If soccer was a joke in the aughts, it oughta been the king of comedy back then. *Cuts? Barely enough players to field a team and we talkin about cuts?* introspected the AI fan. Not to mention Franco's All-County claim. Every team got to elect one player. He slipped in his senior year. Not first team. Not second. Not third. Just honorable mention. The most dishonorable of all the mentions. Franco, too, was thinkin, *Damn.* As he listened to "Everything I Am." Thinkin about everything he was. Delusional. Outmatched. Destined to be a bum.

Franco ran the track back as he ran the petrol tracks. Had to take another listen to the lyrical teachings of this new-school cat, Kanye. What was T tryin to tell him with the tune? Was Franco hearing the words to the song all wrong? Was T saying that everything Franco *isn't*...is what makes him...*great?*

Franco beat feet into Fords. Ran along New Brunswick Ave's one-story brick stores all telling the same story. Of a tough little town no one could hold down. Bustling with business from The Made Man Barber Shop fulla dudes with fresh mops to Ruben's Auto Body to The Flower Shop run by Dotty. Franco then ran past Dotty's biggest customer. A cemetery full of cement flower stations. Just one of the gazillion graveyards that could be found all over the old town. Three hundred fifty years of fallen fathers, mothers, sisters, brothers. Scattered about town in plain sight. The poop of a nest the newly hatched generation would just have to endure. Despite the scatalogy of the analogy, Franco actually breathed a sigh of relief. The masses who had widowed Woodbridge were all definitely too dead to be let down by The Brawler. He had half a mind to wave to the graves. *Nice to see yous!*

Franco trucked along Route 1 as trucks roared past. He on Woodbridge Township's Fords borough side. Edison Township on the other. Named after the Wizard of Menlo Park himself. As Franco hauled past Menlo Mall, he tried to remember that thing Edison said. He didn't fail a million times? He found a million ways not to make a light bulb? Was that it? And what the fuck did that mean? Goddamn it why didn't Franco pay more attention to Mr. Ertz in his Earth Science class? Oh that's right. Cuz him and Joey were too busy cracking up. Calling it *Ertz* Science. Jesus Christ. Why couldn't Edison build a goddamn time machine for Franco?

Now that would be useful. Franco was sure to stay on the Woodbridge Township side of the road. Fuck Edison.

But as Franco beat feet out of Fords, his feelings flipped. *He* had a light bulb moment. Maybe *none* of his life had been a failure. Maybe it was all a prelude to him turning on his own light the following night. Finally illuminating exactly the life he set out to live.

As Franco's mind was in fifth gear, his feet hit the fifth borough of his township run. Sucking wind as he entered Iselin. His gills enflamed as he turned on Gill Lane. The road laid on a land once full of teepees was now full of Indian joints all over again. Only Columbus would've been correct in his ethnic assessment this time around. Franco pushed through Merrill Park as the track was a-changin. To "The Times They Are a-Changin." Franco's ankle straight killin. As he listened to Dylan. "Get him, Franco," said an old Indian man wearing a sari. Franco shrugged—a prepaid sorry. A couple of high fives he barely mustered. For two Guindians eating pretzels n mustard. It took all he had to pick up a cricket ball batted his way. He handed it over to a pursuant little squirt. In a Yankees t-shirt. The name on the back put some juice in Franco's meter. The kid repped Jeter.

Franco continued past the three generations of family picnicking at the park. Continued on his own. To "Like a Rolling Stone." Like the fallen hero in the song, Franco, too, had nothing to lose. Maybe that would give him comfort in defeat. He chugged down Chain O' Hills Road in his nine-year-old Nikes. Nikes he vowed to wear until he wore The Belt. Nine-year-old Nikes he feared would see ninety. Nine-year-old Nikes he'd be buried in. As he groveled past yet another graveyard, he had half a mind to hop the fence and get right to it.

But another Bob kept the fire lit. "Get Up, Stand Up."

Franco listened to the commands from Marley as he followed a Harley. Through winding roads that ranged from centuries-old single lanes to overhauled highways. Past a mishmash of houses that varied in size, style, and century built. Across yet another traffic bottleneck of a township that wasn't properly planned. Rather, sprawling in ways and directions as variable as the times it had been through. An unpredictable, divergent town that was either a cancer cell. Or. A diamond in the rough.

Franco was five of nine boroughs done and hearing The Wood's most famousest son. Halfway there. Hearin "Livin' On a Prayer." Franco cruised into Colonia. Sure, it was the crown jewel of the township with its lush woods and single lanes that snaked past acre lots older than America. Past colossal colonials built in better days. Past the country club that served as a reunion hall for those outtie in their Audis. "FRANCOOO!" yelled a thirtysomething doing fortysomething in a car worth fiftysomething. Franco threw a neutral nod to the pilot of the A6. Unsure if he was fuckin with The Brawler still crawlin in Asics. Franco couldn't trust Colonia either. Even there, the picturesque gave way to the grotesque. Aging all-brick apartments. Drags of drab strip malls. Shut-down shops. They were all over Woodbridge, weren't they? Caldor. Woolworth. Rickel's. Burned-out stores as old as Don Rickles.

The Prince, meanwhile, was the properly planned exurb of Franco's dreams. Literally of Franco's dreams. Franco had never seen the mansions of Millburn. The landscaped lawns of Livingston. The unbridled colts of Colts Neck. He'd only heard his lawyer chat about Chatham. Only got a glimpse of Glen Ridge from a Parkway bridge. Only once stopped at a Montclair park on a lark. Until county officers asked what his business was. Told him *keep it moving, 'cous.* And of course.

The crown jewel of Jersey. Princeton. Literally fuckin means Prince Town. Franco imagined The Prince as one of them gothic campus buildings. His fight team the landscapers who kept the grounds prim and proper. The contractors ever-expanding the campus. The hired hands weatherproofing and burglar-proofing The Prince from any and all intrusions. The Prince's manager was the city planner at large who mapped out a grid of parallel and perpendicular roads with ample width. And underground electricity of course. His sponsors the corporations that inhabited buildings downtown and spread wealth uptown. The campus donors that endowed The Prince with any and all resources. The Prince's entourage the cops and firefighters that kept him safe at all times. His groupies, his VIP rooms, his penthouses the parks, pools, and golf courses he had all to himself before being chauffeured home to the wives and kids.

Franco scaled yet another bridge that barely stitched his township together. He tried to garner a glimpse—through wires stitching utility poles together, down more train tracks that seemed to cross at every seam, past the marshland maybe home to Hoffa—of Giants Stadium. While he couldn't quite make out the arena, the words of the G-Men's defensive captain came to him clear as a bell. Strahan had said the famous phrase only a month before. After the G-Men pulled off the biggest upset in the world's biggest game. Against what would've been the undefeated, greatest NFL team of all time. *Everybody's got a plan until they get hit in the mouth.* Strahan's requote of words originally spoken by the real deal Brooklyn brawler himself. Words that lit a fire up under the buns of The Bunns Lane Brawler.

Franco accelerated from the apex of the bridge and caught speed into Avenel. Into stomping grounds with a grit that made the fighter feel more at home. The utility poles as crooked as his past. The lots as little as his own. The Route 1 joints as rundown as himself. But still plugging along. Better yet, the broken hero had some extra juice. Thanks to another track from Bruce. "Thunder Road" as he thundered down the road. But something was wrong as he heard his wedding song. What kind of backwards fucking life did Franco live that entering Avenel made him feel better? The American Dream ran the other way. Into Colonia. Into a colossal colonial. Into the country club. So what the fuck was Franco running? Past potholed roads. Run-down ranches. Mobile homes for the downwardly mobile. The fear gave Franco another gear. He went into overdrive as he did a loop around The Loop. The motel of heart-shaped tubs and sauna showers. For lovers by the hours.

Franco ran along Rahway Prison. Rahway. Ha. The iconic green-domed fortress of *Ocean's Eleven* and *He Got Game* fame sat entirely on Woodbridge Township property. Worse. One of Franco's favorite movies, *Rounders*, did something even more preposterous to the prison's position. When Mikey McD himself rolls into Woodbridge and picks up Worm at the prison's gates, what did the movie makers put on the prison's sign? Some fake-ass name across an image of the state of New York! It ain't enough that New York claimed the Jets and Giants from Jersey. They had to jack the jail, too! As Franco ran around the grounds and onto Rahway Ave, he had another wonder altogether. Why the fuck did he even care if Woodbridge got credit for a fuckin jail? How twisted was that? It was enough to give him the Folsom Prison Blues. Until he remembered. That he had cut ties with The Frog. And any chance of ever hopping into incarceration. Franco found yet another gear as he cashed in on a different Cash song from T. For T. "I Walk the Line."

Franco trucked past the prison. Destined for another

cage. Then got some extra hops. From "When the Music Stops." As Em had him feeling froggish, Franco forgot all about the toad. He fuckin blazed down Blair Road. Trucked parallel to trucks on the Turnpike. Along the edge of borough seven. Port Reading. Yeah, there were stretches of brush that would brush him onto the busy road. Yeah, the other side had a sidewalk. Yeah, he had homies over on the Carteruff side. But he was just. He was feeling his town today. Woodbridge. The Wood. The W. Feeling *trim* as he listened to Slim. As he motored past immobile mobile homes. As he made his way along more where-the-fuck-am-I industrial outskirts. One plant after another. Combining one chemical or another. Mixin up swamps in the swamps of Jersey.

Franco pushed forward as the ancient township and its Washington memorials and Jefferson Streets gave way to Omar Avenue and the Oros Wildlife Preserve. On a gray day, the preserve looked like it preserved whacked wiseguys. But on this morning, with the sun shimmied up over the forest and shining upon the lake, Franco had half a mind to rent a fuckin canoe. No need to row to the Wu. He could just chill in that nifty lake right in his hometown. Maybe after the fight. Yeah. Definitely. He'd sit out there in a canoe one way or the other. Maybe as a champ who could reclaim his princess. Stand there with Julie at the edge of the canoe like he was fuckin Leo in *Titanic*. Or as a total loser. As Fredo getting one last look at God's green earth. Before it all went black.

Franco revved his engine to a gear he didn't know he had. He clocked the digital clock on the Turnpike billboard. *8:02.* Eight-o-fuckin two! Even before the cracked ankle, he never cracked 8:05. *8:02 mothafucka. Fierce as the Wu mothafucka. Listenin to Em mothafucka.* Franco hit a runner's high on his eighth mile. Pumped by the man from *8 Mile.* As the music made him feel uplifted, his mind drifted. Many times, the victor was just the one who wanted it more, wasn't it? Broadway Joe and the Jets, *18-point underdogs*, finding a way to outball Baltimore in Super Bowl III. The Amazin Mets down to their last out, refusing to be eighty-sixed in '86. The Rangers' Mark Messier messing up the Canucks for the Cup in '94—the ex-Oiler able to go to the well once more. *Right at Franco's age no less.* The about-to-be-down one game to three underdog Yanks who yanked the Series back—outbraving the Braves in '96. And those Jersey G-Men. The ones Joey never stopped believin in. Not this year. Not ever. Just last month. Greatest upset of all time.

And the fight game was a whole other level. Fuck who wants it more. Who *needs* it more. Who even gets into the fight game to begin with? Dudes with no other options. Dudes that are willing to walk into a cage with a killer. *And be the killer.*

But what about The Prince? An exception to the rule. Born with it all. On the outside. On the inside, a giant hole in his soul. Franco knew a lot about that. Knew The Prince had a lot to prove. His baba was a bear of a man who built the Saudi fight game with his bare hands. Not to mention his expansion of their oil empire as the Middle Easterner found mad West Side love. And The Prince's mother. Twice the medals and degrees. How the fuck could he please? The Prince poured his rage into the cage. A mixed martial artist born with a lethal mix. The brood n brawn of Baba. The sleek frame n strategic brain of Mama. That Kanye cat crept back in Franco's brain. Those bars. How everything you're not. Makes you everything you are.

Franco ran along the dock where he had the nighttime talk with T. His sweats as wet and salty as the sea. The morning light illuminated the empty trash. No sign of Franco getting trashed. The morning light illuminated the projects he put the Wu at. Illuminated Sewaren's nifty marina full of boats. Flanked by oil tanks. *Only in Woodbridge.* Franco fired some punches. Threw in some dekes and ducks. Dodged a family of ducks. The shadowboxer smiled as he reminisced on that young and drunk night. When Joey was encouraging him to take his fighting skills and marry them with martial arts training. Three (hundred) sheets to the wind, Franco leaned in all glassy-eyed, all dead serious, and recited the riff currently playing on his CD. About how he should mix Shaolin shadowboxing. With the Wu-Tang sword style. Sure, Young Franco was dropping a joke to crack his and Joey's drunk asses up. But he also signed up for Muay Thai the next morning.

Franco crossed himself as he crossed the patch where his pony passed. Then crossed the parking lot of the VFW and soldiered on past a couple soldiers. A long-haired old-timer from Nam and a crew-cut newbie from Fallujah. Vets sharing a smoke and a hallelujah. They made fists in salute to the fighter.

"Get im, Franco," said old man Ernest in earnest.

"Whadaya say now, Wood!" hooted the newbie. Who be. Lookin like Miles. Boobie.

The fighter sent a salute back as Creedence crooned their creed. About how when the wars come. They're the ones. Cuz they weren't no. Fortunate Sons. Franco turned and set his sights on the one and only Woodbridge Ave. A dead shot west. Back to Woodbridge borough. Aka Proper. The sun ablaze at Franco's back in perfect counterbalance to the cool. The local road illuminated. The town's inhabitants in their cars carting this way and that. Backing out of driveways set between green grass. Green grass whose spring smell was springing for the first time this morning. Green grass that ran around cozy Cape Cods glowing in the morning sun. Green grass that boasted budding trees. Oaks and maples the main staples. Green grass that gave way to petite parking lots of quaint corner stores. A camp worthy of Mellencamp. Franco breezed past little pink houses. Hearin a little "Pink Houses." As The Bunns Lane Brawler made his way back to Proper, the townsfolk gave him a sendoff proper. A bus driver beeped her horn. A couple contractors wished him luck from their truck. Families waved hands from minivans.

Franco's fight team did him one better. Joey, Brazil, Taz, and even Lama, who ran like a llama, were all waiting for him at the final high point. The apex of the bridge back to his home borough.

Franco trucked up the bridge lined with armed forces flags that forced his arms faster. His feet flew over the final hill. He was far from over the hill. As he headed back. From the FISH PACK. (The acronym every kid from The Wood learns to remember the eight other boroughs. Fords. Iselin. Sewaren. Hopelawn. Port Reading. Avenel. Colonia. Keasbey.)

"Nigga wait up!" wailed Joey, petty.

But all Franco heard was Petty. "Learning to Fly" as he flew toward his old high school. His whole crew behind him.

A police car pulled out. Franco slowed his roll as the sirens rolled. Was some crooked shit he did for The Frog coming back to bite him? Wait—the cop wasn't stopping him. The cop was *escorting him.* Toward the hundreds of high school kids waiting with Coach Nelson.

"You weren't gonna run without us, were you?" wondered Nelly as he bellied up to Franco, carrying right along.

"Don't you got some athletics to direct?" huffed Franco.

"And what's lesson one of my athletic program?"

Franco grinned. "Woodbridge Pride."

"Woodbridge Pride, baby." Nelly slapped his fighter's back. "Whadaya say now, *WOOD!*"

Five hundred high school kids, *"WHADAYA SAY NOW, WOOD!"*

Franco and Nelly led the congregation past the tennis courts. A steamroller rolled a fresh pave of them.

"What's that about?" floated Franco.

"You didn't hear? Richie Sambora's dumping a ton of money into the school," noted Nelly.

"No shit." Franco picked up the pace. As he looked back to the passing courts, he saw T. "Ay!" Franco's face lit up. "Get up here!"

T breezed past the high schoolers high on freedom and his father's fledgling fame. He dashed alongside Dad.

The heavy Rocky bells ringing in Franco's ears gave way to the song they were sampled into. "Victory." Featuring who else? The Notorious. Franco pointed to his headphones, gave T a fist bump. "Dope." He now had hope. Nothing better than those bells. At once ominous and auspicious. Nothing better than those bells save for Big and Puff belting out bars over them. Nothing better than those bells with Big and Puff belting out bars save for it all being on a bomb-ass CD from T.

Franco ran with all his heart past Pearl Street Park. Past the Cross Keys landmark. Ran right through St. John's on a lark. Those praying to the Holy Spirit in Mass found it in Franco and followed en masse. And fuck beeping, cars began to *park*. Passengers spilled out and ran after Franco and the hundreds of high schoolers. The whole town tailed him as he sprinted past Parker's Printing Press. The landmarked cottage sittin there like it was 1776. Like it was ready to crank out another edition of the colonies' first newsletter. *The New America.*

Franco hit top speed right down the middle of Main Street. In his home borough. The granddaddy of them all. Like he was the Grand Marshall. Of The Granddaddy of Them All.

Franco's buns were ablaze as he blazed down Bunns Lane. Had cramps in his quads as he passed the quads. All on calves unstable as a newborn calf's. Still, he was much enjoying the run. Much enjoying running behind the cops rather than the reverse. Much enjoying the town running with him. Much enjoying throwing clean lefts and rights with equal ease. Thanks to his old man making him a righty when he was really a lefty. Much enjoying that he actually appreciated his old man as he passed his old apartment. Much enjoying wrapping his run in record time as he doubled over on the double yellows. Right in the middle of the road. Right in front of his humble abode. Much enjoying the swarming coaches, kids, and countless other neighbors. Much enjoying a second listen of Fitty. As his town rallied around him, all in a fitty.

Cuz if Franco couldn't do it. It couldn't be done.

TRACK 14. BATTLE OF NEWARK

TWO TONIO FRANCOS walked out the front door that day. The younger set a screen on the screen. The elder shuffled out with a duffel. Closed the warped wood door.

The two Tonio Francos walked into yet another winter wind brought about by the bipolar month. March madness. Behind them, the screen screamed shut. They continued under a down comforter of cumulus. Covering up what The Dealer had in store for Franco's final hand. The down comforter clouds shoulda been downright discomfiting. Especially when a fresh fleet of sleet flew in. But nah. The two Tonio Francos just threw up their hoods up and walked their hood. It was their weather. The badder the better. Smoke fumed from the pitbulls' mouths as they walked in-step. The duo so wired, even their brains were wired. Like an Na and Cl unknowingly held together by invisible bonds far stronger than any physical phenomena. An Na and Cl that, when alone, were unstable and incomplete. But when together were part of something bigger. Father and son's invisible bonds blared an obscure track through both their brains. One with an incessant piano key. A synth as stressed as a boiling kettle. With bass and drums that made it all hum. "Winter Warz" as they marched toward their winter war.

The two Tonio Francos crossed to the Cross Keys Tavern. They rolled up on the Washington memorial as they both harkened back in their bonded brains. Back to all the Jersey battles they had learned about in elementary. In fifth-grade Social Studies. The year designated for Jersey history. The last time Franco earned an A outside gym. The year Joey Yo crossed out JERSEY on his book's cover and Sharpied in JOISEY.

Washington and his ragtag crew. Got their asses handed to them battle after battle across the Tri-State. Pushed back to Pennsy. Starvin n freezing. Ill n injured. Plenty to grieve on Christmas Eve. Could've spent all Christmas morning in mourning. But yo. Fuck that. They crossed the icy Delaware with ice in their veins. Packed boats for pig iron with wills of iron. Ran ashore on Jersey in their tattered jerseys.

The two Tonio Francos planned on patting the memorial and moving on. But. There was an envelope taped to it. Handwritten in all caps: FOR FRANCO.

The elder pulled the handwritten letter out. A scan of it told him it was from G-Dub.

> *Yo. Franco. The way we came up we don't never talk about our feelins or nothin. I don't know if you even know but I was their the night Youngin OD'd.*

Franco. G-Dub. Youngin. The three OGs. The three soccer team refugees. Back of the bus blastin Fugees.

> *And I was watching the night The Prince ended your career. Or so I thought if I'm keepin it real. Outta the three of us I*

always thought you were the one with the chance to really do somethin. End then to see you lose Julie. Your family.

As Franco stood before the memorial of his nation, he had finally found that Jersey Haitian. As he read the letter from his guy, he was hearing "No Woman, No Cry."

But here you are. The man of the hour.
It's time to do work. See you in Newark.

Franco unslung his duffel. The one he had to dust off after giving the other away the other day. The one from his high school soccer days. The one with the broken zipper. The one with Youngin's Asics Aggressors looking right at him.

Franco placed G-Dub's envelope next to Youngin's Asics. With emotions like he was age six. Franco and TJ then patted the memorial together. Something T wanted to do since age six. As they walked away, Franco wiped a tear from his eye. Under the gray sky. Still hearing "No Woman, No Cry."

At the Woodbridge train station, Joey, Coach Nelly, Brazil, Taz, and Lama all joined the revolution. A militia ready to overthrow The Prince. Their own general looking like Prince. They his band. The Revolution.

Lama lofted, "Where's the Stang?"

But it didn't sting. Wasn't a second ominous sign. The two Tonios wanted to take the Transit train. Wanted to walk along the linoleum tiles splitting the peanut pleather seats. Wanted to sit among pardoned prisoners from Rahway and those sentenced to The City grind. Wanted to sit in the seats with the rockable backs that allowed the Francos to rock back. And sit right across from each other. Just like back in the day. Back in the day when Franco and Julie would take little T to NYC. They'd arrive at the tracks under MSG. Unfold the stroller. Rock the little feller up to Rockefeller. Little T loved The Tree. Julie the Macy's sprees. Franco the Big East Tourney. All three the Statue of Liberty. Julie talking about her Ellis Island heritage like a preacher. Followed by watching the Bombers from the bleachers. Where Dad became the teacher.

As the Transit train lifted past Linden, the Francos' melded mind drifted. To all the events they couldn't see. The Knicks tickets too big a nick in the pockets. The Rangers hockey tickets hocked for hundreds. The common man Billy Joel jams the common man couldn't afford. They almost went crazy. When they couldn't see Jay-Z. But not tonight. The Francos were the show and the front row. The brawn ready for anything his opponent could bring. The brains having plotted the whole thing. The premonition personified.

The conductor made his way through.

"I got us. What do I owe ya?" said Franco as he grabbed a money clip from his bag with the broken zip.

"One of those," said the conductor, pointing to Franco's chest. A *W*. The conductor made a fist. Went on conducting his business.

General Franco and his fight team crossed the freezing Rahway River. A river run black in the dusk. A dusk that accentuated the harshness of the marsh. A dusk that deepened the rust on the refineries they rolled by. The brick Budweiser plant churned out smoke. Brewed Bud Heavy as the sky grew heavy. The General and his son shared a look. *Optimal conditions. To make a run on royalty.*

The train pulled into Penn Station. The *other* Penn Station. The one in Brick City. Perhaps a third ominous sign. That they didn't quite make The City. No way. Where better to get down n dirty? Than in Turnpike Jersey.

The doors opened.

The General and his militia stepped into the frosty New Jersey night. It was time for the Battle of Newark.

The militia stood atop the hill. A path before them cut to the battlefield below. A caged canvas. At the center of an A-plus arena crowded with 20,000 colonists. All who came to see blood. Hoping to witness a revolution. General Franco surveyed the scene. T at his side. In red Adidas pants with the white stripes. As jacked as Jack White. Joey Yo at Franco's other side rockin a star-spangled bandana. Around—not over—his hair of course. Coach Nelly in Woodbridge red from toe to head. Brazil in blue warmups. Lama in a white pantsuit. Taz in a razzmatazz of all of the above.

The General took one last look as he stood in the lucky trunks he always wore. The ones that were white and blue when Julie bought them for him. But that was many bloody battles ago. Now? Now they were red, white, and blue.

As the challenger, General Franco's war drum beat first. Julie may not have been there, but his song remained the same. Their song from the second he heard it. Back in the day. He was on his way home from a double shift down the docks. Spring rain pelted the metal frame of his first Mustang. A 1985 5.0. Ten years old and ready to fold. The washed-out windshield offered a watercolor canvas of Turnpike taillights. Franco himself still soaked as he sulked. He had just started down the docks. Was saddled there all of Saturday. While Joey Yo and a co of coeds were far from the bleakness. Down at Preakness. The bring-your-own-kegs-and-coolers infield shit show at the second leg of the Triple Crown. Joey drinking a triple Crown. In a caravan goin down to Marylan. Living the best part of "Everyday Struggle." While Franco was living the whole fuckin song. And to top it all off, it was a sunny weekend down in Baltimore. Just to bust Franco's balls some more. Right then and there at the red light in the rain. On the corner of Amboy Ave and Main. It hit Young Franco. *This is it.* His job at the docks. The favors for The Frog. A family to support. *The rest of his life.* Nineteen and nuked.

He pulled into the driveway around 5 am. Ready to sleep till 5 am. But Julie bolted out the front door clutching Baby T. Even in the dark, he could make out her eyes. Incredible. Baby T was wailing like Franco never heard. Julie hopped in and told him to head to the hospital. TJ was running a fever. 105.

Franco drove. Turned the station to 105. He was transfixed by the opening piano keys. Even Baby T's wails gave way. To the soothing voice of Mary J. Franco looked into Julie's blues. If Franco was bein honest, he didn't like a lot of songs, even some of his favorites, the first time or two he heard them. But this one. This one went to the top of his list in the first few lyrics. Then the peaceful song went to a whole other level. When Meth blew it up like a rebel. And was that...*Biggie*...in the background? It was an embarrassment of riches.

By the time they pulled into the hospital, the rain had subsided. The pink dawn was peeking. And Mary just kept on peaking. Baby T had stopped crying altogether. He was asleep. With a sweat-streaked forehead that darkened his hairs. His nose stuffed. His toothless mouth. His breathing raspy. His one little hand wrapped around Julie's finger. Franco put his calloused hand around Baby T's other. As if God had sent Franco his own little cloud to clutch.

Julie's blues looked to Franco, much obliged. Thanks to the words of Mary J Blige. Julie could finally see. Franco was her destiny.

Franco and Julie. Hearing Meth and Mary. "I'll Be There For You/You're All I Need To Get By." Franco staring into those blues. His Jewels. Their real fortune bundled in her arms. It was an embarrassment of riches.

General Franco broke the marching protocol. Fuck the formality of war. *Him* and the Americans stormed the battlefield. They had their own method, man, as the arena pumped Method Man.

Franco scaled the cage. Took one last look around The Vault for the Jewels. But. They were nowhere to be found. His song cut out as that other one picked right back up in his head. "No Woman, No Cry." There Franco stood, encased in a cage. The same size and shape as one of those inflatable airplane lifeboats he prayed he'd never have to get into. But there he was. Surrounded by sharks circling. In the front row. Arturo. With his petite princesa. To his right in a tight dress. Perfectly postured in Prada. To Arturo's left was his dough boy, Boy George. As white n soft as the Pillsbury Doughboy. As tickled as him, too, as he downed a dirty martini with glee. Across the cage sat The Queen. The Prince's mother. The medalist once again draped in precious metals. On hand to see her son retain his belt full of them. And who was that sitting somewhere between El Jefe and The Queen? A chinny man. With a full head of gray hair. And a tie. Was that...? And who the hell was with him? Wasn't his goomar from Belmar. Was that...*his wife?* Hair cut. Dress cut. Ready to cut a rug. *What the fuck?* Franco was as shook as Shakespeare. *Fair is foul and foul is fair.* What did the idiot say when Miss Lane taught his remedial class that quote? Oh yeah. *Ay Miss Lane. Is Shakespeare tryin ta invent baseball?* Good one, Franco. That's when Franco heard the drums. As something wicked this way comes.

The lights went down on the sharks. Illuminated an even more imposing threat. The army from across the Atlantic. Standing stalwart in row formation. Three rows of five. Fourteen soldiers committed to a victory for His Majesty. All of them donning red. Warmups for the warriors. A robe for the royalty.

Their battle song blared. Almost broke Franco's eardrums. Not the noise level. The lyrics. Somethin about *Mansionnns. Ferrariis. Diamond ringsss.* Bling. Bling. Bling. Please, somebody ring the bell. Ding. Ding. Ding. No, of course not. The Prince has to lead the Redcoats on a deliberate march. His Highness and his Hessians from his father's homeland. Mercenaries now loyal to the Crown. To the almighty pound.

The motley crew of revolutionaries circled the wagons around Franco. They, too, loyal to the pound. The one in Franco's chest.

With every march-step forward, the Redcoats grew more and more imposing.

"We shoulda hid in the crowd. Ambushed their asses," offered Joey.

"Think we'd get disqualified," floated Franco.

"Least we'd win."

A fourth ominous sign? Was Joey insinuating that they *weren't* about to win? Nah...

Franco met The Prince in the middle as the ref meddled. Franco was flat-footed while The Prince popped up and down like a popcorn kernel about to pop. And why not? He had three inches of height and three less pounds of fat. Fat that Franco had packed on in advanced years. Confirming his concern about what DeNiro had said in *Cape Fear.* Somethin about how a man past his prime starts puttin on a pound of fat per year. The Prince also had two A-plus ankles. And who knows what coursing through his veins. Franco's last physical meanwhile. High fuckin cholesterol. Ate healthy as hell. Didn't drink. Didn't smoke. Still. There was something innate inside him that couldn't be changed. Reminded him of an old tone. "Bad to the Bone."

As the ref said what refs say, Franco tracked the pristine Prince popping from side to side. Intermittently revealing his coach father and his metallic mother. Back and forth. It was then that Franco realized why he was so taken by The Prince at the beginning of their last fight. Going into the fight, on paper, Franco had felt good at five-nine 170. A nice size for a welterweight back in '01. The Prince was listed at six-foot 170. A twig that Franco's tree-trunk arms would snap. Then the actual sight of The Prince in the cage. Taller with just as much muscle. What he took in vertical inches, he wasted at the waist. The first of these new wave fighters Franco had fought a few times since. Taller, leaner, stronger. Ripped from shin to shoulder.

And there again the two were at the center of the cage. Franco. And The Man of Franco's Dreams. Franco at five-nine, nine percent body fat. The Prince at six feet, four percent. Making Franco look like a fat midget. Or worse. Like The Prince's lesser brother. Every pair of brothers Franco ever met, the one with the extra height got to stretch out all that predetermined DNA. While the shorter one got the extra snub of stub. But Franco and The Prince didn't have the same parents, did they? And maybe that was the only difference, Franco figured as he eyed the army of trainers behind The Prince. Headed by his father. His decorated mother in the front row right behind them. *That's* why Franco's roll was slowed the first time he stepped into the cage with The Prince. He was everything Franco could've been. If he had grown up with proper parents. Nutrition. Sleep. Guidance. Mental health. Money. Franco was feeling that new cat Kanye more and more. Thinking, *Damn.* Hearing "Everything I Am."

While Franco was feeling forlorn, his town was jacked from Fords to Hopelawn. Everyone in Woodbridge was rooting for The Bunns Lane Brawler. Errryone. From the cops crowded around the big screen at Big Times to the small-time crooks crowded around Screws's hospital bed. From the Colonia country clubbers in the clubhouse to the Poor Billy's night clubbers packing the house. From the Indians screening it in an Iselin temple. To the Sewaren salts flocked on a docked yacht. From Port Reading heads hyping the fight on Facebook. To Avenelers replying: *Franco by left hook!* From the crazies at the Elks in Keasbey. To the crowd in the Bunns Lane projects. Crowdin around the projector projectin the fight. Right off the bricks of The Brawler's old apartment. Cuz everyone in Woodbridge could ascertain. That Franco was gonna bring the pain.

The fight was on. Franco stepped to the center of the cage. The Prince danced around like a merry-go-round. One that could go in either direction on a dime. Yet Franco was the one dizzied. An old axis creaking as it kept up. The dazzling merry-go-round with its dashing speed. Muscular horses. Flawless bobbing. The ride didn't last long before there was a foot to Franco's face. A move so rarely successful on Franco that he wasn't even sure if it was a left or a right. He tucked like Chris Tucker. But The Prince was more a fan. Of Jackie Chan. He rushed forward with a flurry of fists and feet. Franco deflected six of them. Absorbed a half dozen of the other. But he had nowhere to run. No one to run to. No father, no mother, no sister, no brother. Only his betta meta-brother. The Prince. The strapping foreigner. Franco his pudgy Jersey brother. Like they were Schwarzenegger and DeVito in *Twins*.

Franco tied The Prince up against the cage. Stood in one of his least favorite moves. The pummel clinch. Not the wrestler's clinch that afforded opportunities to free up his fists and give his opponent the business. Not the Muay Thai clinch where he could throw knees to abs above. Just the pummel fuckin clinch. The all-in tie up that bored the hell out of boxing and MMA fans alike. A neutral position at best. Just so Franco could grab a rest. Take some breaths. For his heaving chest. While The Prince was like Young Franco at his very best. His kick had caught Franco so bad, Franco was already gushing blood from a gash ten times worse than T's. The boot caused a swell to boot. Left Franco's left eye as blind as the condom-covered eye of Lisa "Left Eye" Lopes.

Franco countered with a couple kicks. The Prince swatted the first. Caught the second. Stepped on *Frank's* jank ankle. Tipped him like a pole vault. Franco slipped his foot free, fell into the cage, then did something he never did. Ran. On his now hyperextended ankle. He backpedaled with the grace of an excavator on uneven terrain. He deked. Ducked. Then trucked the other way. An outmatched hero in some kinda *Terminator* movie. Being attacked by a new, improved version of himself. Younger, faster, stronger. Franco 2.0. Hunting down the one that used to drive a 5.0.

With Franco unwilling to engage, The Prince's fists and feet began to fall short. So. He shot on Franco. The Prince's wrestling-since-he-was-six paid dividends like it was his trust fund. He picked Franco up by the legs and planted him on the canvas. Then split his forehead with a hammer punch. Franco shouldn't've groomed that morning— The Prince busted his unibrow for him. Franco reached up and once again wrapped up. From his back. The jumbotron above might as well have fell. Drilled him straight to hell. But Franco was saved by the bell. Like he was Zack v Slater in *Saved by the Bell*. Franco unfurled from the fetal position. Austin Powers unfrozen for the first time. He lumbered to his feet. His forehead rupture erupted lava flows of blood. Flows that fell to the canvas as Franco fell into his stool.

"The FUCK was that!" wondered Joey.

"You have to dictate the terms," said Nelly like he was Miss Lane reviewing vocab.

"From the guard," zaid Brazil.

Franco spit out his mouthpiece. Sucked wind and blood with every breath. Clutched his stool like he could sit on it forever. He had forty more seconds.

Nelly backed up Brazil. "He's got your number standing up. Give the guard a go."

"And...fuckin fight this time!" injected Joey.

Franco's nose leaked like an everlasting jelly donut. "Good idea."

Taz had been tidying him up. He ironed Franco's eyes. Toweled the blood from his head. Tried to stop the nose bleed once. Twice. Thrice. No dice. He plugged it with a cotton ball.

"Mind if I get some of that?" mustered Franco.

Joey was mid-sip of Franco's water. Staring across at The Prince. Sitting upright and unscathed. Chiseled from chin to shin. Bobbing his head. Listening to his team like he was listening to a tune. Joey squirted the water in Franco's gasping mouth. "Ya know. He kinda looks like you. Like you but in high school."

Franco shook his head. Tried to shake the cobwebs as he trotted out. Tried to dictate the pace in round two. He had the success of a white teacher in the hood. In one of them movies. The teacher-in-over-his-head threw punches. The precocious pupil evaded. Smirked over the authority's effort. The teacher escalated the issue to takedown attempts. The pupil skirted them like a homeboy told to go to the office. Not gonna happen, teach. Before long, the pupil straight-up took over the class. Put the teacher on his ass.

"The guard!" yelled Brazil.

After some opening pops by The Prince and a well-timed takedown, Franco fell into his least favorite form of MMA fighting. The guard. Yeah, he'd worked on it a brazillion times with Brazil. Yeah, there was the added edge of there not being footage of him on the offensive from the guard. But still. If a street fight was a barn-burning brawl that scattered this way and that, fighting from the guard was its opposite. A counter to aggression. Immobile. A slow burn that required precision. The slip of an arm, the tuck of a knee enough to swing a fighter from submitter to submitted. So any move made by Franco also opened the door for him to be moved on. The Bunns Lane Brawler was used to *coming forward. Throwing fists. Scoring takedowns.* Now? He lay on his back. On guard from the guard. Knees and elbows up like a baby about to have his diaper changed. Or worse. Like an old man trying to stop the coffin from closing.

The Prince rained hammer fists on Franco like a Hammer Bro on Mario. He zapped any Flower Power Franco had then shrunk him down to a shell of himself. Franco on his last man in the Video Game of Life. So Franco, feeling shrunk to a baby, pulled The Prince in and gave him a big huggie. Yeah, Franco tried to make it look good with the occasional arm bar attempt. But The Prince evaded and countered with pounding punches. While Mario Franco had shrunk, the Hammer Bro grew as big as Bowser. Fired punches like fireballs.

Still, Franco saw the engagement as a relative win considering how round one went. The Prince had proved so potent on his feet that there was no need for him to go to his back. Instead, it was Franco on his back. Shifting from snake position to rubber position to the alleged Damn Good Guard position.

Franco even lost ground with the crowd. Heard something he *never* heard before. Boos. *From a Jersey crowd, no less. Damn.* It was a good reminder. Who the fuck was he? The locals even booed Jeter once. Back in '04 when he showed his first signs of age. Same year Bernie Williams said he was done and ended the Core Four's run. And maybe the round two bell that had just rung was announcing the end of Franco's. He headed to his corner with Metallica on his mind. "For Whom the Bell Tolls."

Franco kept his head down. Twenty thousand let down. And that was just in the arena. Not to mention he couldn't even bear a glance with T. T had saved him over and over in his life. T the inspiration for Franco to get his ass in gear over the years. T's yoking of Yogi. T's coming up with the plan to get Franco out of the fix. The premonition personified. *T gave Franco this shot.* This shot at the life Franco always dreamed. Only now, in the cage, it wasn't about the brains. It was about the brawn. Franco now the king. And T the pawn. It was on Franco now. He finally snuck a glance at T. Through his eyes beat to daylights. His son was a deer in headlights.

Even Franco's team was defeated after round two. Brazil took Nelly's usual front and center position, "Man, come on! You've submitted *me* from the guard!"

"You didn't beat my fuckin face in first," Franco managed between breaths.

Nelly stepped in. Said all the right things. *You're getting your wind. Fight your fight. Hang in there.* Taz and Joey did all the right things. The eye iron. The wipe down. The water. All of them clapped it up as Franco stood. Still, Franco didn't need Skylar's magic eight ball to know: *Outlook not so good.*

Franco, with a round off his feet, was ready to give the stand-up game another go. Nothing to lose. The Brawler came forward true to form. Jabbed. The Prince parried. Landed a counter-cross to the kisser. The shot rocked Franco. Like he was Frisco. In an 8.0.

Everybody's got a plan until they get hit in the mouth. Well. That was true for Franco, too. So much for the Warning in Joey Yo's apartment. So much for the run. Rocky fuckin lost the original flick, didn't he? Everyone forgets that. All he did was go the distance. Forty years and forty million hours of media ago. Good luck being a heroic loser these days. Franco was either gonna leave the fight a champ. Or a chump. The allegedly non-ominous signs—the weather, the dead car, the second-rate city, Joey's candid comment—were ominous after all. Four foreshadowings that flew right over Franco's head. Miss Lane, wherever she was, was probably havin a good laugh. Probably on her couch with a big ole tub of popcorn. Why read a book tonight? When she could watch the kid who flunked her class fail one last test. For every one of those underdog wins Franco waxed about, there were five favorites who took care of business as usual. From Jeter and the Yanks to the Cards and Stan Musial. Fuckin Franco. In the cage and thinkin about baseball. *Fair is foul and foul is fair.* Shook as Shakespeare all over again.

Franco covered up on the canvas as he wondered what the fuck he was thinking all these years. Last time, he was in his prime and caught a 22-year-old Prince in his third fight for The Show. And Franco *still* couldn't get the W. Yet ever since, he didn't stop believin, like the Soprano family in their final scene. Nowhere like standing in a cage with a killer to realize that maybe that scene was also ironical. Everyone's always caught up in their own shit, ain't they? The Prince deserved it too, didn't he? His privilege was either earned by his parents or their parents before them—*who are all him*—when ya get right down to the DNA. The Prince could probably lay out his whole fuckin family tree. Dust off some giant scroll from his oak fuckin library. Unravel the shit at some grand podium and tell you all about this royal Saudi line and this angelic Anglo line and so on. He probably put on glasses and a pipe and told you awl about it. What the fuck did Franco know about his ancestry? What the fuck! One fuckin thing. That he learned just last year from Church. Eric fuckin Church. He's from a line of *Sinners Like Me*. Not The Prince. His proud people were reaping what they sowed. Watering their seed since birth. Steered him right into mixed martial arts. And as Franco was witnessing firsthand, His Highness had honed the fuck out of his craft.

Franco almost let his guard down right then and let The Prince get it over with. All these years. While Franco was dancing around deluding himself with lines from *36 Chambers*, The Prince was sleepin in a fuckin hyperbaric chamber. While Franco was doing prison workouts, The Prince had a gym the size of a prison ta work out. While Franco was eating two-buck canned tuna, The Prince was eating fresh catch. While the possibly part-Roman ate ShopRite romaine, the True Caesar feasted on organic kale. ShopRite. Ha. Franco shopped at a store that couldn't even spell its name rite. The Prince meanwhile was one of those holier than thou Whole Foodies. You are what you eat. The Prince. And The Pauper.

The Prince landed punishing blows while The Pauper accounted for the pennies of his life. The final blow was a showstopper. Franco was on the defensive. But The Prince leaped off the fencing. He cracked Franco with a foot flush across the face. With such force and follow-through that The Prince spun into his landing. Like Ryu landing a Hurricane Kick. His street-fighter opponent as done as Rubin "Hurricane" Carter. Another promising Jersey fighter who wound up in Woodbridge. Rahway Prison to be exact.

Franco was amazed by what can pass through one's mind in a moment. He floated to the canvas like that feather in *Forrest Gump*. And took inventory of his life's box of chocolates. The good old days. Five years old with Joey Cano in kindergarten. Gone. His parents—biological and otherwise. Gone. His relationship with The Frog. Gone. His prime as a fighter. Gone. The guys at the docks. Gone. His Mustang. Gone. A lost T who needed him. Gone. His Julie. *Gone Baby Gone*. Franco's life's box of chocolates was empty. It was time to go to sleep.

The General hit the canvas and it all went black as fast as *The Sopranos* finale. The Battle of Newark was his Battle of Yorktown. The final battle of the Revolution. When the World Turned Upside Down. Only this time. The American was turned upside down.

Franco lay there. On his stomach. His face sideways. After seven years of sideways.

Though he was seeing black, his eyes must've been cracked. Because he saw them. Tucked ten rows back. Those two jewels. Amid nothing but black. Big and blue. And staring right back. Glowing like they used to. Way back. Franco stared for what felt like an eternity. At those jewels that stopped time and stood the world still. Those majestic jewels of such exalt. More powerful. Than smelling salt.

Franco reached in their direction. Grabbed the cage. Climbed himself upright. Unsure if ten milliseconds or ten years had passed. "Julie!" Franco kept the pursuant Prince at bay with a couple of back kicks. Like a philly not wanting to be phucked. "Julie!"

The bell rang as the ringside fight commentators tried to make sense of the situation. The bald Bull gushed into his headset. "Take a look at this replay! Franco gets kicked *flush* across the face. Look at his eyes. It's lights out. His legs collapse right out from under him. His arms are spaghetti— he's defenseless! It's over! All The Prince has to do is pound for what, a few seconds, until the ref calls it?"

"The Prince saw what we saw! That it was over!" began the mustachioed Mercer. "Look at this replay. Franco is DOA." Mercer shook his head. "Then boom! He's up!"

"What was he screaming?" begged The Bull. *"Julie?"*

"He should've been screaming HELP!" mused Mercer.

"He's gonna need a lot of it. There's no question he's down all three rounds. His only chance is a finish," The Bull said as he shook his head.

"A finish? *He's* finished!" burst Mercer. "Have you *ever* seen a beating like this? This is... This is The Assault at The Vault!" decried the unmerciful Mercer.

Franco zig-zagged to his corner like Baby T's first walk across the carpet. Only this time son caught father.

"You guys see that? Julie's here!" is how it sounded in Franco's head.

His fight team heard, *Yuhgaseeat? Jews here.*

"What! *Jews are here?"* exclaimed Joey. "Of course they are! It's fuckin Jersey!" continued Joey with his arms out.

"The Prince is here, too!" roared Nelly.

Taz got to work on Franco's claymation face. But no enswell was gonna end the swell. And that roundhouse kick. Oof. Left Franco's nose as crooked as some of the fans in the front row.

"Good news bad news," tallied Taz as he plumbed Franco's nostrils. "Bad news. Your nose is broken."

"What's the good news?" wheezed Franco. *Wuzagoodnew?*

"You already ugly."

Franco's laugh launched bits of blood. Added to the tapestry of Taz's razzmatazz getup. The whole team helped Franco get up. *What the hell were they all so worried about?* Franco tried reassuring them. *"Igahdis. Jews here."*

TRACK 15. EVERYTHING I'M NOT

FRANCO STAGGERED OUT for Round Four. He might've looked like hell but he had found his heaven. His Jewels. The Prince's flurries. His blizzards. His hurricanes. Any storm was manageable. When you had The Jewels. And Franco knew all about fighting in shitty conditions. Knew how to hobble his way through a return fight on a reattached ankle. Knew how to take haymakers and make hay on counters. Knew how to take knees and 'bows. From the kidneys to the nose. The pain and numbness custom to him. All the way back to first grade. In that Adidas-sandaled walk through winter slush that turned his toes purple. All the way back to that second-grade bathroom fight. When he caught a concussion from the porcelain sink. Then sunk into his classroom seat like nothing happened. All the way back to third grade when his foster father showed up tuned up to his basketball game and yelled, *Shoot the fuckin ball.* Then under his Jim Beam breath, *Bastard.* Little Franco went on the hunt like Will Hunting—had the best game of his life. Cuz fuck the old man. That's why. The Prince had never been beyond round three. Franco's whole life was a five-round fight.

Everyone knows about the Boston Tea Party. Paul Revere's ride. The Shot Heard Round the World.[5] But Franco's favorite part of the Revolution? What happened after Yorktown. The alleged last battle of the Revolution. Ha. Not in Jersey. In true Jersey fashion, the fighting went past the bell. In true Jersey fashion, there was no formality to it. Just a bunch of down n dirty scraps. Bloody messes that never had the prestige of being called "Battle." The Skirmish at Manahawkin. The Ambush of Amboy. The Long Beach Island Massacre.

There Franco stood. Beyond the bell of the third round for the first time in his career. Into the championship rounds. The fellas on the undercard could call it a night after three. But The Prince and The Patriot? They were gonna keep it going in true Jersey fashion. With a little down n dirty scrap beyond the bell.

That last flying foot from The Prince? Nothing more than a little tap on the shoulder to wake Franco up. While Franco got his motor going for the first time, he could see the invisible battery above The Prince's head. And he wasn't keepin it one hunid. Franco used his extra bit of heft to pull The Prince into a wrestler's clinch. They exchanged intimate blows. Franco's chipped away at The Prince's pristine conditions. While The Prince's returns only tired his taut arms further as the beefy Brawler absorbed them.

But. A knee to the balls backed Franco off. And why not? The Prince was in no danger of losing by points. Bollocks to the boos from the dirty people in Dirty Jersey.

The ref broke them up. Franco waved off his right to a minute and staggered about the canvas. He waved his fists at The Prince. _Let's go._ The fans in The Vault cheered Franco for

[5] Whether it be the shot that started the Revolution. Or as little Franco knew it, the Bobby Thompson home run.

the first time since the fight started. And Franco was with them lockstep the whole time. What did Jeter say when he got booed? Fuck the fans? Helll no. He said, *I'd boo me, too.* Then went to the well and came back with some of the best baseball of his life.

Franco was ready to do the same. Only that shot to the balls. Oof. This was new territory. Even Bunns Lane outlawed blows to the balls. Franco went for another wrestler's clinch, mainly to prop himself up until his balls dropped back in his sack.

The Prince slipped the clinch and kneed Franco below the belly button. And *just* above the unacceptable area. A wise hammering that hampered Franco. Franco doubled over for a millisecond, which might as well be a million in MMA. The Prince thundered down a haymaker at Franco's exposed face. Franco defended in the nick of time.

Once again, Franco was on the run. Any optimism that inflated The Vault was now gone. Like the first breaths into an inflatable raft that proves too big to blow up. The Prince jabbed. Jabbed again. Threw a hook. Franco's defensive arms took the heat. The Prince kicked at Franco's calf. At his knee. His quad. The Prince changed stance and chopped away at the other tree. A lumberjack working toward timbering Franco.

Franco engaged just enough to keep it going. A counter punch here. A spin kick there. A shoot there. If there were disadvantages to his advanced age, there were some advantages, too. If he could keep the phenom before him focused on yet another finish, maybe The Prince would wear himself out. Their last bout, it was Franco who looked past the safe W. The ambition of youth. Now it was his opponent in his prime. And primed to maintain his finishing streak. Forget being a champ. Franco's opponent wanted to be an all-timer. After all, he was *THE* Prince.

They continued to spar. Franco figured the invisible battery above The Prince's head was at 80 percent. Damn. Had to wear him out some more. Franco fought every instinct to go in for the kill. It was one thing for Franco to show restraint in his last fight when he was winning. Dictating terms from the get-go. Dishing it out in little doses to sweat out the Ulsa in Tulsa. But this fight? He was behind with no chance of taking a decision. He *had* to finish The Prince. Or he was finished.

The Prince lurked along the edge of the cage. Glancing the fencing as he went. Franco ready to move in like a crab that couldn't resist the bait. Then sentenced to death in a cage. Muhammad Walid. Ready to rope-a-dope Franco Foreman.

But did Franco Foreman have it in him? To hold off? The bigger kids on Bunns Lane that wanted to tussle? The best defense was offense. Get after them before they get you. Take them out at the legs. The courts where the big men planted themselves in the post and imposed their will? Not Franco. Kid weaved through traffic in turbo mode. Fuck a cruise. It was his Days of Thunder, and he was Tom Cruise. Fast n furious before there ever was a *Fast n Furious*. Same on the soccer field. And the baseball diamond. Someone better bat Franco in before the crazy fuck tries to steal home, too. Same for the summer weight room. The kid who ran himself skinny all school year would put on incredible bulk. Like he was the Incredible Hulk. Came back to the soccer team jacked. Before there ever was that Brazilian player. Hulk.

Then. There were those tennis matches. Julie's one sport. She honed her game for her college résumé. Worked part-time at the pizza place to pay for private lessons. One eight-hour shift for every one-hour lesson. Franco offered a helping hand. Someone to practice against. Julie would stand on one end ready to serve, looking the part in her skirt and visor. (Secondhand, shh.) Franco would stand ready to return. His shoulders swelling out of his beater. Holding his racquet like a caveman carryin a club. He didn't even have a forehand. Crushed every ball with his baseball swing. Holding that old wooden racquet. Ready to bang like Michael Chang. He'd either hit a winner or an unforced error. At first. He picked up the game over time. Learned to how to keep a rally going so Julie could get her reps. By the time they decided to keep score, he could've beaten her 6-0 every time. But he lobbed his serves over. Played her balls sailing long. Hit it right at her when she went to the net. Their points turned into epic rallies. Ones that gave Julie butterflies as she fluttered across the court. Epic rallies that turned into epic matches. Matches that always seemed to leave Franco on the losing end. Anything for his Jewels.

Franco declined Muhammad Walid's invitation and held back. The temp wasn't much of a Foreman. As Franco hobbled on his ailing Achilles, he worked on The Prince's. A tortoise pretending to keep up with the hare. The Prince kept up the pace. But his breathing also crept up. His chest heaved as he heaved punches. He shot at Franco's legs. But with Franco on the defensive and The Prince a shade slower than in round one, The Prince couldn't get it done. The Prince resorted to punches and kicks. Some landing but most defended.

The Prince waved his gloves. "Let's have at it!"

Franco waved his gloves back. *"Let's!" Leszz.*

The bell rang. Another round for The Prince.

While The Prince sat and sucked wind in one corner, Franco moseyed over to his militia. They tossed the punch-drunk puncher in his chair. Taz landscaped his bloated face.

Joey squirted water that ran back out of Franco's fist-frozen mouth. Nelly tried to talk some sense into his man beaten senseless. "Keep letting the game come to you. Just going the distance. Breaking his streak. You'll get another contract." Franco glanced over at Arturo. Sipping mai tais with the misses. Then looked back to his coach. Right into his emerald eyes this time. "I don't fight for contracts."

However it sounded to Thomas Nelson the Ninth, a Son of the Revolution, he heard all he needed to hear. He open-fisted his own chest twice. "Woodbridge Pride."

General Franco closed-fisted his own twice. "Woodbridge." Then marched on to the final round of battle.

The militiaman with the mug of welts, bruises, and blood addressed the picture-perfect Prince before him. "Ay Your Majesty. When ya gonna hit me?" *Ayuhmahjsteewehyagohimme?*

Despite the speech impediment, The Prince heard the message loud and clear. His stiff jab split Franco's lip before it even finished flapping. But. It was The Prince who scowled. While Franco smiled. With blood erupting out of his lower lip like it was Mt. Saint Helen's. That extra weight he'd put on in his advanced age was suddenly paying dividends like those stocks he never bought. Sure, him and The Prince had both weighed in at 170 the day before. But that was after Franco's run. After fasting. He'd put on fifteen pounds of food and water weight since. The Prince, not an ounce to spare, was still at a buck seventy. Franco had taken blows from 200-pound gorillas in unsanctioned MMA cages and unsanitary Jersey clubs alike. The more the petite Prince pummeled, the more Big Franco smiled. Especially when a revelation unraveled. *There were still things he needed to teach T.* Yeah, Julie had the main things on lock. The do good in school. The plan for your future. The watch who you hang with. But Franco, too, had a few he just couldn't eschew. The find your passion. The never say die pursuit of it. The be the best version of yourself you can be. Fuck Franco the Hustler. He was Franco the Father. *Franco the Fighter.* He'd been working toward this moment his whole life. Since 22, when he formally trained for his first figh— No. Since 19, when his best bros were teaching him boxing and wrestling, not to mention all his lifting, so he could bring the heat on the stree— No. Since seven. That first fight. The bathroom concussion. Ever since, the orphan fought his way through the Lane. Trying to build a base for that needs pyramid. The one he saw on his program therapist's wall. He'd been building that pyramid. Brick. By brick. By brick. Ever since. And it was time to put a capstone on it. The Great Pyramid of Franco. A million sandstorms and still standing.

Franco put everything he had into a jab. His previous half-ass attempts slowed The Prince's reaction time down. It was like seeing Mo Rivera's fastball after ten changeups. Good luck. Franco caught The Prince on his nifty nose. Followed it with a combo. The Prince ate the first hit. Defended the next two. *But the royalty was on the run.*

"Whadaya say now, *WOOD!*" roared Nelly.

Franco heard the battle cry from the head of his crew. Say what you want about them. A bunch of unknowns. Local friends as much as they were professionals. Small in number. But big in heart. Distinguished in each of their disciplines. A Woodbridge-grown garden. With roots all over Earth. From Bunns Lane to Bangkok. It was Lama who sold The Show on this fight. It was Brazil who got Franco here with juiced-up Jiu-Jitsu. It was Taz who had him ready for any blow n stopped all the blood flow. It was his good ole bro, Joey Yo, who taught him how to throw. Who had his back since kindergarten. And it was Coach Nelson. Who went out of his way to take on The Brawler. And turn him into a top-shelf crawler. Franco's team. *His motherfuckin team.* Either a bunch of nobodies from nowhere. Or. The Americans from everywhere. Helping their guy in the game forged from all corners of the earth. Mixed martial arts. M. M. A. Made in the U. S. A.

The Prince meanwhile only hired men from his father's homeland. For all his money, he had drained his team's talent pool from oceans around the world to a gulp of the Persian Gulf. His group-thinking goons still shouting in support of The Prince's streak. "You've got him!" "Finish him!"

Franco and The Prince went toe to toe. Blow for blow.

The crowd, all walks of life, yet all True Jersey mahfuckas who'd been calling for this rematch from jump street, *OOOHED* the surgical strike that landed on Franco's surgery-needing nose. Then cheered Franco's slug to The Prince's now messying mug. The whole crowd on their feet. Praying Franco could pull off the feat. Backwards-hatted dudes wrapped arms as Franco got rapped in the face. Then jumped up and down as Franco went up and down—a jab followed by a body blow. Flat-brimmed homies held their main squeezes. As their main man squeezed The Prince. Power-bombed him to the ground.

When Franco erupted with a trademark ground and pound, the whole place erupted. Freight-trucking fathers and sunnier-prospect sons. Young bucks who put forth their hard-earned bucks. Along with does who made their own dough. Newlyweds. Dudes with dreads. Gals on ladies' nights. Some for the fights. Others for men in tights. Jersey Janes and Joes of all throws. Firefighters and cops next to ex-cons. Dudes that work at Exxon. From the gas pump to the penthouse. Ready to pump the roof off this house.

But the Prince's heel kick interrupted. The plan corrupted.

Franco and The Prince circled despite sucking wind. Despite their heads a hundred pounds. Despite lava flows from their faces to their feet. Like two T. Rexes that got buried in the Big One. Then dug their way out.

That's when he heard it. "Fran-co! Fran-co! Fran-co!" The fans of The Vault. Giving *The Pauper* the exalt. For once, Franco was the one getting his due. Which reminded him of another advantage. Straight-up Jersey hustle. Wasn't Franco busy doing his nightly sit-ups when he sat up and saw The Prince on *Letterman*? Promoting a movie. The Prince must've spent a good month on that role. While Franco was doing Jiu-Jitsu rolls. And wasn't Franco busy busting out another prison workout when The Prince was getting *sent* to prison? Domestic violence. A KO unaccounted for on his win streak. His win streak that never took him this far. Into round five. Into the deep blue sea. With nowhere to go. Just him. And Big Franco.

Franco tied The Prince up and served him a dish of Muay Thai. Pumped his knees into The Prince's body like he was Greg LeMond. And when The Prince dropped his arms to protect his abs, Franco treated him to some of America's famed Southern Hospitality and threw dem 'bows. And in case he was feeling homesick, Franco split The Prince's cheek as wide as the English Channel.

Despite the newfound advantages for Franco, there was still one big one for The Prince. Father Time. And this time, he was telling Franco exactly how many ticks were left. 1:02. 1:01. 1:00. Yeah, Franco was finally winning his first round. Yeah, a few more rounds and he might knock The Prince out. But Franco only had a minute. And The Prince, for all his prettiness, was one tough motherfucker. Franco knew going in that The Prince was the most skilled fighter he ever fought. And he now had to admit. He was the toughest, too.

229

That's when Joey yelled it. "One Minute Man!" Shouting, in the biggest moment of Franco's life, the name of a song by Missy "Misdemeanor" Elliot. Franco knew the cue as Joey's inside jokey way of saying: *Time to be a minuteman.*

If the colonial militia and the conditions they overcame was one level of tough, the minutemen were a whole other level. They were the Navy SEALS of the Continental Army, as Young Franco would drunkenly drum to Joey back in the day. Ready at all times to get done whatever needed to get done. No matter the weather. No matter the lack of supplies. No matter the chance of demise. Franco's favorite minutemen? The Blues. From where? Woodbridge. Motherfuckin. New Jersey.

:49... :48... :47...

The Jersey Blue galloped around the canvas with the kick of his old pony. As if the old pony was carrying the minuteman while he dug deep into the recesses of his brain. The minuteman dug and dug. And excavated a final advantage. Wisdom. Franco had been in enough barn burners to know the shared consciousness that comes across two fighters exchanging brutal blows. And the shared consciousness of him and The Prince concurred. This one was gonna be a to-the-bell slug-out. And that's when Franco pulled the rug out. The thirtysomething able to hear the voice in his head a little more loud and clear with every year. The twentysomething before him still too much of a raging bull to see the way forward in full.

Franco absorbed a jab, ducked a hook, and shot on The Prince's legs.

As they fell to the canvas, that chinny man in the front row fell into Franco's view. The sight was enough to allow the pliable Prince to twist. And it was he who landed on top. While Franco fell to his back. Back to the guard. The Prince couldn't believe his royal fortune. Thirty seconds to go, the fight won on all cards, and he had the wanker lying there like an itty-bitty baby.

:29... :28... :27...

The Prince pounded Franco to a pulp as the seconds wound down. It was so bad, those blue jewels recoiled into their cases. Like pearled oysters slamming shut as a shark attacked.

:13... :12... :11...

Ten. The hand The Dealer had dealt Franco coming into the match. Dealt him a mix of twos and aces over the past four rounds. Franco was sitting at 16. The shittiest hand he could have.

Meanwhile, the chap who once cracked his own wife beat Franco down likewise. To the very last card in the deck. Clubbed him like the king of clubs. Punched as hard as a queen's diamonds. Spaded him like the jack of spades.

Then. That last card. One that Franco was watching from his back the whole time. The one at the bottom of The Dealer's deck as he dealt The Prince royal cards left and right.

Words from Brazil rolled around Franco's head. From countless times rolling on the mats. *When your opponent attacks, he's at his weakest point.* Franco tried to capitalize on The Prince being five rounds in and on the attack. But Franco was spent, too. He wrapped his legs around the guy grounding and pounding him to a pulp *with every last ounce he had.*

Franco ran one leg along The Prince's neck. Secured the hold with his other. A triangle to choke the bloke. Just one problem. It was secured by Franco's ailing ankle. His ailing fuckin ankle that could never hold The Prince. Unless. Franco didn't give a fuck about that ankle. Franco pressed. And pressed. And pressed. Well past the POP. An MMA first. A fighter who finished himself. Only Franco didn't tap.

Didn't even let up. Only pushed it farther. Like that time he pushed his pony onto a snow-covered road. Barely avoided a wreck in Québec. *Had to make the fight that night. For a night like this.*

:06... :05... :04...

Franco looked out at his Jewels and only understood then what she went through the night she birthed their son. His queen of hearts. Watching her suicide king. As he pressed and pressed. Not even sure if he still had a hold on his ankle, it so infested with adrenaline. He did. Despite the astronomical mix of excitement and fear. Like the last time he held something this tight. When the doc handed him his baby boy. Franco's triangle strangulation closed in like a satellite triangulation.

:03... :02... :01...

Franco looked to his corner. Through the haze of his hazels. TJ. Joey. Nelly. Brazil. Taz. All hanging over the cage. Shouting. Waving. Five racing hearts. Watching as the final card fell. The five of hearts. It touched down on the canvas along with The Prince's submitting hand. Twenty-one. *Franco had won.*

As the 21 brought down the house...

All of Woodbridge went Insane in the Brain. From Colonia to Bunns Lane. From the project projector where Dragon and Lenore shared hugs with hundreds more. To the country club crew outtie in their Audis. Celebrating like it was a banger in Franco's basement. Back in the day.

Franco took one step on his separated ankle, "Julie!" then went down like a ton of bricks in the middle of Brick City. He tried to army crawl. But he had given the fight his awl. Franco turned on his side. Raised his gloved fist to the sky. *Damn.* Of all the jams. He heard "Everything I Am."

Franco's 20,000 accomplices celebrated the heist at The

Vault. They jumped up and down. Hugged it out. Chanted. "Fran-co! Fran-co! Fran-co!" There was an upper deck row of brothers. Who looked nothing like brothers. They hugged and high-fived as one of their own. Claimed the throne. There was the decked lady across the deck who buried her bawling eyes in her husband's arms. After a final look at her son's shoes. The red Asics slung over the champ's corner. And there was the dyed blonde who put forth a day's pay to watch one of her old students. Of *awl* her students over *awl* her years. It was him living her story. The story of little Shirley Lane. From Bunns Lane. She took off her designer glasses. Chalked it up as quite a twist. As she watched Woodbridge's own...Oliver Twist. She wiped away a tear. And began to cheer.

There was the lady in the tenth row who was ten minutes late to seeing the tenth-ranked fighter. She had come to Newark. Straight from work. Her big blues blewn away by what they just saw. There was that chinny man in the front row whose wife hopped all over him. As if her own son had won. That chinny man who took out a nickel. Hard to say what year it was. It was turned to tails. He was amphibious like that. Across the cage stood an applauding man tall, dark, and handsome. He respected the fighter. And already had his king's ransom. Next to him was a doughy man downing another dirty martini. As incoherent as the crippled cage fighters. Until a little brown security guard told him, *Pay your fuckin check, mate.* Then dragged his ass out. Put him in checkmate.

As his militia rushed in, General Franco looked to the hill he stood upon before the battle. He thought he was delirious. Thought he was seeing things. But no. Right there upon the hill. It was definitely him. The man himself. *George Washington.* Holding...a Dunkin' Donuts cup.

Washington watched as the five patriots fell on their general. The American victory secured, he turned on his heel and headed home. For another night's rest in Woodbridge. Somewhere other than the Cross Keys this time. Somewhere indoors. On his way out, Washington tossed his fuckin coffee cup. He was more in the mood for tea. Everyone in The Wood would be celebrating and so would Washington. Maybe he'd call up some old friends. Rent Room 112. Throw a little Woodbridge Tea Party.

Franco's brothers-in-arms wrapped up in arms as they fell on him.

"That's! My! Brother!" barked Joey as he embraced his brother. "You got more heart than Derrick from the *Real World Road Rules Challenge!*"

Franco lay on his back. His battered face about to pop. "Nah bro. You do."

"You're a bad man!" exclaimed Nelly as he wedged his way in. "In a good way."

"That's kinda what I been goin for," moaned Franco.

Coach Nelson hugged the hell out of his guy.

"The kid from the Lane!" gushed Brazil.

"Looking like dee biggest bum on it," teased Taz.

TJ made his way in front of Dad. But for the first time since he learned to talk, he was speechless. He finally eked out a "Dad…"

"Son." Franco pulled T in by the back of his head. Held him tight.

"Are you setting me up for a finish?" joked T.

Franco smiled. Tightened the stranglehold on his boy.

The Bull charged in the cage for the post-fight interview. Franco's fight team lifted him on his foot. Joey Yo again Franco's human crutch.

The Bull spoke into the mic amid the continued chants.

Fran-co! Fran-co! Fran-co! "You come into this fight a monster underdog. Not even a week's notice. Up against the greatest finishing streak the fight game has ever seen. Tell us, how did you pull off the heist at The Vault?"

The lights went up on the crowd. Franco's eyes were so swollen, he had to tilt his head to spot his lady. He leaned into the mic. "I just had to find the jewels." Franco then motioned to his own two moon-sized bruises. "Look at me, Jewels. I finally got big beautiful blue eyes. Just like you!"

Julie's Pacific blues emitted oceans of tears. Into an inlet of laughing lips. It had been so long since she laughed like that. Like how Young Franco used to make her laugh in high school. She laughed and laughed. And cried and cried.

The Bull tried to move on. "As far as the fight—"

Franco held his hands over The Bull's, held the mic firm. "Look at her laughin. I think I'm ready for *The Tonight Show.*"

The Bull leaned into the shared mic. "Or how about a next fight?"

The crowd erupted. *Fran-co! Fran-co! Fran-co!*

"Look at me," the mauled man motioned. "Think I got a better shot at *The Tonight Show.*"

The Prince watched as Franco delighted the fight night fans. He shooed away his sheik father. Watched as Franco's fight team stood with him arm-in-arm. A team that included his son and every walk of life under the sun. A visceral bond between them. Between them and the whole arena, The Prince reckoned. Twenty thousand blokes with cheers and tears. That's when it hit The Prince after all these years. He finally sorted what had struck him about the lad from across the Atlantic. He had a toughness that couldn't be taught. Born of something far more motivating than money. Or fame. Or parental rivalry. The Prince shook his head. Wished he'd had the privilege.

The Prince caught Franco's eye. Gave a tip of his crown. General Franco sent him a salute back.

The British Invasion was over. Sgt. Pepper and his Lonely Hearts Club Band hit the road. Back to Abbey Road. The sergeant left the general amid the 20,000 celebrating like it was Independence Day. Twenty thousand Yankees. Celebrating like they were the New York Yankees.

Julie made her way to the edge of the cage while Lama Drama smoothed it over with the security guards.

Franco hopped across the canvas on one foot to meet her. Like a pogo stick pulled by a magnet.

Lama was already on her cell, probably settin up a promotion, Franco figured. She pointed at him as she slipped away— "Just like we planned in my office!" Franco shook his head. Smiled. *Back in the day.*

Franco's hands and forehead pressed into the fencing. Jewels was taken by the up-close look at her mauled man. Franco took note of the fencing between them. "Least it ain't prison," shrugged Franco as his hazels gazed into her blues for clues. Julie burst into laughter. Just like the first time he met her. The Female of Fall. His Goddess had made the fight after all. "Well, whadaya think of my big blues?"

Julie wiped tears from hers. "I like mine better."

"Me too," smiled Franco.

That's the last thing Franco remembered. Staring up-close into Jewels' blues. Diving into them like they were oceans of calm. Oceans of calm that killed his adrenaline. And dropped him to the canvas. It was all over. He had hit the game winner like he was Larry Bird. With no time left. In his Larry Bird year. With no days left.

TJ saw him on the ground. Rushed to his father's aid. Face down and spent. Like Jordan on Father's Day.

TRACK 16. LIFE AFTER DEATH

FRANCO CAME TO sometime the next day. Or the next week for all he knew. His battered head bandaged. Hooked up to fluids. Elevated at a 45-degree angle as he looked out at the 45-degree day. Sunny. Windy. Blowing away the winter once and for all. He saw The Vault. Saw the corner he stood on when he cased the place. He was back at the hospital he was born in. The prodigal son. Lying in the house of pain. Hearing House of Pain.

TJ jumped around his chair. Hurried over. "Dad. Are you all right?"

"Look at me. You shoulda never came up with that plan."

TJ's shoulders shrunk.

"I'm kiddin."

"Oh," shrugged T. "But I guess I did almost get you killed."

"You saved my fuckin life." Franco managed a one-arm hug of his boy. "And don't ever start cursin. Terrible fuckin habit."

Franco and T laughed. Pangs of pain shot through

Franco's core. Ran to his head.

"Happy birthday by the way."

Franco motioned to his battered self. "Livin the dream."

"Can I ask you something?" T began. "When you shot on The Prince at the end. You let him turn over on you, didn't you?"

Franco nodded. "I wasn't gonna finish him on a ground and pound. Not enough time."

"What made you think your plan would work? You hate the guard."

Franco took a breath for the current challenge that was saying a few sentences. "When I was a kid. I used to watch *Bugs Bunny*. There was this episode where this little midget mobster poses as a baby in a baby carriage to rob a bank." Franco strained to sit up a bit. "I swear ta God I haven't thought of that episode in twenty, shit, thirty years. But there I was in The Vault. Thirty seconds to go. When I saw a goodfella in the front row. And it hit me like a bolt of lightning. Figured I'd lay on my back like a harmless baby. And pull off a heist of my own."

TJ shook his head. "So you're telling me...that you beat the guy with the greatest finishing streak of all time...with a move from *Bugs Bunny*?"

"That's what I'm tellin you," Franco said with a twinkle in his kaleidoscope eye.

Father and son cracked up. Of all the treatment Franco received that day, their laughter was the best medicine.

"What about you? What are you workin on over there?" Franco nodded to a notebook by T's chair. "A rhyme?"

"Kind of."

"Whadaya mean?"

"It's more like, a mission statement."

"What's it called?"

T twisted like when he was two and too embarrassed to tell his parents something. "The Ten College Commandments."

Franco mustered the delighted laugh of a parent pleased with his child. "Give it to me, Notorious TJF."

TJ read from his paper. *"Rule Numero Uno. Mo homework n less Ill Co. Gotta call up Lance, Alp, n Blanco."*

Franco's busted lips broke into a smile. "Number two. Always gotta plan your next move?"

TJ smiled, *Sure.* *"Three. Study for the SAT. Four. Never save work for the period before."*

"Five..." Franco fizzled out. "I don't know, you tell me. You're the one goin to college."

TJ again smiled. *"Always carry a backpack. I don't care if you're jacked. Buy one that's whack. Six. That extra credit? Better get it. Seven. Keep your classes' notes dated. And completely separated. Eight. Never make teach wait on you. Number Nine. Do everything assigned. And Number Ten. Mess up, do it again...*or something," ended T with a shrug.

"Oh it's somethin." Franco adored his son's big browns. Lit up like they were back in the day. When Franco was at the wheel of his brand-new blue bomber. Little T strapped in the back. The Jersey boys listening to the Jersey Boys. "My Eyes Adored You." And the song *still* as true. As when T was two.

"So how is that Future Problem Solvers goin?" wondered Franco.

The Jersey boy looked to Dad. His eyes adored him. There Franco was. Lying in a hospital bed. Battered from head to toe. A nobody from nowhere. Who just became Champion of the World. And all he wanted to do was talk about his boy. If something larger than life was God. Then Franco was TJ's.

"Good," said TJ, holding back tears in front of Dad. As

he did two weeks before.

BONUS TRACK. THE STREETS

THE NUGGET OF FAME and fortune was enough for Franco and his fight team to open up a multidiscipline gym. On Route 1 along that run of tough little Turnpike towns. Towns chock full of fledgling fighters. It was a day Franco never thought he'd see. Maybe Young Franco never did have Biggie's Juicy moment. But Old Franco had fulfilled Biggie's prophecy. He was living a Life After Death.

And yeah, he loves living an honest life. Teaching young bucks the fight game. But what he really loves. Is sitting in his old lawn chair. On the roof of his brick-faced fight club. He loves staring out at The City. Loves watching the Freedom Tower light up the night something special. Loves that his boy works there. So he stares and he wonders. What it must've been like for T to go off to college. What it must be like for him to live in the big city. What it must be like for him to be young and born to run. Just like Young Franco used to be. Back in the day.

Franco loves to sit back on that lawn chair. On a summer night with a Bud Light and reminisce about after the fight.

Back in the good old days of '08. When him and his fight team buffeted for days. At the Elks. Catered by all the places Franco ever imagined. Those good old days of '08. Back when TJ had so much juice, he took on the toughest mahfucka in town. Forget Ray. Forget Franco. The kid took on Julie. Told her he was quitting basketball to wrestle. She flipped her wig. *No way in hell am I gonna have another fighter! Are you stoopid?* Only for TJ to explain to her how he's going nowhere with basketball. How weight classes level the playing field in wrestling. How he only has to beat one or two guys for a varsity spot. How all the good colleges have wrestling and how he can use it to get a scholarship. He even showed her an article about college wrestlers doing well in the real world and talked about how he wanted to work in The City himself. TJ, in all of two minutes, turned Julie on ten years of policy. What was her response again? Oh yeah. *Well, hurry up and go sign up already!* Franco must've laughed in his lawn chair a hundred times over that one. Man. Those were some good old days.

He also loves sitting on that lawn chair and thinking up how he can help T promote their charity. Blue-Collar Scholars. Set up to help kids of all kinds make their way outta the basement. Become better students. Better people. Not just via college. Tech and trade schools, too. *Skillin insteada illin* the motto for the latter. They'd joke that maybe one day one of their bright minds would go on to invent the Edison Time Machine. That way, Franco and TJ can go back and be the first recipients.

Franco loves sitting on that lawn chair and looking into those beautiful blues that come around once in a while. With a bottle of pinaht griggeo. They love sitting there with their drinks and looking out at the Freedom Tower. Adoring their boy like it was back in the day. When they took him to the cloud maker.

Franco loves sitting there and turning his attention to his town. His town full of history, culture, industry. Any kinda person you'll ever see. And he loves watching those streets. The cars carting along Routes 1 and 9. Headlights headed one way. Taillights hightailing it the other. The pitched Parkway entrance one way. The turnoff to the Turnpike the other. Four Forty pushin in to Shaolin. Two Eighty-Seven behind the 7-Eleven. All in his tough little town. Woodbridge. With streets that can take you anywhere.

Like when Franco took that trip with T. A few months after the fight. In a brand-new blue Mustang. When they hopped the Turnpike straight outta Jersey. Filled up on Philly cheesesteaks. Listened to rap, rock, and country as they crisscrossed the country. Back to the Cross Keys and the Father of Our Country. In a Woodbridge state of mind.

ABOUT THE AUTHOR

Tom grew up in Jersey. On streets that show no mercy. Like the sun on a Hershey. Then he got a degree. Magna cum laude. From Rutgers. University.

After college, Tom worked in NYC. As an Analyst and Assistant VP. But had to flee. Apply his creativity—

At the UCLA School of Theater, Film and TV. Where Tom earned a Master's degree. Then wrote for Sony and Disney. Turned pitches into screenplays. He writes novels these days.

Tom's also busy leading his tutoring organization. Educating the next generation.

Tom otherwise spends time with his wife Tammi. Their kids. And friends & family. Whether that be on a sunny South Bay day. Or a trip. To NJ.

THE NUTSHELL

A mixed martial artist has an upcoming fight. That can make things right. He just wants to train. Hop an NJ Transit train. Do some work in Newark. Rep his fight team and fans across the nation. Outlast that international sensation. Hopefully raise a victorious glove. Maybe get back with his love. But he's feelin the heat. On Jersey's streets. They docked his dock job. He owes a favor to The Frog. And his teen son T's bein bullied. His plan's all gettin sullied. Not to mention dealing with issues of class. Race. The mirror's reflecting face. It's like there's no escapin '08. But wait. Let the haters hate. Franco's goin for great.

Fightin straight outta Woodbridge. Aka Hoodbridge. The Wood. The Hood. By any name, a town. Too small to be a city. Too broke to be a burb. Too rough to be rural. Just a tough little Turnpike town. Older than America yet representative of today's America. Connecting north to south. Red to blue. Old to new. Either a perfect alchemy. Or an insane stew. In March of '08 it was looking like the latter. One that would swallow up Franco and T both.

LP Novel: (n.) Lyrical Prose novel. A novel that is written lyrical. At times. In its usage of wordplay. And rhymes.

Made in the USA
Coppell, TX
28 June 2020